NORA ROBERTS

LATE SUMMER LOVE

Includes *The Best Mistake* & *Irish Rebel*

Silhouette Books

SILHOUETTE™

Late Summer Love

ISBN-13: 978-1-335-45283-2

Copyright © 2023 by Harlequin Enterprises ULC

The Best Mistake
First published in 1994. This edition published in 2023.
Copyright © 1994 by Nora Roberts

Irish Rebel
First published in 2000. This edition published in 2023.
Copyright © 2000 by Nora Roberts

For questions and comments about the quality of this book, please contact us
at CustomerService@Harlequin.com.

Silhouette
22 Adelaide St. West, 41st Floor
Toronto, Ontario M5H 4E3, Canada
www.Harlequin.com

Printed in U.S.A.

CONTENTS

THE BEST MISTAKE

Chapter 1

No one answered the door. Coop glanced at the scrawled note in his hand to make sure he had the right address. It checked out, and since the tidy two-story Tudor in the neat, tree-lined neighborhood was precisely what he was after, he knocked again. Loudly.

There was a car in the drive, an aging station wagon that could use a good wash and a little bodywork. Somebody was in there, he thought, scowling up at the second-floor window, where music pumped out—high-volume rock with a thumping backbeat. He stuffed the note and his hands in his pockets and took a moment to survey the surroundings.

The house was trim, set nicely off the road behind clipped bayberry hedges. The flower garden, in which spring blossoms were beginning to thrive, was both colorful and just wild enough not to look static.

Not that he was a big flower lover, but there *was* something to be said for ambience.

There was a shiny red tricycle beside the driveway, and that made him a little uneasy. He wasn't particularly fond of kids. Not that he disliked them. It was just that they always seemed a kind of foreign entity to him, like aliens from an outlying planet: they spoke a different language, had a different culture. And, well, they were short, and usually sticky.

Still, the ad had talked of quiet, privacy, and a convenient distance from Baltimore. That was exactly what he was looking for.

He knocked again, only to have a thundering wave of music wash out the window over him. The rock didn't bother him. At least he understood it. But he wasn't a man to kick his heels outside a closed door for long, so he tried the knob.

When it turned, he pushed the door open and walked in. In an old habit, he pushed back the dark hair that fell over his forehead and scanned the none-too-neat living room he'd entered.

There was a lot of clutter, and he, a bachelor who'd spent a great deal of his thirty-two years living alone, wondered over it. He wasn't fussy or obsessive, he often told himself. It was simply that everything had a place, and it was easier to find if it had been put there. Obviously his prospective landlord didn't agree.

There were toys that went along with the tricycle

outside, piles of magazines and newspapers, a pint-size fielder's cap that declared for the O's.

At least the kid had taste, Coop decided, and moved on.

There was a small powder room done in an amazing combination of purple and green, and a den that had been converted into a makeshift office. File drawers were open, papers spilling out. In the kitchen dishes waited in the sink to be washed, and lurid drawings, created by a child with a wild imagination, decorated the front of the refrigerator.

Maybe, he thought, it was just as well no one had answered the door.

He considered backtracking and wandering upstairs. As long as he was here, it made sense to check the rest of the place out. Instead, he stepped outside to get the lay of the land. He spotted open wooden steps leading to a short deck. The private entrance the ad had mentioned, he mused, and climbed.

The glass door was open, and the music rolling through it was overwhelming. He caught the smell of fresh paint, one he'd always enjoyed, and stepped inside.

The open area combined kitchen and living space cleverly enough. The appliances weren't new, but they were gleaming. The tile floor had been scrubbed recently enough for him to identify pine cleaner beneath the scent of paint.

Feeling more hopeful, he followed the music, snooping a bit as he went. The bathroom was as scrupulously clean as the kitchen, and, fortunately, a plain glossy white. Beside the sink was a book on home repair, open to the plumbing section. Wary, Coop turned on the tap. When the water flowed out fast and clear, he nodded, satisfied.

A small room with definite office potential and a nice view of the yard was across the hall. The ad had claimed two bedrooms.

The music led him to it, a fair-sized room that fronted the house, with space enough for his California king. The floor, which seemed to be a random-width oak in good condition, was covered with splattered drop cloths. There were paint cans, trays, brushes, extra rollers. A laborer in baggy overalls and bare feet completed the picture. Despite the hair-concealing cap and oversize denim, Coop recognized a woman when he saw one.

She was tall, and the bare feet on the stepladder were long and narrow and decorated with paint splotches and hot-pink toenails. She sang, badly, along with the music.

Coop rapped on the doorjamb. "Excuse me."

She went on painting, her hips moving rhythmically as she started on the ceiling border. Stepping across the drop cloths, Coop tapped her on the back.

She screamed, jumped and turned all at once. Though he was quick on his feet, he wasn't fast enough to avoid the slap of the paintbrush across his cheek.

He swore and jerked backward, then forward again to catch her before she tumbled off the ladder. He had a quick, and not unpleasant, impression of a slim body, a pale, triangular face dominated by huge, long-lashed brown eyes, and the scent of honeysuckle.

Then he was grunting and stumbling backward, clutching the stomach her elbow had jammed into. She yelled something while he fought to get his breath back.

"Are you crazy?" he managed, then shot up a hand as she hefted a can, slopping paint over the sides as she prepared to use it as a weapon. "Lady, if you throw that at me, I'm going to have to hurt you."

"What?" she shouted.

"I said, don't throw that. I'm here about the ad."

"What?" she shouted again. Her eyes were still wide and full of panic, and she looked capable of anything.

"The ad, damn it." Still rubbing his stomach, Coop marched to the portable stereo and shut it off. "I'm here about the ad," he repeated, his voice loud in the sudden silence.

The big brown eyes narrowed with suspicion. "What ad?"

"The apartment." He swiped a hand over his cheek, studied the smear of white on it, and swore again. "The apartment."

"Really?" She kept her eyes glued to his. He looked tough, she thought. Like a brawler with those broad shoulders, lean athletic build and long legs. His eyes, a light, almost translucent green, looked anything but friendly, and the faded Baltimore Orioles T-shirt and battered jeans didn't contribute any sense of respectability. She figured she could outrun him, and she could certainly outscream him. "The ad doesn't start to run until tomorrow."

"Tomorrow?" Nonplussed, he reached into his pocket for his scribbled note. "This is the right address. The ad was for this place."

She stood her ground. "It doesn't run until tomorrow, so I don't see how you could know about it."

"I work at the paper." Moving cautiously, he held out

the note. "Since I've been looking for a place, I asked one of the girls in Classifieds to keep an eye out." He glanced down at his note again. "Two-bedroom apartment on second floor, private entrance, quiet neighborhood convenient for commuters."

She only continued to frown at him. "That's right."

Realizing his inside track wasn't strictly ethical, he winced. "Look, I guess she got a little overenthusiastic. I gave her a couple of tickets to a game, and she must've figured she'd do me a favor and pass the information along a little early."

When he saw that her grip on the can had relaxed, he tried a smile. "I knocked, then I came around back." Probably best not to mention he'd wandered through the house first.

"The ad didn't run the address."

"I work at the paper," he repeated. He was taking a good look at her now. There was something vaguely familiar about her face. And what a face it was. All slashing cheekbones and liquid eyes, that creamy porcelain skin women's face cream ads always raved about. Her mouth was wide, with an alluringly full lower lip. At the moment, the face continued to frown.

"They had the address for billing," he continued. "Since I had a couple of hours, I thought I'd come by and check it out. Look, I can come back tomorrow, if you'd feel more comfortable. But I'm here now." He shrugged. "I can show you my press pass."

He pulled it out for her, and was pleased when she narrowed her eyes to study it. "I do a column. J. Cooper McKinnon on sports. 'All in the Game'?"

"Oh." It meant nothing to her. The sports page wasn't

her choice of reading material. But the smile had appeased her. He didn't look so much like a thug when he smiled. And the smear of paint decorating the lean, tanned face added just enough comedy to soothe her. "I guess it's all right, then. I wasn't expecting to show the apartment for a couple of days yet. It's not ready." She held up the can, set it down again. "I'm still painting."

"I noticed."

She laughed at that. It was a full-throated, smoky sound that went with the natural huskiness of her voice. "Guess you did. I'm Zoe Fleming." She crouched down to dampen a rag with paint remover.

"Thanks." He rubbed the rag over his cheek. "The ad said immediate occupancy."

"Well, I figured I'd be finished in here by tomorrow, when the ad was scheduled to run. Are you from the area?"

"I've got a place downtown. I'm looking for something with a little more space, a little more atmosphere."

"This is a pretty good-sized apartment. It was converted about eight years ago. The guy who owned it had it done for his son, and when he died, the son sold it and moved to California. He wanted to write sitcoms."

Coop walked over to check out the view. He moved fluidly, Zoe thought, like a man who knew how to stay light and ready on his feet. She'd had the impression of wiry strength when her body tumbled into his. And good strong hands. Quick ones, too. She pursed her lips. It might be handy to have a man around.

"Is it just you, Mr. McKinnon?" She thought wistfully how nice it would be if he had a family—another child for Keenan to play with.

"Just me." The place felt right, he decided. It would be good to get out of a box that was just one more box in a building of boxes, to smell grass now and then. Barbecue smoke. "I can move in over the weekend."

She hadn't thought it would be so easy, and she nibbled her lip as she thought it through. She'd never been a landlady before, but she'd been a tenant, and she figured she knew the ropes. "I'll need first and last months' rent."

"Yeah."

"And, ah, references."

"I'll give you the number of the management company that handles my building. You can call Personnel at the paper. Have you got a lease for me to sign?"

She didn't. She'd checked out a book from the library, and she'd meant to type up a scaled-down copy of a lease from it the next morning. "I'll have it tomorrow. Don't you want to look at the rest of the apartment, ask any questions?" She'd been practicing her landlady routine for days.

"I've seen it. It's fine."

"Well." That deflated her a bit. "I guess I can cancel the ad."

There was a sound like a herd of rampaging elephants. Zoe glanced toward the open door and crouched to intercept the missile that hurtled through.

It was a boy, Coop saw when she scooped the child up. He had glossy golden hair, red sneakers, and jeans that were streaked with some unidentifiable substance that looked like it would easily transfer to other surfaces. He carried a plastic lunch box with a picture of some apocalyptic space battle on it, and a sheet of drawing paper that was grimy at the edges.

"I drew the ocean," he announced. "And a million people got ate by sharks."

"Gruesome." Zoe shuddered obligingly before accepting his sloppy kiss. She set him down to admire the drawing. "These are really big sharks," she said, cagily distinguishing the shark blobs from the people blobs.

"They're monster sharks. Mutant monster sharks. They have teeth."

"So I see. Keenan, this is Mr. McKinnon. Our new tenant."

Keenan wrapped one arm around Zoe's leg for security as he eyed the stranger. His eyes were working their way up to Coop's face when they lit on the T-shirt. "That's baseball. I'm gonna learn. Mama's getting a book so's she can teach me."

A book. Coop barely checked a snort. As if you could learn the greatest game invented by Man from a book. What kind of nerd did the kid have for a father?

"Great." It was all Coop intended to say. He'd always thought it wise to avoid entangling himself in a conversation with anyone under sixteen.

Keenan had other ideas. "If you're going to live here, you have to pay rent. Then we can pay the mortgage and stuff and go to Disney World."

What *was* the kid? An accountant?

"Okay, old man." Zoe laughed and ruffled his hair. "I can handle it from here. Go on down and put your stuff away."

"Is Beth coming to play with me tonight?"

"Yes, Beth's coming. Now scoot. I'll be down in a minute."

"'Kay." He made a dash for the door, stopping when his mother called him. It only took one look, the raised brow for him to remember. He looked back at Coop, flashed a quick, sunny grin. "Bye, mister."

The herd of elephants rampaged again, then there was the crash of a door slamming. "He makes an entrance," Zoe said as she turned back to Coop. "The dramatic flair comes from my mother. She's an actress, off-off-Broadway." Tilting her head, Zoe rested one bare foot on the bottom rung of the stepladder. "You look like you're ready to change your mind. You have a problem with children?"

"No." The kid might have thrown him off, but Coop doubted it would be a problem. The boy would hardly be beating a path to his door. And if he did, Coop thought, he could send him off again quickly enough. "No, he's, ah, cute."

"Yes, he is. I won't claim he's an angel, but he won't make a nuisance of himself. If he gives you any trouble, just let me know."

"Sure. Look, I'll come by tomorrow to sign the lease and give you a check. I'll pick up the keys then."

"That'll be fine."

"Any special time good for you?"

She looked blank for a moment. "What's tomorrow?"

"Friday."

"Friday." She closed her eyes and flipped through her messy internal calendar. "I'm working between ten and two. I think." She opened her eyes again, smiled. "Yeah, I'm pretty sure. Anytime after two-thirty?"

"Fine. Nice meeting you, Mrs. Fleming."

She took his offered hand. "It's Miss," she said easily. "I'm not married. And since we'll be living together, so to speak, you can make it Zoe."

Chapter 2

No one answered the door. Again. Coop checked his watch and saw that it was quarter to three. He didn't like to think he was a man obsessed with time, but as his living centered around deadlines, he did respect it. There was no rusting station wagon in the driveway this time, but he walked around the back of the house, hoping. Before he could start up the stairs to the apartment, he was hailed from across the chain-link fence.

"Young man! Yoo-hoo, young man!" Across the yard next door came a flowered muumuu, topped with a curling thatch of brightly hennaed hair that crowned a wide face. The woman hurried to the fence in a whirl of color. It wasn't just the dress and the improbable hair, Coop noted. The face itself was a rainbow of rich red lipstick, pink cheeks and lavender eye shadow.

When she reached the fence, she pressed a many-ringed hand over the wide shelf of her breasts. "Not as young as I used to be," she said. "I'm Mrs. Finkleman."

"Hi."

"You're the young man who's going to live upstairs." Mrs. Finkleman, a born flirt, patted her curls. "Zoe didn't tell me you were so handsome. Single, are you?"

"Yeah," Coop said cautiously. "Miss Fleming was supposed to meet me. She doesn't seem to be home."

"Well, that's Zoe, flying here, flying there." Mrs. Finkleman beamed and leaned comfortably on the fence, as if she were settling in for a nice cozy gossip. "Got a dozen things on her plate at once, that girl does. Having to raise that sweet little boy all alone. Why, I don't know what I'd have done without my Harry when our young ones were coming up."

Coop was a reporter, after all. That, added to the fact that he was curious about his landlady, put him in interview mode. "The kid's father doesn't help out any?"

Mrs. Finkleman snorted. "Don't see hide nor hair of him. From what I'm told, he lit out the minute he found out Zoe was expecting. Left her high and dry, and her hardly more than a child herself. Far as I know, he's never so much as seen the boy. The little sweetheart."

Coop assumed she was referring to Keenan. "Nice kid. What's he, five, six?"

"Just four. Bright as a button. They grow them smarter these days. Teach them faster, too. The little love's in preschool now. He'll be home any minute."

"His mother went to pick him up, then?"

"Oh, no, not her week for car pool. Alice Miller— that's the white house with blue trim, down the block?—

it's her week. She has a boy and a girl. Little darlings. The youngest, Steffie, is Keenan's age. Now her oldest, Brad, there's a pistol for you."

As she began to fill Coop in on the neighborhood rascal, he decided it was time to draw the interview to a close. "Maybe you could tell Miss Fleming I was by? I can leave a number where she can reach me when—"

"Oh, goodness." Mrs. Finkleman waved a hand. "I do run on. Nearly forgot why I came out here in the first place. Zoe called and asked me to look out for you. Got held up at the flower shop. She works there three days a week. That's Floral Bouquet, down in Ellicott City? Nice place, but expensive. Why, it's a crime to charge so much for a daisy."

"She got held up," Coop prompted.

"Her relief had car trouble, so Zoe's going to be a little late. Said you could go right on into the kitchen there, where she left the lease and the keys."

"That's fine. Thanks."

"No problem at all. This is a friendly neighborhood. Always somebody to lend a helping hand. I don't think Zoe mentioned what you did for a living."

"I'm a sportswriter for the *Dispatch*."

"You don't say? Why, my Harry's just wild for sports. Can't budge him from in front of the TV when a game's on."

"That's what makes this country great."

Mrs. Finkleman laughed and gave Coop's arm an affectionate bat that might have felled a lesser man. "You men are all the same. You can come over and talk sports with Harry anytime. Me, if it's not baseball, it isn't worth talking about."

Coop, who'd been about to retreat, brightened. "You like baseball?"

"Son, I'm a Baltimore native." As if that said it all. "Our boys are going to go all the way this year. Mark my word."

"They could do it, if they heat those bats up. The pitching rotation's gold this year, and the infield's tight as a drum. What they need—"

Coop was interrupted by a cheerful toot. He glanced over to see Keenan burst out of a red sedan and rocket across the side yard.

"Hi, mister. Hi, Mrs. Finkleman. Carly Myers fell down, and there was blood." The big brown eyes gleamed wickedly. "Lots and lots of it, and she screamed and cried." He demonstrated, letting go with a piercing yell that had Coop's ears ringing. "Then she got a Band-Aid with stars on it." Keenan thought it would have been worth losing some blood for such a neat badge of honor. "Where's Mama?"

"Little lamb." Mrs. Finkleman leaned over the fence to pinch Keenan's cheek. "She's working a little late. She said you could come stay with me until she gets home."

"Okay." Keenan liked his visits next door, since they always included cookies and a rock on Mrs. Finkleman's wonderfully soft lap. "I gotta put my lunch box away."

"Such a good boy," Mrs. Finkleman cooed. "You come on over when you're done. Why don't you show the nice man inside so he can wait for your mother?"

"Okay."

Before Coop could take evasive action, his hand was

clutched by Keenan's. He'd been right, he thought with a wince. It was sticky.

"We've got cookies," Keenan told him, cannily deducing that he could have double his afternoon's treat if he played his cards right.

"Great."

"We baked them ourselves, on our night off." Keenan sent Coop a hopeful look. "They're really good."

"I bet." Coop caught the back door before it could slam shut.

"There." Keenan pointed to a ceramic cookie jar in the shape of a big yellow bird on the counter. "In Big Bird."

"Okay, okay." Since it seemed like the best way to appease the kid, Coop reached in and pulled out a handful of cookies. When he dumped them on the table, Keenan's eyes went as wide as saucers. He could hardly believe his luck.

"You can have one, too." He stuffed an entire chocolate chip deluxe in his mouth and grinned.

"That good, huh?" With a shrug, Coop sampled one himself. The kid, Coop decided after the first bite, knew his cookies. "You'd better get next door."

Keenan devoured another cookie, stalling. "I gotta wash out my thermos, 'cause if you don't, it smells."

"Right." Cooper sat at the table to read through the lease while the boy dragged a stool in front of the sink.

Keenan squirted dishwashing liquid in the thermos, and then, when he noticed Coop wasn't paying any attention, he squirted some more. And more. He turned the water up high and giggled when soap began to bubble and spew. With his tongue caught between his teeth, he jiggled the stopper into the sink and began to play dishwasher.

Coop forgot about him, reading quickly. The lease seemed standard enough, he decided. Zoe had already signed both copies. He dashed his signature across from hers, folded his copy, then set the check he'd already written on the table. He'd picked up the keys and rose to tuck his copy in his pocket when he spotted Keenan.

"Oh, God."

The boy was drenched, head to foot. Soap bubbles dotted his face and hair. A good-sized puddle was forming on the tile at the base of the stool.

"What are you doing?"

Keenan looked over his shoulder, smiled innocently. "Nothing."

"Look, you've got water everywhere." Coop looked around for a towel.

"Everywhere," Keenan agreed, and, testing the opposition, he slapped his hands in the sink. Water and suds geysered.

"Cut it out! Jeez! Aren't you supposed to be somewhere else?" He grabbed a dish towel and advanced, only to be slapped in the face by the next geyser. His eyes narrowed. "Look, kid—"

He heard the front door slam. Like mother, like son, he thought.

"Keenan?" Zoe called out. "I hope you haven't been into those cookies."

Coop looked at the crumbs on the table, on the floor, floating in the soapy water.

"Oh, hell," he muttered.

"Oh, hell," Keenan echoed, beaming at him. He giggled and danced on his stool. "Hi, Mom."

Zoe, her arms full of day-old irises, took in the scene with one glance. Her son was as wet as a drowned dog, her kitchen looked as though a small hurricane had blown through. Hurricane Keenan, she thought. And her new tenant looked damp, frazzled, and charmingly sheepish.

Like a boy caught with his hand in the cookie jar, she noted, glancing at the telltale crumbs.

"Been playing dishwasher again?" With a calm that baffled Coop, she set the flowers down. "I'm just not sure it's the right career choice, Keen-man."

Keenan fluttered his long, wet lashes. "He wanted cookies."

Coop started to defend himself, then simply scowled at the boy.

"I'm sure he did. Go on into the laundry room and get out of those wet clothes."

"Okay." He jumped from the stool, splashing more water before he zoomed away. He stopped only long enough to give his mother a wet kiss before he disappeared into an adjoining room.

"Sorry I'm late," Zoe said easily, yanking the stopper out of the sink then walking to a cupboard to get a vase.

Coop opened his mouth. He started to explain what had gone on in the past ten minutes, but realized he wasn't at all sure. "I signed the lease."

"I see that. Would you mind putting some water in this?" She held out the vase. "I need to get a mop."

"Sure."

She was probably going to wallop the kid with it,

Coop thought, and felt a quick tug of regret and guilt. But the sounds from the laundry room where she'd disappeared weren't those he associated with corporal punishment. They were a young boy's giggles, a woman's lusty laugh. Coop stood, a vase of water in his hands, and wondered at it.

"You're standing in a puddle," Zoe commented when she came back with a mop and pail.

"Oh, right." Coop glanced down at his wet hightops, shifted. "Here's your vase."

"Thanks." She tended to her flowers first. "You met Mrs. Finkleman, I hear."

"News travels fast."

"Around here it does." When she handed him a dishcloth to dry his face with, he caught her scent—much more potent, much more colorful, than the flowers. She was wearing jeans and a baggy T-shirt with Floral Bouquet across the chest. Her hair, he noted, was some elusive shade between brown and blond. She wore it tied back in a jaunty ponytail.

When she lifted her brows, he realized he'd been staring. "Sorry. I mean—I'm sorry about the mess."

"Were you playing dishwasher, too?"

"Not exactly." It was impossible not to smile back, to ignore the quick pull of attraction.

It wouldn't be so bad, he mused, having a pretty landlady, sharing the house with her, maybe an occasional meal. Or an occasional—

"Mama!" Keenan stood in the doorway, wearing nothing but skin. "I can't find my pants."

"In the basket by the washing machine," she told him, without taking her eyes from Coop's.

He'd forgotten about the kid, let himself fantasize a little before remembering she didn't come as a single. He took a long mental step backward and jingled the keys to his new apartment.

"I've got some boxes out in the car," he told her. "I'm going to move some things in this afternoon."

"That's fine." It was silly to feel disappointed, Zoe thought. Foolish to have felt that fast feminine flutter when she recognized interest in his eyes. More foolish to feel let down because the interest had blanked out when her child called her. "Do you need any help?"

"No, I can handle it. I've got a game to cover tonight, so I'm going to move the rest in tomorrow." He backed toward the door. "Thanks."

"Welcome aboard, Mr. McKinnon."

"Coop," he said as he stepped outside. "It's Coop."

Coop, she thought, leaning on the mop handle. It had seemed like such a good idea to make use of the apartment upstairs. The extra income would take some of the pressure off, and maybe add a few bonuses. Like that trip to Disney World that Keenan wanted so badly.

It had been a risk to buy the house, but she'd wanted her son to grow up in a nice neighborhood, with a yard, maybe a dog when he was a little older. The rental income would take away some of the risk.

But she hadn't realized it could add another, more personal risk. She hadn't realized how awkward it might be to have a tenant who was male, single, and absolutely gorgeous.

She laughed at herself. Dream on, Zoe, she thought. J. Cooper McKinnon was just like the rest, who ran like a hound when they heard the patter of little feet.

Something crashed in the laundry room. She just shook her head.

"Come on, sailor," she called to Keenan. "It's time to swab the deck."

Chapter 3

"Pretty good digs, Coop. Really, pretty good." Ben Robbins, a staff reporter for the *Dispatch,* sipped a cold one while surveying Coop's apartment. "I didn't think much of it when we hauled all your junk up here, but it ain't half-bad."

It was a lot better than not half-bad, and Coop knew it. He had everything exactly where he wanted it. The living room was dominated by his long, low-slung sofa of burgundy leather and his big-screen television, so perfect for viewing games. A couple of brass lamps, a nicely worn coffee table scuffed from the heels of the dozens of shoes that had rested on it and a single generous chair completed the formal section of the room.

There was an indoor basketball hoop, small-scaled, for practice—and because shooting a little round ball helped him think. A used pinball machine called Home Run, a stand that held two baseball bats, his tennis racket and a hockey stick, a pair of old boxing gloves hanging on the wall and a scarred Fooz Ball table made up the recreation area.

Coop wouldn't have called them toys. They were tools.

He'd chosen blinds, rather than curtains, for the windows. Blinds, he thought, that would close out the light if a man decided to treat himself to an afternoon nap.

The bedroom held little other than his bed, a nightstand and another TV. The room was for sleeping—or, if he got lucky, another type of sport.

But it was his office that pleased him most. He could already imagine himself spending hours there at his computer, a game playing on his desktop TV. He'd outfitted it with a big swivel chair, a desk that had just the right number of scars and burns, a fax, a dual-line phone and a VCR—to play back those controversial calls or heart-stopping plays.

With all the plaques and photos and sports memorabilia scattered about, it was home.

His home.

"Looks like the neighborhood bar," Ben said, and stretched out his short, hairy legs. "Where the jocks hang out."

Coop considered that the highest of compliments. "It suits me."

"To the ground," Ben agreed, and toasted Coop with his bottle of beer. "A place where a man can relax, be himself. You know, since I started living with Sheila, I've got little china things all over, and underwear hanging in the bathroom. The other day she comes home with a new bedspread. It's got *flowers* all over. Pink flowers." He winced as he drank. "It's like sleeping in a meadow."

"Hey." With all the smug righteousness of the unencumbered, Coop propped his feet on the coffee table. "Your choice, pal."

"Yeah, yeah. Too bad I'm nuts about her. And her an Oakland fan, too."

"Takes all kinds. Talk is the A's are trading Remirez."

Ben snorted. "Yeah, yeah, pull the other one, champ."

"That's the buzz." Coop shrugged, took a pull on his own beer. "Sending him to K.C. for Dunbar, and that rookie fielder, Jackson."

"They got to be crazy. Remirez hit .280 last season."

".285," Coop told him. "With twenty-four baggers. Led the team in errors, too."

"Yeah, but with a bat like that… And Dunbar, what's he? Maybe he hit .220?"

"It was .218, but he's like a vacuum cleaner at second. Nothing gets by him. And the kid's got potential. Big, strapping farm boy with an arm like a bullet. They need new blood. Most of the starting lineup's over thirty."

They argued baseball and finished their beers in complete male harmony.

"I've got a game to cover."

"Tonight? I thought the O's were in Chicago until tomorrow."

"They are." Coop pocketed his tape recorder, his pad, a pencil. "I'm covering the college game. There's a hot third baseman who's got the scouts drooling. Thought I'd take a look, cop an interview."

"What a job." Ben hauled himself to his feet. "Going to games, hanging around locker rooms."

"Yeah, it's a rough life." He slung an arm over Ben's shoulders as they headed out. "So, how's the story on neutering pets going?"

"Stuff it, Coop."

"Hey, some of us hang around the pound, some of us hang around the ballpark."

And a hell of a day it was for it, too, Coop thought. Balmy and clear-skied. He could almost smell roasting peanuts and hot dogs.

"While you're hanging around a bunch of sweaty college boys in jockstraps, I'll be snuggled up with a woman."

"Under a flowered bedspread."

"Yeah, but she says flowers make her feel sexy. And I'm here to tell you— My, oh, my..."

When Ben's small, square face went lax, Coop turned. He felt his own jaw drop. And, if he wasn't mistaken, his tongue landed on his shoes.

She was wearing what had to be the shortest skirt ever devised by man. Beneath it were a pair of endless legs that were molded into black fishnet hose. She swayed when she walked. How could she help it, when she stood in black skyscraper heels?

A tiny white bustier exposed a delicious amount of cleavage. Around her neck was a shiny black bow tie that, for reasons utterly inexplicable to Coop, made every male cell in his body sizzle.

Her hair was down, falling straight as a pin to her shoulders in a melding of tones that made him think of wild deer leaping through a sunlit forest.

She stopped, smiled, said something, but his mind had checked out the moment his eyes landed on her legs.

"...if you've settled in okay."

"Ah..." He blinked like a man coming out of a coma. "What?"

"I said I haven't had a chance to check and see if you've settled in okay."

"Fine." He folded his tongue back in his mouth and got a grip on himself. "Just fine."

"Good. Keenan came down with a cold, so things have been hectic. I caught a glimpse of you hauling things up the steps a couple of days ago."

"Hauling," he repeated. "Yeah. Ben," he said when his friend jabbed him. "This is Ben. He's been giving me a hand moving."

"Hi, Ben. I'm Zoe."

"Hi, Zoe," Ben said stupidly. "I'm Ben."

She just smiled. It was the outfit, she knew. As much as she hated it, she couldn't help but be amused by how it affected certain members of the species. "Do you work at the paper, too?"

"Yeah, I'm, ah, doing a story on neutering pets."

"Really?" She almost felt sorry for him, the way his Adam's apple was bobbing. "I'll be sure to look for it. I'm glad you're settling in okay. I've got to get to work."

"You're going out?" Coop said. "In that?"

Her lips twitched. "Well, this isn't my usual outfit when I'm carpooling, but I thought I'd wear it to work tonight. At Shadows? I'm a waitress. Nice meeting you, Ben."

She walked to her car. No, Coop thought, swayed to it, in those long, lazy strides. They were both still staring when she pulled out of the drive and cruised down the street.

"Your landlady," Ben said in a reverential whisper. "That was your landlady."

"I think it was." She hadn't looked like that when he signed the lease. Beautiful, yes—she'd been beautiful, but in a wholesome, unthreatening sort of way. She hadn't looked so...so... Words failed him. She was a mother, for God's sake, he reminded himself. She wasn't supposed to look like that. "She's got a kid."

"Yeah? What kind?"

"Human, I think."

"Come on."

"A boy," Coop said absently. "This high." He held a hand, palm down, about three feet from the ground.

"She may have a kid, but she's also got legs. This high." Ben waved a hand in front of his own throat. "You got a charmed life, Coop. My landlord's got arms like cinder blocks, and a tattoo of a lizard. You got one who looks like a centerfold."

"She's a mother," Coop said under his breath.

"Well, I wouldn't mind coming home to her for milk and cookies. See you at the sweatshop."

"Sure." Coop stood where he was, frowning at the quiet street. Mothers weren't supposed to look like that, he thought again. They were supposed to look...motherly. Safe. Comfortable. He blew out a breath, willed away the knot in his stomach.

She wasn't *his* mother, he reminded himself.

By midnight, Zoe's feet were screaming. Her back ached, and her arms felt as though she'd been hauling boulders rather than drink trays. She'd deflected six propositions, two of them good-hearted enough to amuse, one of them insulting enough to earn the gentleman in question a bruised instep, courtesy of one of her stiletto heels. The others had been the usual, and easily ignored.

It went with the territory, and it didn't bother her overmuch.

The lounge earned its name from the shadowy effect of neon and all the dim corners. The decor was fifties tacky, and the waitresses were dolled up like old-fashioned mindless floozies to match.

But the tips were excellent, and the clientele, for the most part, harmless.

"Two house wines, white, a Black Russian and a coffee, light." After calling out her order to the bartender, Zoe took a moment to roll her shoulders.

She hoped Beth had gotten Keenan to bed without any fuss. He'd been cranky all day—which meant he was nearly over his sniffles. He'd put up quite a fuss that morning, Zoe remembered, when she'd nixed the idea of him going to school.

Didn't get that from me, she thought. She'd never fussed about not going to school. Now, at twenty-five, she deeply regretted letting her education slide. If she'd applied herself, tried for college, she could have developed a skill, had a career.

Instead, she had a high school diploma she'd barely earned, and was qualified for little more than serving drinks to men whose eyes tried to crawl down her cleavage.

But she wasn't one for regrets. She'd done what she'd

done, and she had the greatest prize of all. Keenan. In a couple of years, she figured, she'd have saved enough that she could turn in her bustier and take a night course. Once she had a few business courses under her belt, she could open her own flower shop. And she wouldn't have to leave Keenan with sitters at night.

She served her drinks, took an order from another table and thanked God her break was coming up in five minutes.

When she saw Coop walk in, her first thought was Keenan. But the sick alarm passed almost as quickly as it had come. Coop was relaxed, obviously scoping the place out. When his eyes met hers, he nodded easily and made his way through the scattered tables.

"I thought I'd stop in for a drink."

"This is the place for it. Do you want to sit at the bar, or do you want a table?"

"A table. Got a minute?"

"At quarter after I've got fifteen of them. Why?"

"I'd like to talk to you."

"Okay. What can I get you?"

"Coffee, black."

"Coffee, black. Have a seat."

He watched her head toward the bar and tried not to dwell on how attractive she looked walking away. He hadn't come in because he wanted a drink, but because she seemed like a nice woman in a tight skirt—spot, he corrected. A tight spot.

Get hold of yourself, Coop, he warned himself. He knew better than to let a pair of long legs cloud his judgment. He'd only come in to ask a few questions, get the full story. That was what he did, and he was good at it. Just as he was good at dissecting a game, any game, and finding those small triumphs and small mistakes that influenced the outcome.

"We've been busy tonight." Zoe set two coffees on the table before sliding onto a chair across from Coop. She let out a long, heartfelt sigh, then smiled. "This is the first time I've been off my feet in four hours."

"I thought you worked in a flower shop."

"I do, three days a week." She slid her cramped feet out of her shoes. "Around Mother's Day, Christmas, Easter—you know, the big flower days, I can squeeze in more." She sipped the coffee she'd loaded with sugar and let it pump into her system. "It's just a small shop, and Fred—that's the owner—only keeps on a couple of part-timers. That way he doesn't have to pay any of the bennies, like hospitalization, sick leave."

"That's lousy."

"Hey, it's a job. I like it. It's just Fred and Martha—she's his wife. They've taught me a lot about flowers and plants."

Someone pumped quarters into the jukebox. The room heated up with music. Coop leaned over the table so that she could hear him. For a moment he lost the thread somewhere in her big brown eyes.

"Have I met you somewhere before?" he asked her.

"In the apartment."

"No, I mean…" He shook his head, let it go. "Uh, why here?"

"Why here what?"

"Why do you work here?"

She blinked, those long lashes fluttering down, then up. "For a paycheck."

"It doesn't seem like you should be working in a bar."

"Excuse me?" Zoe wasn't sure if she should be amused or insulted. She chose the former simply because it was her nature. "Do you have a problem with cocktail waitresses?"

"No, no. It's just that, you're a mother."

"Yes, I am. I have a son to prove it." She laughed and leaned her chin on her fist. "Are you thinking it would be more appropriate for me to be home baking cookies or knitting a scarf?"

"No." Though it embarrassed him that he did. "It's that outfit," he blurted out. "And the way all these men look at you."

"If a woman's going to wear something like this, men are going to look. Looking's all they do," she added. "If it makes you feel better, I don't dress like this for PTA meetings."

He was feeling more ridiculous every second. "Look, it's none of my business. I just have a habit of asking questions. Seems to me you could do better than this. I mean, you've got the flower job, and the rent—"

"And I have a mortgage, a son who seems to outgrow his clothes and shoes every other week, a car payment, grocery bills, doctor bills."

"Doctor? Is the kid sick?"

Zoe rolled her eyes. Just when she was starting to get irritated, he deflated her. "No. Kids Keenan's age are always bringing some germ or other home from school. He needs regular checkups with his pediatrician, with the dentist. Those things aren't free."

"No, but there are programs. Assistance." He

stopped, because those big brown eyes had turned fierce.

"I'm perfectly capable of earning a living, and of taking care of my child."

"I didn't mean—"

"Maybe I don't have a college degree or any fancy skills, but I can pay my own way, and my son doesn't lack for anything." She jammed her feet into the backbreaking heels and stood. "We've been doing just fine on our own, and I don't need some nosy jock reporter coming in here and telling me how to be a mother. Coffee's on the house, you jerk."

He winced as she stormed away from the table, then let out a long breath. Handled that one *real* well, Coop.

He wondered if there would be an eviction notice on his door in the morning.

Chapter 4

She didn't kick him out. She had thought of it, but had decided the satisfaction she'd gain didn't quite equal the rental income. Besides, she'd heard it all before.

One of the reasons she'd moved from New York was that she'd grown impossibly weary of friends and family telling her how to run her life. How to raise her son.

Baltimore had been a clean slate.

She'd had enough money put aside to afford a nice two-bedroom apartment and invest the rest. And because she was willing to work at any job, and work hard, she'd rarely been unemployed. It had been difficult for her to put Keenan in day care. But he'd thrived. He had his mother's knack for making friends.

Now, two years after the move, she had a house, and

a yard, in the kind of neighborhood she wanted for her son. And she'd paid for every bit of it on her own.

Too many people had told her she was crazy, that she was too young, that she was throwing her life and her chances away. With a grunt, Zoe shoved the lawn mower around and began to cut another strip of grass. *Her* grass, she thought with clenched teeth.

She'd proved them wrong. She'd had her baby, kept her baby, and she was making a decent life for him. She and Keenan weren't statistics. They were a family.

They didn't need anyone to feel sorry for them, or to offer handouts. She was taking care of everything, one step at a time. And she had plans. Good, solid plans.

The tap on her shoulder made her jump. When she whipped her head around and looked at Coop, her hands tightened on the mower. "What?"

"I want to apologize," he shouted. When she only continued to glare at him, he reached down and shut off the engine. "I want to apologize," he repeated. "I was out of line last night."

"Really?"

"I'm sort of addicted to poking into other people's business."

"Maybe you should go cold turkey." She reached down to grab the pull cord. His hand closed over hers. She stared at it a moment. He had big hands, rough-palmed. She remembered the impression she'd gotten of strength and energy. Now the hand was gentle and hard to resist.

She hadn't felt a man's hands—hadn't wanted to feel a man's hands—in a very long time.

"Sometimes I push the wrong buttons," Coop continued. He was staring at their hands, as well, thinking how small hers felt under his. How soft. "It's earned me a fist in the face a time or two." He tried a smile when her gaze slid up to his.

"That doesn't surprise me."

She didn't smile back, but he sensed a softening. The roar of the mower had awakened him. When he'd looked out and seen her marching along behind it in baggy shorts, a T-shirt and a ridiculous straw hat, he'd wanted to go back to bed. But he'd been compelled to seek her out.

It was only a flag of truce, he told himself. After all, he had to live with her. More or less.

"I didn't mean to be critical. I was curious about you. And the kid," he added quickly. "And maybe seeing you in that outfit last night pushed a few of my buttons."

She lifted a brow. That was honest enough, she thought. "All right. No permanent damage."

It had been easier than he'd expected. Coop decided to press his luck. "Listen, I've got to cover the game this afternoon. Maybe you'd like to come along. It's a nice day for baseball."

She supposed it was. It was warm and sunny, with a nice, freshening breeze. There were worse ways to spend the day than in a ballpark with an attractive man who was doing his best to pry his foot out of his mouth.

"It sounds like fun—if I didn't have to work. But Keenan would love it." She watched his jaw drop, and smothered a smile.

"Keenan? You want me to take him?"

"I can't think of anything he'd rather do. Some of the kids play in their yards, and they let him chase the

ball. But he's never seen the real thing, except on TV."
She smiled now, guilelessly, and held back a hoot of
laughter. She could all but see Coop's mind working.

"I don't know too much about kids," he said, back-
pedaling cautiously.

"But you know about sports. It'll be great for Keenan
to experience his first real game with an expert. When
are you leaving?"

"Ah…a couple of hours."

"I'll make sure he's ready. This is awfully nice of
you." While he stood staring, she leaned over and kissed
his cheek. After one hard tug, she had the mower roar-
ing again.

Coop stood planted like a tree when she strolled
away. What the hell was he supposed to do with a kid
all afternoon?

He bought popcorn, hot dogs and enormous cups of
soft drinks. Coop figured food would keep the kid quiet.
Keenan had bounced on the seat of the car throughout
the drive to Camden Yards, and since they had arrived
he'd goggled at everything.

Coop had heard "What's that?" and "How come?"
too many times to count. Nervous as a cat, he settled
into the press box with his laptop.

"You can watch through the window here," he instructed Keenan. "And you can't bother anybody, because they're working."

"Okay." Almost bursting with excitement, Keenan
clutched his hot dog.

There were lots of people in the press box, some with
neat computers, like Coop, others with headphones. A

few of them had smiled at him, and all of them had said hello to Coop. Keenan knew Coop was important. As his mother had instructed, he kept close and didn't ask for any presents. Even though there had been really neat stuff at the stands. His mother had given him five whole dollars and told him he could buy a souvenir. But there'd been so many he didn't know which to pick. And Coop had walked so fast he'd hardly been able to look.

But it didn't matter, because he was at a real ball game.

Wide-eyed, he stared down at the field. It was bigger than anything he'd imagined. He knew where the pitcher would stand, and he recognized home plate, but he wasn't sure of anything else.

The big scoreboard exploded with pictures, and words he couldn't read. Circling it all were the stands, filled with more people than he'd ever seen.

When they announced the lineup, he looked down at the players with naked admiration. The national anthem began, and, recognizing it, Keenan stood up, as he'd been taught.

Coop glanced over, saw the boy standing, with a hot dog in one hand and a big, dazzling grin on his face. Suddenly he remembered his first time at a ballpark. His eager hand gripping his father's, his eyes trying to see everything at once, and his heart so full of the excitement, of the game, of just being a boy.

As the players took the field, Coop reached over and tugged on Keenan's bright hair. "Pretty cool, huh?"

"It's the best ever. Those are our guys, right?"

"Those are our guys. They're gonna kick butt."

Keenan giggled and leaned closer to the glass to watch the first pitch. "Kick butt," he said with relish.

He didn't, as Coop had expected, fidget, whine or make a general nuisance of himself. Because he was accustomed to working under noisy and confusing conditions, Keenan's constant questions didn't annoy him overmuch. At least, he thought, the kid had the good sense to ask.

Between innings, Keenan peered over Coop's shoulder and sounded out the words that were popping up on the computer screen, and he did transfer some mustard from his hands onto Coop's sleeve. But it wasn't the disaster Coop had envisioned.

Coop even felt a quick tug of pride when the play-by-play announcer called Keenan over and let the boy sit in his lap for an inning.

Most kids would've been running around the booth begging for more candy. But this one, Coop thought, had come for the game.

"How come he didn't run all the way? How come he didn't?" Keenan shifted from foot to foot. His bladder was past full, but he couldn't bear to miss a minute.

"The throw went to second, so he was forced out," Coop explained. "See, the second baseman caught the ball and stepped on the bag to retire the side."

"Retire the side," Keenan repeated reverently. "But we're still winning?"

"The O's are up by one going into the top of the ninth. Looking at the batting order, I'd say they'll put in a southpaw."

"Southpaw," Keenan repeated, as if it were gospel.

"A left-handed reliever. Probably Scully." He glanced

over and noted that Keenan was holding his crotch. "Uh, got a problem?"

"Nuh-uh."

"Let's hit the john—the bathroom." He took Keenan's hand and hoped it wasn't too late. As they passed through the door, Scully was announced as the relief.

"Just like you said." Keenan looked up at Coop with dazzling admiration. "You're smarter than anybody."

Coop felt a grin break out over his face. "Let's just say I know the game."

When they arrived home, Keenan was wearing a new Orioles jersey and carrying an autographed baseball in a pint-size baseball glove. He waved a pennant in his other hand as he scrambled up the steps.

"Look! Look what Coop got me!" He barreled into his mother who'd barely walked in the door herself. "We went into the locker room with the real Orioles, and they signed the baseball for me. To keep."

"Let's see." She took the ball and examined it. "This is really special, Keenan."

"I'm gonna keep it forever. And I got this shirt, too, like they wear. And a glove. It even fits."

Emotion backed up in her throat. "It certainly does. Looks like you're all ready to play ball."

"I'm gonna play third base, 'cause it's the...the..."

"Hot corner," Coop supplied.

"Yeah. Can I go show Mr. Finkleman? Can I show him my baseball?"

"Sure."

"He's gonna be surprised." He turned and threw his arms around Coop's legs. "Thanks, thanks for taking me. I liked it best of anything. Can we go again, and take Mama?"

"Uh, yeah, I guess. Sure." Feeling awkward again, he patted Keenan's head.

"Okay!" Giving Coop one last squeeze, Keenan raced out the door to show off his treasures.

"You didn't have to buy him all that stuff," Zoe began. "Taking him was enough."

"No big deal. He didn't ask for it, or anything." Coop stuck his hands in his pockets. "He got such a charge out of meeting the players, and one thing kind of led to another."

"I know. I hear our team won."

"Yeah. Clipped them by one. I had to stop by the paper and file the story, or we'd have been here sooner."

"I just got in myself." On impulse, she walked over, wrapped her arms around him and hugged. Coop's hands stayed paralyzed in his pockets. "I owe you. You gave him a great day. He won't forget it." She drew back. "Neither will I."

"It's no big deal. He just hung out in the press box."

"It's a very big deal, especially since I trapped you into it." She laughed and tossed back her hair. "You were so transparent this morning, Coop. The idea of having a four-year-old tagging along terrified you. But you did good, real good. Anyway— Sorry," she said when the phone rang. "Hello? Oh, hi, Stan. Tonight? I'm not scheduled." Letting out a breath, she sat on the arm of a chair. "I'll have to let you know. No, Stan, I can't tell you now. I have to see if I can find a sitter. An hour, then. Yes, I understand you're in a jam. I'll call you back."

"Problem?"

"Hmmm… Two of the waitresses called in sick for tonight. They're short-staffed." She was already dialing the phone. "Hi, Mrs. Finkleman. Yeah, I know. He had a great time. Mmm-hmm…" Zoe's gaze flicked up to Coop as Mrs. Finkleman told her how important it was for a boy to have a man in his life. "I'm sure you're right. I was wondering if you're busy tonight. Oh. That's right, I forgot. No, it's nothing. Have a good time."

Zoe hung up and pursed her lips. "It's their bingo night," she told Coop. "Beth's got a date. Maybe Alice." She reached for the phone again, shook her head. "No, she's having her in-laws over for dinner." Her eyes lit on Coop and narrowed in speculation. "You didn't have any problem with Keenan today."

"No," Coop said slowly, wary of another trap. "He was cool."

"Stan doesn't need me in until nine. Keenan goes to bed at eight, so you wouldn't have to do anything but hang around, watch television or whatever."

"Hang around here, while you work?" He took a step back. "Just me and the kid—like a babysitter? Listen…"

"I'll pay you. Beth gets two an hour, but I can up the ante."

"I don't want your money, Zoe."

"That's so sweet." She smiled, took his hand and squeezed. "Really, so sweet of you. If you could come down about eight-thirty."

"I never said—"

"You can help yourself to anything in the kitchen. I'll make some brownies, if I have time. I'd better call Stan back before he pulls out what's left of his hair."

She picked up the phone, beamed at Coop. "Now I owe you two."

"Yeah, right." He hurried out before she could find some way to owe him three.

Chapter 5

For the next couple of hours, Coop immersed himself in "All in the Game," his weekly syndicated column. The kid had given him the hook, he thought. The first visit to a ball game, the passing on of tradition, and the bond that was forged over the cheers, the crack of the bat, the peanut shells.

It was a good piece, Coop decided, and wrote easily. He supposed since he owed the idea to Keenan the least he could do was hang around downstairs and eat brownies while the kid slept.

He wandered back down just as Zoe came through the kitchen door.

She hadn't been sure he'd come. She knew she'd hustled him, and after she'd finished being amused by it, she felt guilty. But here he was, right on time, standing at the foot of the steps.

"I pushed you into a corner..." she began.

"Yeah, you did." She looked so somber, he had to smile. "You've got a real talent for it."

She shrugged her shoulders and smiled back at him. "Sometimes being pushy's the only way to get things done, but I always feel bad about it after. I did bake brownies."

"I could smell them all the way upstairs." When she didn't move, he tilted his head. Funny, though she was wearing that sexy waitress rig again, she didn't seem so outrageous. Except for that bow tie, he thought. Something about that black tie around that slim white throat shot straight to his libido.

"You going to let me in, or do you want me to stand out here?"

"I have this guilt thing," she explained, "whenever I have to ask anyone for a favor. And it was so sweet of you to take Keenan to the game, especially when..."

"When I'd been asking you out?"

She shrugged her shoulders again, let them fall. He was looking at her that way again, and something in her body was reacting helplessly. Better, she thought, to set the rules quickly. "I don't go out with men. I should have told you straight out."

He had to force himself not to lift a hand to that neat little bow and tug. "At all?"

"It's just easier not to. They're not interested in Keenan, or they pretend they are so they can talk me into bed." When he rocked back on his heels and cleared his throat, she laughed. "What they don't know is that they're clear as cellophane. You see, Keenan and I are a team. As a sportswriter, you should know what that means."

"Sure. I get it."

"Anyway, you gave him a really wonderful day, and I feel like I'm twisting your arm about tonight."

He decided, after a moment, that she wasn't doing it on purpose. There was just too much sincerity in that glorious face for a con. And if there was a twinge of guilt because he had given considerable thought to talking her into bed, that was his problem.

"Look, he's asleep, right?"

"Yes. All the excitement wore him out."

"So, I'll eat your brownies and watch your TV. No big deal."

Her smile came easily now, beautifully, and made his mouth water. "I left the number of the club by the phone, just in case. The Finklemans should be home by eleven. She'd come over and relieve you if you want."

"We'll play it by ear."

"Thanks, really." She stepped back into the kitchen to let him in. "My shift ends at two, at closing."

"Long day for you."

"I've got tomorrow off." After grabbing her purse, she took a quick look around. "Make yourself at home, okay?"

"I will. See you."

She hurried out, those incredibly sexy heels clicking across the tile. Coop let out a long breath and told himself to settle down. The lady had just set the ground rules. Fun and games were out.

She had the face of a siren, the body of a goddess,

and legs designed to make a strong man whimper—but deep in her heart she was Betty Crocker.

Coop took a deep sniff and decided to content himself with a plate of double fudge brownies.

The storm rolled in just before midnight. Coop had taken Zoe at her word and made himself at home. He was stretched out on her couch, sunk deep in the cushions, with his feet propped comfortably on her coffee table. He was dozing in front of an old war movie, his only regret being that he hadn't thought to bring a couple of beers down with him.

Zoe's selection ran to milk, juice and some unidentified green liquid.

He'd poked around a little—it was simply in his nature. The clutter ran throughout the house, but he began to see a pattern to it. Obviously she wasn't a detail person, but the general lack of order made the house comfortable, even cozy. Coop wasn't sure if the result was by design or simply because she was a woman who worked two jobs and had a kid to raise.

And from the library books he'd found stacked here and there, it seemed she spent most of her free time reading up on flowers, car repair, tax laws and time management.

He couldn't help but think it was a waste of a perfectly stunning woman, this voluntary burial of self in books and nowhere part-time jobs.

But it wasn't his problem.

The crash of thunder from outside harmonized nicely with the artillery barrage on the TV screen. Coop had just decided that this baby-sitting racket was a snap.

Then he heard the wailing.

Marines didn't wail, he thought fuzzily, especially when they were battling Nazi scum. He yawned, circled his neck until it cracked, then spotted Keenan.

The boy stood at the base of the stairs in Batman pajamas, a battered stuffed dog clutched in one arm and tears pouring down his face.

"Mama!" His voice sharpened like an ice pick, then hitched. "Where's my mama?"

"She's at work." Coop straightened on the sofa and stared helplessly. "Something wrong?"

A flash of lightning lit the room. By the time the thunder rolled in answer, Keenan screamed like a banshee and launched himself into Coop's lap.

"I'm scared. There's monsters outside. They're coming to get me."

"Hey…" Coop gave the head buried in his chest an inadequate pat. "Hey, it's just a thunderstorm."

"Monsters," Keenan sobbed. "I want Mama."

"Well, she's—" He started to swear, caught himself. The poor kid was shaking. With an instinct he didn't recognize, Coop cuddled Keenan in his lap. "You don't like storms, huh?" All Keenan could do was shake his head and burrow deeper. "They're just like fireworks. You know, on the Fourth of July, or after your team wins the pennant? They probably just had a big game up there. They're celebrating."

"Monsters," Keenan repeated, but he'd calmed enough to lift his head and look at Coop. "Big black monsters with sharp teeth." He jolted at the next clap of thunder. Fresh tears started to roll. "They want to eat me."

"Nah." Experimentally, Coop tested Keenan's biceps. "You're too tough."

"I am?"

"You bet. Any monsters who looked in here would see you and run for their lives. They'd never take on Coop and the Keen-man."

Keenan sniffled, rubbed a fist over his eyes. "Really?"

"Absolutely." Coop saw Keenan's lower lip tremble when thunder grumbled. "Home run," he said, and Keenan's trembling mouth curved in a hesitant smile.

"Can I stay out here with you?"

"Sure. I guess."

Keenan, an expert in such matters, settled himself comfortably in Coop's lap, laid his head against Coop's heart and sighed.

Zoe was swaying with fatigue by the time she let herself in. It was nearly 3:00 a.m., and she'd been up and going for twenty hours straight. All she wanted was to fall facedown on her bed and sleep.

She saw them in the gray light of the snowy television screen. They were curled together on the couch, the boy snuggled deep against the man. Something shifted inside her at the sight of them, both sleeping deeply, Keenan's tousled golden hair beneath Coop's broad, tanned hand.

She set her purse and her keys aside without taking her eyes off them.

How small her son looked, and how safe.

She slipped out of her shoes and walked to them on stockinged feet. In a natural gesture, she brushed a hand over Coop's hair before gently lifting her son. Keenan stirred, then settled against her.

"Mama."

"Yes, baby," she murmured. She nuzzled him as she carried him away, caught the scent of man mixed with boy.

"The monsters came, but we scared them away."

"Of course you did."

"Coop said the thunder's just fireworks. I like fireworks."

"I know." She laid him in his bed, smoothing the sheets, his hair, kissing his soft cheeks. "Go back to sleep now."

But he already had. She watched him a moment longer in the faint glow of his night-light, then turned and went back downstairs to Coop.

He was sitting up now, his head in his hands, the heels rubbing against his eyes. She switched off the buzzing television set, then sat on the arm of the couch. Any man who could sleep so comfortably with a child, to her mind, had unlimited potential.

She wondered, just for an instant, what it would feel like to curl up beside him.

"The storm woke him?"

"Yeah." His voice was rusty. He cleared it. "He was pretty spooked."

"He said you chased the monsters away."

"Seemed like the right thing to do." He turned his head to look at her. Those big brown eyes were sleepy and smiling. The quick hitch in his heartbeat warned him to be on his way. But he lingered. "He's okay now?"

"He's fine. You'd make a good daddy."

"Oh, well…" That had him moving. He stood, working out the kinks. "That's not my line. But it was no big deal."

"It was to me." She'd embarrassed him, she noted, and she hadn't meant to. "Why don't I fix you breakfast tomorrow?"

"Huh?"

"Pay you back with pancakes. Mrs. Finkleman tells me you bring in a lot of pizza and Chinese, so I don't imagine you cook. Do you like pancakes?"

"Who doesn't?"

"Then let me know when you're up and around. I'll flip some for you." She lifted a hand, brushed the hair from his brow. "Thanks for helping me out."

"No problem." He took a step away, swore under his breath and turned back. "Listen, I've just got to do this, okay?"

Before she could respond, he took her face in his hands and closed his mouth over hers.

The kiss was quick, and it was light, and it sent sparks snapping down her nerve ends.

When she didn't move a muscle, he lifted his head, looked at her. She was staring at him, her eyes heavy and dark. He thought he saw the same stunned reaction in them that was curling somewhere in his gut. She opened her mouth as if to speak, but he shook his head and kissed her again. Longer, deeper, until he felt her bones begin to melt. Until he heard the small whimper of pleasure purr in her throat.

Her hands slid up his arms, gripped, then moved up to tangle in his hair. They stood there, locked against each other.

One of them quivered, perhaps both. It didn't seem to matter as the warm taste of her seeped into his mouth, into his blood. It was like a dream that he hadn't yet shaken off, one that tempted him to sink back in, to forget reality.

She'd forgotten it. All she knew for one glorious moment was that she was being held in strong arms, that her mouth was being savored wonderfully, and that needs, so long dormant, were swimming to the surface and breaking into life.

Touch me. She wondered if she said it, or if the words simply whirled hazily in her head. But his hand, hard and sure, ran once down her body, kindling fires.

She remembered what it was to burn, and what it was like when the flames died out and left you alone.

"Coop." Oh, she wanted, so badly, just to let it happen. But she wasn't a young, reckless girl this time. And she had more to think of than herself. "Coop. No."

His mouth clung to hers for another moment, his teeth nipping. But he drew back. He was, he realized, as breathless as a man who'd slid headfirst into home plate.

"Now I'm supposed to say I'm sorry."

She shook her head. "No, you're not. I'm not."

"Good." The hands that were resting on her shoulders kneaded once, then slipped away into his pockets. "Me neither. I've been thinking about doing that since I first saw your feet."

Her brows rose. Surely she'd heard him wrong. "My what?"

"Your feet. You were standing on the ladder, painting. You weren't wearing any shoes. You've got tremendously sexy feet."

"Really?" It amazed her that he could tie her into helpless knots one minute, then make her laugh the next. "Thanks. I think."

"I guess I'd better go."

"Yeah, you'd better."

He nodded, started out. This time, when he stopped, she braced, and she yearned. But he simply turned and looked at her. "I'm not going to try to talk you into bed. But I want you there. I figured I should let you know."

"I appreciate it," she said in a shaky voice.

When the door closed behind him, she let her weak legs fold and sat down on the couch. What, she asked herself, was she supposed to do now?

Chapter 6

When Coop dragged himself out of bed, it was nearly noon. He stumbled into the shower and nearly drowned himself before both of his eyes opened. Wet and out of sorts, he rubbed himself down, gave a moment's thought to shaving, then dismissed the idea.

He tugged on gym shorts and a T-shirt before heading directly to the coffeemaker. While it brewed, he opened his front door and let the full power of the sun shock him the rest of the way awake.

They were in the yard, Zoe and Keenan, laughing as mother tried to help son hit fungoes with a plastic bat. The kid wasn't having much luck, Coop noted. But he was sure having fun. He started to step back inside before either of them spotted him. But the jock in him had him kibitzing.

"He'll never hit anything standing that way," Coop called out, and had two pairs of big brown eyes looking up in his direction.

"Hi, Coop. Hi. I'm playing baseball." Thrilled to have an audience, Keenan waved his bat and nearly caught his mother on the chin.

"Watch it, champ," she said, and shifted out of range. "Good morning," she called out. "Want your breakfast?"

"Yeah, maybe."

Keenan took another pathetic swing and had Coop muttering under his breath. Swung like a girl. Somebody had to show the kid how to hold a bat, didn't they? he asked himself as he started down.

"You're choking it too much."

Zoe's brows drew together. "The book I got said—"

"Book." He cursed automatically. Keenan echoed him. "Sorry," he muttered when Zoe gave him a narrow-eyed look. "Now listen, you learn how to add and subtract from books. You don't learn baseball. Just like a girl." He crouched down and adjusted Keenan's hands.

Zoe had been ready to concede to the expert, but the last statement stopped her. "Excuse me? Are you implying that females can't play sports?"

"Not what I said. Swing from the shoulders," he told Keenan. Coop might have been grouchy, but he wasn't stupid. "There are plenty of terrific female athletes. Keep your eye on the ball, kid." He kept one hand around Keenan's and lightly tossed the ball up in the air with the other. The bat connected with a hollow thud.

"I hit it! I hit it really, really hard!"

"Major league stuff." Coop slid his eyes back up to Zoe's. "I thought you were making pancakes."

"I was— I am." She blew out a breath. "I guess you're taking over."

"Well, I don't know diddly about pancakes, and you don't know squat about baseball. Why don't we both do what we know'?"

"Like it's a big deal to hit a stupid ball with a stupid bat," she muttered as she strode to the back door.

"You can't do it."

She stopped dead in her tracks, eyes narrowed, turned. "I certainly can."

"Yeah, right. Okay, Keenan, let's try it again."

"I believe it's my turn." Challenge in her every movement, Zoe slipped the bat from her son's hands.

"Are you going to hit it, Mama? Are you?"

"You bet I am." She held out a hand for the ball Coop was holding. She tossed it up, swung, and batted the ball to the chain-link fence bordering the side yard. Keenan let out a cheer and raced to retrieve it.

Coop sniffed, smiled. "Not bad, for a girl. But anybody can hit a fungo."

"Keenan's too young for anything but a plastic ball."

"No, a fungo's when you toss it up yourself and hit it."

"Oh."

"I'm gonna throw it, Coop. You catch."

"Sure, zip it in here."

It took Keenan three tries, running in closer each time, to send the ball anywhere near Coop.

"I suppose you don't think I could hit it if you threw it at me..." Zoe began.

"Pitch it to you," Coop said patiently. "I would pitch it to you."

"All right, pitch it to me, then." She raised the bat.

"Fine, but you might want to turn a little more to the side. That's it," he said, backing away. "Zoe, you're holding the bat like you're going to use it to hammer a nail. Okay, here it comes."

He tossed the ball soft and underhand, but she still had to grit her teeth to keep herself from jerking away. Because her pride and her son's respect for women were at stake, she swung hard. No one was more stunned than Zoe when she connected. Coop snatched the ball an instant before it could smash his nose.

"Well." Zoe handed the bat back to a wide-eyed Keenan, dusted her hands. "I'll go see about those pancakes."

"She hit it really hard," Keenan said admiringly.

"Yeah." Coop watched the back door swing shut behind her. "Your mother's really...something, kid."

"Will you pitch to me, Coop? Will you?"

"Sure. But let's work on that stance, huh? You gotta look like a ballplayer."

When Zoe finished flipping the last pancake on the stack, she looked out the window and saw her son swing the bat. The ball didn't go far, but Coop made a pretense of a diving catch, missing, while Keenan danced gleefully in place.

"Too hot to handle," Coop claimed, and Keenan jumped on top of him. "Hey, there's no tackling in baseball. Football's out of season." He scooped the wriggling boy up and held him upside down. Somewhere along the line, his sour mood had vanished.

* * *

It became a habit to spend time with the boy. Nothing planned, just playing a little catch in the yard or showing Keenan how to dunk baskets in the apartment. It wasn't as though he were attached to the kid, Coop assured himself. But when he had some free time and the boy wanted to hang around, what was the harm? Maybe it was sort of nice to see those big eyes all full of hero worship. And maybe it wasn't so much of a hardship to listen to that rollicking belly laugh Keenan burst into when something struck his fancy.

If the boy sometimes came along with the bonus of his mother, it wasn't exactly a hardship.

The fact was, he had seen a great deal more of Keenan than Zoe since the night of the thunderstorm. She was friendly enough, but she'd been careful—or so it seemed to Coop—not to be alone with him.

That was something he was going to fix, he decided as he shut down his computer.

He grabbed a couple of miniature race cars, some of the flotsam and jetsam of boyhood that Keenan had left in his apartment. If Coop knew Zoe as he thought he was beginning to, the toys would be an easier entry than a bouquet of long-stemmed roses.

Jiggling the cars in his hand, he strode down the steps to knock on her kitchen door.

In the laundry room, Zoe slammed down the lid on the washer. "Who is it?"

"It's Coop."

She hesitated, started the machine. "Come on in. I'll be right out." She hefted a basket of clean laundry, as much out of defense as out of necessity, and went into the kitchen.

God, he looked good. She had really, really tried not to dwell on how good the man looked. So damn male, she thought, the rangy, athletic body, the muscles, the dark, untidy hair, and those wonderful pale green eyes. She wished her heart wouldn't always stutter when he aimed one of his cocky grins in her direction.

"Hi." She plopped the basket on the kitchen table and immediately began busying her hands folding socks.

"Hi." The kitchen was cluttered, as always. She really needed someone to help her organize, he thought. God, she smelled fantastic. "Keenan left these upstairs." Coop set the cars on the table. "I thought he might be looking for them."

"Thanks."

"So where is he?"

"In school."

"Oh, right." Coop knew Keenan's schedule as well as he knew yesterday's box scores. "You just get in from the flower shop?"

"Mmm-hmm… Business is picking up. We've got a couple of weddings. Actually, I could work full-time for the next three weeks, but it just doesn't fit Keenan's schedule."

"What do you mean?" Idly he plucked a shirt from the basket.

"Well, the spring weddings. The arrangements take a lot of extra hands, so Fred asked if I could put in full days for a while."

"So, that's good, right?"

"The school Keenan goes to is really more of a preschool than day care. It doesn't stay open after three. And I have the car pool next week, anyway. Plus, I promised to take him and some of the other kids swimming at the community center on Friday. He's really looking forward to it."

"Yeah, he mentioned it." About twenty times, Coop recalled.

"I don't want to let him down."

"So, I'll do it."

She looked back up, socks dangling from her hands. "What?"

He couldn't believe he'd said that. He stared at her for another moment, then shrugged. "I said I'd do it. It's no big deal. He can hang with me when he gets home from school."

She tilted her head. "Don't you have a job?"

"That's what I call it, since they pay me." He smiled, finding the idea went down easily. "I do most of my writing here, and he could tag along when I go in to the paper or on an interview. He'd probably get a kick out of it."

"I'm sure he would." She narrowed her eyes. Why couldn't she get a handle on J. Cooper McKinnon? "But why would you?"

He wasn't sure he had the answer to that, so he punted. "Why not? He's not that much of a pest."

With a laugh, she went back to her laundry. "Maybe he's not, but you forgot the car pool."

"I can drive. What's the big deal about hauling a bunch of kids to school and back?"

"I can't begin to tell you," she murmured. It was,

perhaps, something every adult should experience for himself. "And the swimming."

"I was captain of the swim team in college. All-state."

She glanced up at that. "I thought you played baseball. Uh, Keenan mentioned it."

"Yeah, I did. Two hundred and twelve RBIs my last season. I played basketball, too, averaged forty-two points a game." He was bragging, Coop realized. Like some gawky teenager trying to impress the head cheerleader. He frowned down at the little cars, began to slide one over the table.

"Keenan says you make great engine noises."

"Yeah, it's a talent."

He'd embarrassed himself, Zoe realized, and she wanted to hug him. "Tell you what. Why don't we take it a day at a time? If you decide you can't handle it—"

His eyes flashed up at that. "I think I can handle one scrawny kid and a few of his pals."

"Okay. If you decide you don't *want* to handle it, no hard feelings."

"Fine. When do you want to start?"

"Tomorrow would be great."

"Okay." That was settled. Now, he thought, it was on to other business. "How about dinner?"

Her eyes widened in surprise. "Um…sure. We're just going to have chicken. I'll probably fry it."

"No." He stepped closer. She stepped back. "I mean, why don't we have dinner? Out. You and me."

"Oh, well…" Good answer, she thought foolishly. Very succinct. She took another step in retreat. "I have to work tonight."

"Tomorrow."

"I don't really go out."

"I've noticed. What are you backing away from, Zoe?"

"You." Annoyed with herself, she held up a hand. And found it pressed against his chest. "I don't want to date anyone. Start anything. I have very good reasons."

"You'll have to tell me about them sometime." He reached up, combed a hand through her hair and loosened the band that held it back.

"You're not going to kiss me again."

"Sure I am." He touched his lips to hers to prove it. His eyes remained open as he drew her lower lip into his mouth, as he used his tongue, his teeth, to tease and seduce. "You've got an incredible mouth."

She couldn't get her breath. Even as she gasped for it, her vision dimmed. It was all she wanted. It seemed her life depended on keeping her lips against his. This wasn't fair, she thought dimly as she began to sink into the glory of sensation. Too long, she told herself. Surely she was reacting this way only because it had been so terribly long since she'd allowed herself to feel only as a woman.

She was melting against him like wax. He hadn't known how painfully erotic it would be to feel that long, lean body go fluid. He'd only meant to kiss her, to test them both, but his hands were already reaching, stroking, exploring.

His touch, those hard, callused hands against her bare skin, all but brought her to her knees.

"I have to think."

"Think later." He pressed his mouth to her throat.

Oh, it was glorious, glorious to ache again. But she knew too well what came from soothing that ache. "Coop, we can't do this."

"Yes, we can. I'll show you."

With a laugh that came out half moan, she turned her head away. "My head's spinning. You have to stop. God, do you have any idea what you're doing to me?"

"I haven't even started. Come upstairs, come upstairs with me, Zoe. I want to feel you under me. I want to feel myself inside you."

"I want to." She trembled, the needs exploding inside her like firebombs. "Coop, I need to think first. I have to think. I haven't been with anyone in five years."

His mouth stopped its desperate journey over her throat. Slowly he drew back to look at her. Her eyes were clouded, and her mouth was swollen and ripe. "No one?"

"No." She swallowed and prayed for her system to level before she gave in to the urge to rip off his clothes and cut loose. "Since before Keenan was born. I feel like all those needs dried up—like old leaves. You've set a match to them, and I don't know how to handle it."

"The kid's father," Coop said carefully. "You're still in love with him."

"No." She might have laughed at that, if she weren't so shaken. "He has nothing to do with it. Well, of course he does, but… I have to sit down." She walked unsteadily to a chair. "I knew this was going to happen. I think I knew it the first time I saw you. There's been no one, because I didn't want anyone. Because Keenan was all that mattered to me. I have plans." That came out as an accusation, and her eyes darkened. "Damn it, I have plans. I want to go back to school. I want to have my own flower shop one day." Her voice began to catch, alarming him.

"Zoe—"

But she barreled right over him. "And everything was going along fine. I got the house. I wanted him to have a house, and a yard, and neighbors. Everyone said I was crazy, that I'd never be able to do it, that I'd be sorry I'd given everything up to raise a child on my own. But I'm not sorry. He's the best thing that ever happened to me. And I've done a good job. Keenan's happy, and he's bright and funny and wonderful. We have a good life, and I know I can make it even better. I haven't needed anyone. And… Oh, God, I'm in love with you."

The hand he'd lifted awkwardly to pat her head froze. "What?"

"Oh, what a mess. What a mess." She plucked a tiny sock out of the laundry basket and wiped her eyes. "Maybe it's just hormones. It could be, you know. But I walked in and you were sleeping with him on the couch. It was so sweet. Then you were kissing me and everything went crazy. Then you're out in the yard looking so smug and male, showing Keenan how to hit that silly ball. And you're eating pancakes and looking at me. I can hardly breathe when you're looking at me."

Somewhere along the line, his mind had gone blank. "I think I missed a step."

"No, you didn't." She sniffled and struggled to get herself under control. "I've just taken too many. It's my fault. You've been nice to Keenan, and you've been honest with me." She sighed, dropped the damp sock in her lap. "Believe me, I know my emotions are my responsibility." Because he was still staring at her, like a man who'd just had the friendly family dog lunge for his throat, she smiled. "I'm sorry, Coop. I shouldn't have dumped all that on you. I didn't even know it was all bottled up."

This time he took a step back. "Zoe, I like the kid. Who wouldn't? And I'm attracted to you. But—"

"There's no need to explain." Steady now, she rose. "Really, there isn't. I don't expect anything from you, and I'm sorry if I made you uncomfortable. But I feel a lot better." And, oddly enough, she did. "When I go to bed with you, we'll understand each other."

"When you—"

"I think we both know that's going to happen," she said calmly. "We both want it to, and it's smarter to face that than to live with all this tension. Keenan's been wanting to spend the night with a friend of his. I'll arrange it." She laughed a little at Coop's expression. "It's a little hard to be spontaneous with a four-year-old around. I hope you don't mind planning out a night together."

"No, I mean, I don't— God, Zoe."

"If you'd rather not, or if you want some time to decide, that's all right."

He studied her face, felt that same greedy tug, and a flare of something entirely different. Entirely new. "No, I want you. Whenever."

"How about Monday night?"

"I've got a twilight doubleheader on Monday." He couldn't believe he was standing here planning out a wild night of love like a dentist's appointment.

"Ah… Wednesday?"

He nodded. "Wednesday's good for me. Do you want to go out somewhere?"

It was sweet, she thought, really sweet of him to ask. "It's not necessary." She laid a hand on his cheek. "I don't need flowers and candlelight. I'll come upstairs after Keenan's settled."

"Good. Fine. I…better get back to work."

"Do you still want to have Keenan tomorrow?"

"Yeah, no problem. Tell him to come on up." Coop backed toward the door as Zoe began folding laundry again. "I guess I'll see you."

She listened to him walk up the steps. He was certainly a mistake, she told herself. But she'd made others. Life got too mundane when you avoided all the wrong turns.

Chapter 7

"He shoots, he scores!" Coop made apropriate crowd noises as Keenan dunked the basket.

"I can do it again! I can, okay?" From his perch on Coop's shoulders, Keenan swung his sneakered feet.

"Okay, you've drawn the foul." Coop scooped the palm-sized ball up and passed it into Keenan's eager hands. "It's game point, kid, ten seconds to play. This free throw is all-or-nothing. Got it?"

"Got it!"

"A hush falls over the crowd as Fleming steps up to the line. He's played the game of his life tonight, but it all comes down to this one shot. He eyes the basket. You eyeing the basket?"

"Eyeing it," Keenan said, with his tongue caught between his teeth.

"He sets…and shoots." Coop winced as the little rubber ball circled the rim, then watched through squinted eyes as it tipped in and dropped through the net.

"And the crowd goes wild!" Coop danced around the sofa while Keenan hooted and clapped on his shoulders. When he dumped the boy on the cushions of the sofa, Keenan let go with one of the rolling belly laughs that always made Coop grin. "You're a natural."

"You shoot it, Coop! You!"

Obliging, Coop executed a quick turnaround jump shot. This wasn't such a bad way to spend a rainy afternoon, he decided. And it helped keep his mind off how he was going to spend the rainy night ahead.

It was Wednesday.

"Okay, time out. I've got to finish up my piece on the track meet."

"Are we going to go to the paper again? It's neat there."

"Not today. I'm going to fax it in when it's done. You watch some tube." Coop hit the remote, then handed it over.

"Can I get a drink?"

"Yeah, there's some of that juice your mom sent up for you. Stay out of trouble, right?"

"Right."

When Coop headed into his office, Keenan scrambled up from the couch. He liked it best when he got to stay with Coop after school. They always got to do something neat, and Coop never asked if he'd washed his hands or said too many cookies would spoil his appetite.

Best of all, he liked when Coop picked him up. It

was different than when his mother did. He liked when she held him, nuzzled him after his bath or rocked him when he had a bad dream. But Coop smelled different, and felt different.

He knew why, Keenan thought as he wandered into the kitchen. It was because Coop was a daddy instead of a mom.

He liked to pretend Coop was his daddy, and figured that maybe if he didn't do anything bad, Coop wouldn't go away.

After a couple of tugs, Keenan had the refrigerator open. He was proud that Coop had hung the pictures he had drawn for him on the door. He peered inside, saw the jug of juice his mother had bought for him. And the green bottles Coop liked.

"B-E-E-R," Keenan said to himself. He remembered that he'd asked Coop if he could have a taste from the bottle, and that Coop had told him he couldn't until he was big. After Coop had let him sniff the beer, Keenan had been glad he wasn't big yet.

There was a new bottle in the fridge today, and Keenan knit his brow and tried to recognize the letters. *C-H-A-R-D-O-N*— There were too many letters to read, so he lost interest.

He took out the jug, gripping it manfully and setting it on the floor. Humming to himself, he dragged a chair over to get cups from the cabinet. One day he'd be as tall as Coop and wouldn't need to stand on a chair. He leaned forward on his toes.

The crash and the howl had Coop leaping up, rapping his knee hard against the desk. Papers scattered as he raced out of the office and into the kitchen.

Keenan was still howling. A chair was overturned, juice was glugging cheerfully onto the floor, and the refrigerator was wide open. Coop splashed through the puddle and scooped Keenan up.

"Are you hurt? What'd you do?" When his only answer was another sob, he stood Keenan on the kitchen table and searched for blood. He imagined gaping wounds, broken bones.

"I fell down." Keenan wriggled back into Coop's arms.

"Okay, it's okay. Did you hit your head?"

"Nuh-uh." With a sniffle, Keenan waited for the kisses he expected after a hurt. "I fell on my bottom." Keenan's lip poked out. "Kiss it."

"You want me to kiss your— Come on, kid, you're joking."

The lip trembled, another tear fell. "You gotta kiss where it hurts. You gotta, or it won't get better."

"Oh, man." Flummoxed, Coop dragged a hand through his hair. He was desperately relieved that no blood had been spilled, but if anyone, anyone, found out what he was about to do, he'd never live it down. He turned Keenan around and made a kissing noise in the air. "Does that do it?"

"Uh-huh." Keenan knuckled his eyes, then held out his arms. "Will you pick me up?"

"Yeah." He didn't feel as ridiculous as he'd expected when the boy's arms went around his neck. "Okay now?"

With his head resting on Coop's shoulder, he nodded. "I didn't mean to do it. I spilled all the juice."

"No big deal." Hardly realizing he did so, Coop

turned his head to brush his lips over Keenan's hair. Something was shifting inside him, creaking open.

"You aren't mad at me? You won't go away?"

"No." What the hell was going on? Coop wondered as unexplored and unexpected emotions swirled inside him. "No, I'm not going anywhere."

"I love you," Keenan said, with the simple ease of a child.

Coop closed his eyes and wondered how a grown man was supposed to handle falling for a four-year-old boy.

Well, here she was, Zoe thought as she stood at the bottom of the steps leading to Coop's apartment. All she had to do was go upstairs, open the door and start an affair. Her stomach clenched.

Silly to be nervous, she told herself, and climbed the first step. She was a normal woman with normal needs. If her emotions were too close to the surface, she would deal with it. It was much more difficult to be hurt when you had no expectations.

She'd had expectations once, but she knew better now.

This was simply a physical attraction between two single, healthy people. She'd nearly backed down a step before she forced herself to move forward. All the practical details had been seen to. Her son was safely tucked away for the night at his sleepover. She'd arranged for birth control—that wasn't an oversight she would make again.

No regrets, she promised herself as she lifted a hand to knock. She knew how useless they were.

He answered so quickly, she nearly jumped. Then they stood and stared at each other.

She'd worn a dress, one of those thin, breezy sundresses designed to make a man give thanks for the end of winter. Her hair was loose, falling over thin raspberry-colored straps and bare, peach-toned shoulders. There were nerves in her eyes.

"Hi." He glanced down to the cordless phone she held. "Expecting a call?"

"What? Oh." She laughed, miserably self-conscious. "No, I just don't like to be out of touch when Keenan's not home."

"He's all settled at his pal's?"

"Yeah." She stepped inside, set the phone on the counter. "He was so excited, he—" She broke off when her sandal stuck to the floor.

Coop grimaced. "I guess I missed some of it. We had a spill."

"Oh?"

"The kid took a tumble, sheared off ten years of my life. No blood lost, though. Just a half gallon of orange juice." When she only smiled, he stepped to the refrigerator. Why in hell was he babbling? "Want some wine?"

"That would be nice." Why, he's as nervous as I am, she realized, and she loved him for it. "Keenan's having a wonderful time staying with you. I have to study the sports pages now just to keep up with what he's talking about."

"He catches on fast."

"So do I. Go ahead," she said as he handed her a glass of wine, "Ask me about stats. I know all about RBIs and ERAs." She took a sip, then gestured with her glass. "I think the Orioles would have taken the second game of that doubleheader the other night if they'd put in a relief pitcher in the second inning."

His lips twitched. "Do you?"

"Well, the starter had lost his stuff, obviously. The guy who was announcing—"

"The play-by-play man."

"Yes, he said so himself."

"So, you watched the game."

"I watch 'Sesame Street,' too. I like to keep up with Keenan's interests." She trailed off when Coop reached out to twine a lock of her hair around his finger.

"He's got a thing for dinosaurs, too."

"I know, I've checked a half dozen books out of the library. We've—" The fingers trailed over her shoulder. "We've been down to the natural history museum twice."

She set the glass aside and fell into his arms.

He kissed her as though he'd been starved for her taste. The impact was fast, deep, desperate. The little purring sounds that vibrated in her throat had his muscles turning into bundles of taut wire.

"I wasn't sure you'd come."

"Neither was I. I—"

"Can't think of anything but you," he said as he swept her off her feet. "I thought we'd take this slow."

"Let's not," she murmured, pressing her lips to his throat as he carried her into the bedroom.

She had a quick impression of Spartan neatness and simple masculine colors and lines before they tumbled onto the bed.

Neither of them was looking for patience. They rolled

together, a tangle of limbs grasping, groping, glorying. The sheer physicality of it, flesh to flesh, mouth to mouth, had Zoe's head reeling. Oh, she wanted to be touched like this, to feel so desperately like a woman, with a man's hand streaking over her, with his lips savoring every thud of her pulse.

So she lost herself. No more nerves, no more fears. And if she loved, it only made the joy of mating more lovely.

She was every man's fantasy. Stunningly responsive, breathlessly aggressive. And so beautiful, he thought. Undraped, the exquisite body was so slim, so perfect, he couldn't believe it had ever carried a child. In the gilded light of dusk, her face was elegant, heart-stopping. Whenever he touched, wherever he touched, he could see the bold echo of her pleasure reflected in her eyes.

He watched those eyes glaze over, felt her body tense, heard her strangled cry of release. Swamped with the power of it, he drove her upward again until they were both panting for air, until she reared up from the bed and wrapped herself around him.

Damp skin slid over damp skin, hungry mouth sought hungry mouth. They rolled over the bed again, moaning, quivering. Then his hands gripped hers, and his mouth crushed her mouth. And he thrust inside her, hard and deep.

She felt the sensation as if it were a lance through her system, painful, glorious. For an instant, neither of them moved, they just stayed tensed and shuddering on the edge.

Then it was all movement, all speed, a wild race that ended with them both plunging deliriously over the finish line.

It wasn't exactly the way he'd imagined, Coop thought. They were sprawled across his bed, Zoe curled against him. The light was nearly gone, and the room was full of shadows.

He'd imagined they would progress to the bedroom by stages. They were both adults and had known that was the ultimate goal, but he'd thought they would move slowly.

Then she'd been standing there smiling, the nerves shining in her eyes... He'd never wanted anything or anyone more in his life.

Still, he thought she deserved more than a quick tussle, however rewarding. But the night was young.

He flexed his arm to bring her head a little closer, brushed his lips over her temple. "Okay?"

"Mmm... At the very least." Her body felt golden. She was surprised her skin didn't glow in the dark.

"I rushed you a little."

"No, perfect timing."

He began to trail a finger up and down her arm. He wanted her again. Good God, his system was already churning to life. A little control, Coop, he ordered himself. "You're going to stay?"

She opened her eyes, looking into his. "Yes."

"I'm going to go get the wine."

"That's good." She sighed as he left the bed. She'd forgotten how to deal with the after, she realized. Or with the before and during, for that matter, she thought with a wry smile. Though she thought she'd done pretty well so far.

She hadn't known how much had been bottled up inside her. Or just how much she'd needed to feel like a woman again. But then, she hadn't known she could love again.

She shifted, slipping under the tangled sheets, automatically lifting them to her breasts when Coop came back with the wine and glasses.

The sight of her in his bed shot to his loins, with a quick detour through the heart. He said nothing, pouring wine, offering her a fresh glass and settling beside her.

"Why haven't you been with anyone?" The moment the question was out, he wished for a rusty knife to hack off his tongue. "Sorry, none of my business."

"It's all right." *Because I haven't fallen in love with anyone before you,* she thought. But that wasn't what he wanted to hear, she knew. Nor was it really what he'd asked.

"You want to know about Keenan's father."

"None of my business," he repeated. "Sorry, it's the reporter in me."

"It was a long time ago—a lifetime ago. I don't mind telling you. I grew up in New York. I think I mentioned that my mother's an actress. I was the result of a second marriage. She's had five. So far."

"Five?"

Zoe chuckled into her wine, sipped. "Clarice falls in love and changes husbands the way some women change hairstyles. My father lasted about four years before they parted amicably. Clarice always has friendly divorces. I didn't see much of him, because he moved to Hollywood. He does commercials and voice-overs mostly. Anyway, I think she was on husband number four when I was in high school. He had some pull with the Towers Modeling Agency. They're pretty big."

"I've heard of them."

"Well, he got me in. I started doing some shoots. And I caught on."

"That's it," Coop said, interrupting her. "I knew I'd seen your face before."

She moved her shoulders. "Five, six years ago, it was hard to avoid it. I did twenty covers in one month, the year after I graduated school."

"Cover of *In Sports,* swimsuit edition."

She smiled. "You've got a good memory. That was six years ago."

He remembered the long, sand-dusted legs, the lush wet red excuse for a bathing suit, the laughing, seductive face. He gulped down wine. "It was a hell of a shot."

"And a long, grueling shoot. Anyway, I was making a lot of money, getting a lot of press, going to lots of parties. I met Roberto at one of them."

"Roberto." Coop grimaced at the sound of the name.

"Lorenzi. Tennis player. You might have heard of him."

"Lorenzi? Sure—took the French Open three years ago in straight sets, then blew Wimbledon in the semis. He's got a bad attitude and likes to race cars and chase women on the side. Hasn't been seeded above twenty-fifth in the last two years. Got some bad press this spring when he tipped back too many vinos and punched out a photographer." Coop started to drink, stopped. "Lorenzi? He's Keenan's father? But he's—"

"A womanizer?" Zoe supplied. "A creep, a rich, spoiled egotist? I know—now. What I saw then was a gorgeous, charming man who sent me roses and jetted me off to Monte Carlo for intimate dinners. I was dazzled. He told me he loved me, that he adored me, worshiped me, he couldn't live without me. I believed him, and we became lovers. I thought, since he was my first, he'd be my only. Anyway, I didn't realize he was already getting tired of me when I found out I was pregnant. When I told him, he was angry, then he was very calm, very reasonable. He assumed I'd want an abortion and agreed to pay all the expenses, even to make the arrangements."

"A real prince."

"It was a logical assumption," Zoe said calmly. "I had a career on fast forward, in a field that wouldn't wait while I put on weight and suffered from morning sickness. He, of course, had no intention of marrying me, and thought, rightly enough, that I knew the rules of the game. I did know them," she said quietly. "But something had changed when the doctor confirmed the pregnancy. After the disbelief, the panic, even the anger, I felt good. I felt right. I wanted the baby, so I quit my job, moved away from New York and read everything I could get my hands on about parenting."

"Just like that?"

"Well, there were some scenes, some dire predictions, and a lot of anger, but that's how it worked. Roberto and I parted less than amicably, but with the agreement that he would stay out of my life and I would stay out of his."

"What have you told Keenan?"

"It's tough." And it never failed to make her feel guilty. "So far I've just told him his father had to go away, that he wasn't going to come back. He's happy, so he doesn't ask a lot of questions."

"Are you? Happy?"

"Yes." She smiled and touched his cheek. "I am. All my life I wanted a home, a family, something solid and settled. I didn't even know it until Keenan. He changed my life."

"No urge to go back and smile for the camera?"

"Oh, no. Not even a twinge."

He cupped a hand behind her neck, studying her. "It's such a face," he murmured. Right now he liked the idea of having it all to himself.

Chapter 8

The concept of car pools obviously had been devised by someone with a foul and vicious sense of humor. Having lived most of his life in cities where public transportation or a quick jog would get a man from his home to his office, Coop had never experienced the adult version.

But he'd heard rumors.

Arguments, petty feuds, crowded conditions, spilled coffee.

After a week as designated driver, Coop had no doubt the kiddie version was worse. Infinitely worse.

"He's pinching me again, Mr. McKinnon. Brad's pinching me."

"Cut it out, Brad."

"Carly's looking at me. I told her to stop looking at me."

"Carly, don't look at Brad."

"I'm going to be sick. Mr. McKinnon, I'm going to be sick right now."

"No, you're not."

Though Matthew Finney made gagging noises that had the other kids screeching, Coop gritted his teeth and kept driving. Matt threatened to be sick twice a day unless he rode in the front seat. After five miserable days Coop had his number. But that did very little to soothe his nerves.

Keenan, who had waited all week for his turn in the front, swiveled in his seat to make monster faces at Matt. This incited a small riot of elbow jabs, howls, screaming giggles and shoves.

"Keenan, turn around!" Coop snapped. "You guys straighten up back there. Cut it out! If I have to stop this car…" He trailed off, shuddered. He'd sounded like his own mother. Now Coop was afraid *he* would be sick. "Okay, first stop. Matt, scram."

Fifteen minutes later, his backseat thankfully empty, Coop pulled into the drive and rested his throbbing head on the steering wheel. "I need a drink."

"We got lemonade," Keenan told him.

"Great." He reached over to unbuckle Keenan's seat belt. All he needed was a pint of vodka to go with it.

"Can we go swimming again soon?"

The idea of taking a herd of screaming kids back to the community pool anytime within the next century had a stone lodging in Coop's heart. "Ask your mother."

Coop started to look in the backseat and realized

he couldn't face it. Earlier in the week he'd made that
mistake, and discovered wads of chewing gum on the
rug, cookie crumbs everywhere, and a mysterious green
substance smeared on the seat.

In his weakened state, even a candy wrapper was
likely to tip the balance.

"Yoo-hoo!" Mrs. Finkleman stripped off her flowered garden gloves and headed across the lawn in a
flowing tent dress and electric-blue sandals. "How was
your swim, little man?"

"We had races, and Brad dunked Carly and made her
cry even though Coop told him not to, and I can hold
my breath underwater for twelve seconds."

"My goodness." She laughed and ruffled Keenan's
hair. "You'll be in the Olympics next." Her shrewd eyes
took in Coop's haggard face. "You look a little frazzled, Coop. Keenan, why don't you run in and tell Mr.
Finkleman you want a piece of that cherry cobbler he
baked today?"

"Okay!" He tugged on Coop's hand. "Do you want
some? Do you wanna come?"

"I'll pass. You go ahead."

Mrs. Finkleman chuckled as Keenan darted away
and scrambled up the steps. "Little angel. We'll keep
him entertained for a couple of hours—or he'll keep us
entertained. You look like you could use a few minutes
in a quiet room."

"Padded room," Coop muttered. "How does anyone
survive kids?"

"It's easier if you go through the stages with them.
Once you've walked the floor all night with a colicky
baby, nothing much fazes you." She sighed. "Except

science projects. Science projects always took me to the edge. And that first driving lesson." She shook her head at the memory. "That can bring you to your knees." She beamed and patted his arm. "But there's years yet to worry about that. And you've been doing a fine job. Why, Harry and I were just saying how nice it is that Zoe and Keenan have a man in their lives. Not that Zoe hasn't been handling everything. Raising that sweet-natured boy all alone, and working two jobs and tending the house. But it does my heart good to see you and that little angel playing ball in the yard, or the way Zoe lights up when you're around. You make a lovely little family. Now, you go and take a nice nap. We'll keep an eye on your boy."

"I'm not— He's not—" But even as Coop stammered, she was drifting away.

Family? he thought as a ball of ice formed in his stomach. They weren't a family. Oh, no, he promised himself as he walked around the house to his steps. He hadn't taken that on.

He liked the kid, sure. What wasn't to like? And he was damn near nuts about the mother. But that didn't make them a family. That didn't make things permanent. Maybe he'd volunteered to spend time with the kid, taught him a few things about ball, pitched him a few, but that didn't make him Daddy.

He headed straight for the refrigerator, popped the top off a beer and took a long pull.

Sure, maybe he enjoyed having the kid around, and Lord knows he enjoyed being with Zoe. He'd even been sort of pleased when a woman at the pool mistook Keenan for his and commented on what a handsome son he had. But that didn't mean he was going to start thinking about family health insurance or college funds.

He was single. He liked being single. It meant coming and going as he pleased, planning all-night poker games, spending all day with the sports channel blaring.

He liked working in his own space—that was why he did the bulk of his writing at home, rather than at the paper. He didn't like people messing with his things or structuring his time or planning outings.

Family life—as he remembered from his childhood—was lousy with outings.

No way was he changing his nice comfortable existence to accommodate a family.

So he'd made a mistake, Coop decided, and stretched out on the couch with his beer. He'd given Zoe and the kid a little too much of his time, a little too much of his attention. It hadn't been anything he didn't want to give, but he could see now that the gesture could be misconstrued. Particularly since Zoe had once brought up the *L* word. Only once, he reminded himself, and he'd like to think that had just been a woman thing.

Still, if he didn't back off, they might start to depend on him. He shifted uncomfortably as the idea flitted through his mind that he might also come to depend on them.

It was time to reestablish himself as the tenant upstairs.

Keenan raced out of the house next door the minute his mother pulled her car in the drive.

"Hi, Mama, hi! I held my breath for twelve seconds underwater!"

Zoe caught him on the fly and swung him twice. "You must be hiding gills in there," she said, tickling his ribs. "Hi, Mrs. Finkleman."

"Hi yourself. We've had ourselves a fine hour. I sent Coop up for a nap when they got home. He looked like he'd had a rough day."

"Thanks." She kissed Keenan's waiting lips, then smacked her own. "Mmm… Cherries."

"Mr. Finkleman baked them, and they were good."

"I bet. Did you say thank you?"

"Uh-huh. Matt almost throwed up in Coop's car."

"Threw up," Zoe said as she carried Keenan inside.

"Uh-huh. 'Cause it was my turn to ride in the front. I had the best time, and Coop helped me to swim without my bubbles. He said I was a champ."

"That's just what you are." She collapsed with him on a chair. The idea of fixing dinner, changing into her uniform and serving drinks for six hours loomed heavily. "Give me a hug," she demanded, then soothed herself with some nuzzling. "Definitely a champion hugger. Why don't you come in the kitchen and tell me what else you did today while I fix dinner?"

A half hour later, as Zoe was draining pasta and Keenan was entertaining himself with crayons and paper on the kitchen floor, she heard the sound of Coop's feet on the stairs. Her heart sped up. The normal, healthy reaction made her smile. Imagine, she thought, believing herself immune to men.

She left the pasta draining in the sink and went to the back door just as he came to the foot of the steps.

"Hi."

"How's it going?" Coop jingled the keys in his

pocket. Did she look all lit up? he wondered. She was smiling, and despite the shadows of fatigue under them, her eyes did have the prettiest lights in them.

"I was just going to call upstairs. I thought you'd like some dinner after a hard day at the pool." She opened the screen door and leaned out to kiss him. The smile dimmed a bit when he eased back. "It's just chicken and pasta."

It smelled nearly as good as she did. He glanced inside—the homey scene, cluttered counters, fresh flowers, steam rising from a pan on the stove, the child sprawled on the floor, the pretty woman offering him food and kisses.

A definite trap.

"Thanks, but I'm on my way out."

"Oh. I thought you had a couple hours before game time." She laughed at his arched brow. "I guess I've been paying more attention to the sports scene. Baltimore versus Toronto, game one of three."

"Yeah." When she starts to take an interest in *your* interests, she's really shutting the cage door. "I've got some stuff to do."

"Can I go with you?" Keenan dashed to the door to tug on Coop's slacks. "Can I go to the game? I like watching them with you best."

Coop could almost hear the locks clicking into place. "I've got too much to do," he said, with an edge to his voice that had Keenan's lips quivering. "Look, it's not just a game, it's my job."

"You said I was good luck."

"Keenan." Zoe put her hand on her son's shoulder to draw him back, but her eyes stayed on Coop's. "Did you forget Beth was coming over to stay with you to-night? She'll be here soon, and you're going to watch a tape of your favorite movie."

"But I wanna—"

"Now go wash your hands for dinner."

"But—"

"Go on now."

The way Keenan's face crumpled would have soft-ened an ogre's heart. Dragging his feet, he headed out of the kitchen.

"I can't take him with me everywhere..." Coop began defensively.

"Of course not. He's just overtired. I couldn't have let him go, in any case." She hesitated, wishing she could ignore her instincts. "Is everything all right?"

"Everything's fine." He didn't know why he shouted it. He didn't know why he felt like something slimy stuck to the bottom of a shoe. "I have a life, you know. I don't need kids climbing up my back or you fixing me dinner. And I don't have to explain myself."

Her eyes turned very cool, her face very composed. "You certainly don't. I appreciate you helping me out the past couple of weeks. Let me know if I can return the favor."

"Look, Zoe—"

"I've got to get dinner on the table, or I'll be late for work." She let the screen door slam between them. "Enjoy the game."

She knew exactly how long he continued to stand there while she worked at the stove. Knew exactly when he turned and walked away.

It wasn't unexpected, she reminded herself. This

backing away was typical, even understandable. Perhaps it had taken Coop a few weeks to completely comprehend that she didn't come as a single. She was part of a pair, a ready-made family, with its share of responsibilities and problems and routines.

And he was opting out.

He might not even know it yet, she thought, but he was in the first stages of a full retreat.

Her eyes blurred, her chest heaved. Resolutely she choked the tears back. She would indulge herself with a nice long cry later, she promised. But for now she had a little boy to soothe.

When he came back in, she crouched down until they were eye-to-eye.

"You had a good time with Coop today, didn't you?"

Keenan sniffled, nodded.

"And he's taken you a lot of places. You've had fun, and done a lot of new things."

"I know."

"You should be grateful for that, baby, instead of pouting because you can't have more."

She straightened again and hoped she could take her own advice.

Chapter 9

"You're spending a lot of time around here." Ben edged a hip onto the corner of Coop's desk. All around Coop's cubicle phones rang, keyboards clattered.

"So?" Without taking his eyes from the computer screen, Coop hammered out the draft of his weekly column.

"I just figured you had it made in that apartment of yours. I mean, great location." He thought of Zoe. "Great view. You didn't spend as much time in here when you lived downtown."

"I needed a change of scene."

"Yeah." Ben snorted and picked up a baseball from Coop's desk. "Trouble in paradise?"

"I don't know what you're talking about. And I've got a column to write."

"Pretty obvious the last few weeks that you've been stuck on the landlady." He tossed the ball from one hand to the other. "I mean, when a man hauls a kid around, buys little baseball jerseys, it follows that he's hooking a line into Mom."

Coop's eyes flashed up. "I like the kid, okay? I don't have to use a four-year-old to get a woman. The kid's cool."

"Hey, I got nothing against rug rats. Might even have a few of my own one day. The thing is, when a woman's got one, a man has to play Daddy if he wants the inside track."

"Who says I have to play at anything to get a woman?"

"Not me. But it was you who couldn't shoot hoop last week because you were taking the family to the aquarium." Ben winked, set the ball down. "Still, I bet you scored better than I did." Ben jerked back as Coop lunged for his throat.

"It's not like that," Coop said between his teeth.

"Hey, hey. Just yanking your chain. I wouldn't have made any cracks if I'd known you were serious about her."

Coop's grip loosened. "I didn't say I was serious. I said it wasn't like that."

"Whatever you say."

Disgusted with himself, Coop dropped back in his chair. He and Ben had been riding each other about women for better than five years. No reason to overreact, he thought. Or to make a fool of himself. "Sorry. I've got a lot on my mind."

"Forget it. What you need's a distraction. You coming to the poker game tonight?"

"Yeah."

"Good. Losing money should put you back on track."

Something had to, Coop thought as he sat back alone in his cubicle to stare at his screen. For the past three days he'd slept little, eaten less, and gone around in a constant state of flux.

Because he was avoiding the issue, he decided. Opting to bunt, when he should be swinging away. The only solution to getting his life back in order was to face the problem head-on.

He flicked off his terminal.

The beautiful thing about an afternoon off, Zoe thought, was the solitude. No customers to talk to, no orders to fill. It meant she didn't have to be salesclerk, or waitress, or Mom, or anything but Zoe.

Sitting on the back stoop, she struggled to understand the assembly instructions for the new barbecue grill she'd bought. She was going to surprise Keenan with hamburgers.

She liked the quiet—her kind of quiet, which meant there was music throbbing from the kitchen radio. She liked the loneliness—her kind of loneliness, which meant Keenan would dash toward her shortly with open arms and chattering voice.

She knew the upstairs apartment was empty, and she tried not to think about that. Tried not to think about the fact that Coop had been away more than he'd been home in the last few days.

Foolish of her to have thought he was different. He'd

wanted her, he'd had her, and now he'd lost interest. Well, she had wanted him, so they were even there. If her heart was suffering it would pass. It had passed before. She and Keenan could get along fine on their own. Just like always.

Her screwdriver slipped, scraped her knuckles, had her swearing.

"What the hell are you doing?"

Eyes hot, she looked up at Coop. "Baking a cake. What does it look like I'm doing?"

"You can't put something together if you're going to spread parts all over the damn place." Automatically he bent down to organize. She rapped his hand away with the rubber grip of the screwdriver.

"I don't need you to put things together for me. I'm not some poor helpless female who needs a man to pick up the slack. I managed just fine before you came along."

Stung, he rammed his hands in his pockets. "Fine. Do it yourself."

"I am doing it myself. I like doing it myself."

"Terrific. And when the thing topples over, you won't have anyone else to blame."

"That's right." She blew her hair out of her eyes. "I accept when something's my fault." She picked up a wrench and locked a bolt in place. "Do you plan to hover over me all afternoon?"

"I want to talk to you."

"So talk."

He had it well planned. He was a writer, after all. "I realize the way I've been hanging around with you and the kid—"

"His name is Keenan," Zoe said between her teeth.

"I know what his name is. The way I've been hanging around the last few weeks might give the wrong impression."

"Oh, really?" She looked up again, tapping the wrench against her palm.

"He's a great kid, he kind of grows on you. I've gotten a kick out of spending time with him."

Though she hated herself for it, Zoe softened. She understood that he was genuinely fond of Keenan. That only made it all the more difficult. "He likes spending time with you. It's been good for him."

"Well, yeah, on the one hand. On the other, I started thinking that he—that you—that both of you might get the wrong idea. I mean, tossing a ball around or taking him to a game, that's cool. I just don't want him thinking it's like—permanent."

"I see." She was calm now, frigidly so. It would help keep the hurt in check. "You're afraid he might begin to see you as a father figure."

"Well, yeah. Kind of."

"That's natural enough. But then, he spends a lot of time with Mr. Finkleman, too, and with Billy Bowers down the street."

"Finkleman's old enough to be his grandfather, and the Bowers kid is eighteen." Coop backed off, realizing there was a touch of jealousy in the defense. "And they don't have the same sort of thing going with you."

She arched both brows. "Thing?"

"Relationship," he said tightly. "Whatever the hell you want to call it. Damn it, we only slept together once."

"I'm aware of that." Carefully she set the wrench aside. It would give her only momentary pleasure to heave it at his head.

"That came out wrong," he said, furious with himself. "It sounded like it didn't mean anything. It did, Zoe." A great deal, he was afraid. A very great deal. "It's just that…"

"Now you're terrified that Keenan and I will trap you into a family. That you'll wake up one morning and be Daddy, with a wife and a mortgage and a small boy who needs attention."

"Yes. No. Something like that." He was burying himself, he realized, and he suddenly didn't know why. "I just want to make myself clear."

"Oh, I think you have. Perfectly." She rubbed her hands on her knees as she studied him. "You needn't worry, Coop. I advertised for a tenant, not a father for my child, or a husband for myself. I slept with you because I wanted to, not because I thought I could lure you to the altar."

"I didn't mean it like that." Frustrated, he dragged a hand through his hair. However well he'd planned this little scene, it was going all wrong. "I wanted you. I still do. But I know how badly you were let down before. I don't want to hurt you, Zoe. Or the kid. I just don't want you thinking I'd slide into the gap."

The anger came back, one swift wave of it that reddened her vision. She was on her feet before either of them realized she'd moved. "Keenan and I don't have a gap. We're a family, as real and as complete and as full a family as any could be." She jabbed the wrench at his chest. "Just because Daddy doesn't make three doesn't mean we're less of a unit."

"I didn't mean—"

"I'll tell you what you mean. You see a woman and a small boy and you think they're just pining away for some big strong man to come along and fulfill them. Well, that's bull. If I needed a man, I'd have one. And if I thought Keenan needed a father to make him happy, I'd find him one. And," she continued, advancing and giving him another jab, "if you think you're at the head of some fictional list, you're wrong. Maybe I'm in love with you, but that's not enough. It's not just me, and it's not just you. Keenan comes first. When and if I want a father for Keenan, he'll be someone with compassion and patience, someone willing to adjust his life to make room for my son. So relax, Cooper. You're in the clear."

"I didn't come here to fight with you."

"Good, because I'm finished."

He grabbed her arm before she could turn away. "I haven't. I'm trying to be straight with you, Zoe. I care about you, okay? About both of you. I just don't want it to get out of hand."

"Out of whose hands?" she retorted. "Yours? Then that's no problem, is it? Because you know how to hold on to everything inside, really tight. Just keep holding on to it, Coop. Don't worry about me or about Keenan. We'll be fine." She jerked her arm free and sat again. Picking up the instruction sheet, she gave it her full attention.

Now why, he wondered, did he feel as though he'd just been rejected? Shaking his head, Coop took a step in retreat. "As long as we're clear."

"We are."

"I've, ah, got a little time, if you want me to help you put that grill together."

"No thanks. I can do it." She slanted him a look. "I'm going to grill burgers later. You're welcome to join us. Unless you're afraid it will lead to a commitment."

She shoots, he thought wryly, she scores. "Thanks anyway. I've got plans. Maybe I could take a rain check."

"Fine. You know where to find us."

He got drunk. Not sloppily, but thoroughly. When Coop poured himself out of the cab and staggered toward the house, he already knew he'd hate himself in the morning. But it was tonight he had to deal with.

He leaned heavily against Zoe's front door and waited for the porch to settle down under his feet. She might think they'd finished, he told himself blearily, but she was wrong. Dead wrong.

He'd thought of a dozen things he had to say to her. There was no time like the present.

Lifting a fist, he pounded on the door. "Come on, Zoe." He pounded again. "I know you're in there." He saw a light flick on inside and kept on pounding. "Come on, come on. Open up."

"Coop?" From the other side of the door, Zoe belted her hastily donned robe. She'd been home from the lounge for barely twenty minutes, and in bed for less than five. "It's after two o'clock in the morning. What do you want?"

"I want to talk to you. Let me in."

"We'll talk in the morning."

"You just said it was morning."

When he pounded again, she flicked off the locks. "Stop that—you'll wake Keenan." Furious, she yanked open the door and had the surprise of a hundred-and-seventy-pound male tumbling against her. "Are you hurt? What happened?" The alarm signals that had screamed on shifted when she caught the scent of beer. "You're drunk."

"Mostly." He started to straighten, then lost himself in the smell of her. "God, you feel good. What d'you wash this in?" He nuzzled her hair. "Smells like moonbeams."

"Really drunk," she said with a sigh. "Sit down. I'll get you some coffee."

"Don't want coffee. Doesn't sober you up, only wakes you up. And I'm awake, and I have something to say to you." He drew away then, and discovered he wasn't as steady as he'd hoped. "But I'll sit down." He did, heavily. "Hate getting drunk. Haven't done it like this since I played minor league. Did I tell you I played minor league ball? Triple A."

"No." Baffled, she stood her ground and watched him.

"Right out of high school. Two years. Thought I'd make it to the show. The majors. But I didn't, so I went to college, and now I write about people who did."

"I'm sorry."

"No." He waved that away. "I like writing. Always did. Like watching the games and seeing all the little dramas. If I'd've played, I'd be nearly washed up now. I'm almost thirty-three. Old man for the game." He focused on her, smiled. "You're the most beautiful woman

I've ever seen in my life. You know, the kid looks just like you. Look at him, see you. It's spooky. I see you all the time. Minding my own business, and pop! There's your face in my head. What d'ya make of that?"

"I don't know." She wanted to be angry with him, really she did. But he was so foolishly drunk. "Why don't I take you upstairs, Coop? Put you to bed."

"I want you in my bed, Zoe. I want to make love with you. I want to touch you again."

She wanted that, too. Very much. But new lines had been drawn. "You said you wanted to talk to me."

"Do you know what your skin feels like? I can't describe it, it's all soft and smooth and warm. I started thinking about your skin when I was playing poker and getting drunk tonight. I won, too. Took a big pot with a pair of sixes. Pulled in over two hundred and fifty dollars."

"Congratulations."

"But I kept thinking about you. You have this little dimple right here." He nearly poked himself in the eye, then dragged a finger down his cheek to the corner of his mouth. "I kept thinking about that little dimple, and your skin, and those big eyes and killer legs. And I kept thinking how I like to watch you with the kid, like I do sometimes from upstairs, when you don't know. Didn't know that, did you?"

"No," she said quietly. "I didn't."

"Well, see…" He gestured wildly. "You've got this way of running your hand over his hair. It gets to me." He shook his head. "It really gets to me. Keenan loves me, you know. He told me he did. So did you."

"I know."

"And I meant everything I said this afternoon."

"I know." Sighing, she walked over to undo his shoe-laces.

"Every word, Zoe. I've got my life set, just like I want it."

"Okay." She pried off his shoes, hefted his legs onto the couch.

"So you can stop popping into my head, 'cause it's not changing anything."

"I'll keep that in mind."

He was asleep before she bent over and kissed his cheek.

Chapter 10

As hangovers went, Coop knew, this would be a champ. He didn't have to open his eyes, he didn't have to move, not when his head was already beating like the Army drum corps.

He wasn't sure how he'd managed to get home and into bed, but the blur of the evening wasn't comforting. Still, he thought it best to wait to tax his brain.

Cautious, close to fearful, he opened his eyes. The little face directly above him had him jerking back, then moaning at the pain.

"Good morning," Keenan said cheerfully. "Did you sleep over?"

"I don't know." Coop lifted a hand to his head. "Where's your mother?"

"She's making my lunch. She said I could come in

and look at you if I didn't wake you up. I didn't wake you up, did I? I was really quiet."

"No." Coop closed his eyes again and prayed for oblivion.

"Are you sick? Do you have a temperature?" Keenan laid a small, light hand on Coop's aching forehead. "Mama can make it better. She always makes it better." Very gently, Keenan replaced his hand with a kiss. "Does that help?"

Oh, hell, Coop thought. Even a hangover didn't have a chance against this kid. "Yeah, thanks. What time is it?"

"The big hand's on the ten and the little hand's on the eight. You can sleep in my bed until you're better, and play with my toys."

"Thanks." Coop made the supreme effort and sat up. When his head rolled, he did his best to catch it in his hands. "Keenan, be a pal and ask your mom for some aspirin."

"Okay." He raced off, and the sound of his sneakers pounding the floor had Coop shuddering.

"Headache?" Zoe asked a moment later.

Coop lifted his head. She was still in her robe. The robe he remembered from the night before. He was beginning to remember quite a bit from the night before. "If you're going to yell at me, could you do it later?"

In answer, she held out aspirin and a glass filled with reddish liquid.

"What is it?"

"A remedy from Joe the bartender. He guarantees it'll take the edge off."

"Thanks."

There was a blast of a horn from outside that cut through Coop's skull like a dulled knife. While he was dealing with the shock of that, Keenan came racing back.

"Bye, Mama, bye!" He gave her a smacking kiss, then turned to hug Coop. "Bye."

As the door slammed behind him, Coop gulped down Joe's remedy.

"Do you want coffee?" Zoe ran her tongue around her teeth and tried not to smile. "Some breakfast?"

"You're not going to yell at me?"

"For barging in here, drunk, in the middle of the night? And for passing out on my sofa?" She paused just long enough to make her point. "No, I'm not going to yell at you. I figure you're suffering enough."

"I am, I promise you." He got up to follow her into the kitchen. "Not just physically. I feel like a total jerk."

"You *were* a total jerk." She poured a mug of coffee, set it on the table for him. "My mother's third husband had a fondness for bourbon. He swore eggs the morning after were the cure. How do you want them?"

"Scrambled would be good." He sat gingerly at the table. "I'm sorry, Zoe."

She kept her back to him. "For?"

"For being a jackass yesterday afternoon, and a bigger jackass last night."

"Oh, that." With the bacon frying, she chose a small bowl to scramble eggs in. "I don't imagine it's the first or the last time you'll be one."

"You didn't..." He shifted miserably. "Ah, you didn't tell Keenan I was..."

"Drunk and disorderly?" A half smile on her face,

she glanced over her shoulder. "I told him you weren't feeling well and went to sleep on the couch. Which was close enough."

"Thanks. I wouldn't want him to think...you know. I don't make a habit out of it."

"So you said last night." She turned the bacon, whipped the eggs.

He watched her, gradually getting past the astonishment that she wasn't going to rub his nose in the mess he'd made of things. Remembering the afternoon before, when she'd stood up to him with all that pride and fury shining in her eyes. And the other night, when he'd fallen asleep on her couch—the way she'd looked when she slipped the boy from his arms into hers and carried him into bed.

A dozen other pictures, captured in so short a time, flitted through his head, until they were whittled down to one. This one. Zoe standing at the stove, with the morning sun streaming over her tousled hair, her robe flowing down, breakfast smells warming the room.

How could he have thought he didn't want this? Just this. And what did he do now that he knew the truth?

"Food should help." She set the plate in front of him. "I've got to get ready for work."

"Can you— Have you got a minute?"

"I suppose." She poured herself another cup of coffee. "I don't have to be in until ten."

He began to eat while thoughts scrambled in his brain. "This is good. Thanks."

"You're welcome." She leaned back against the counter. "Did you want something else?"

"Yeah." He ate more, hoping eggs equaled courage.

Then he put his fork down. It was the ninth inning, he thought, and there were already two outs. "You. I want you."

She smiled a little. "Coop, I doubt you're in any shape for that, and I really have to go to work, so—"

"No, I don't mean that. I mean I do, but not—" He broke off, took a long, deep breath. "I want you to marry me."

"I beg your pardon?"

"I think you should marry me. It's a good idea." Somewhere in the back of his mind, he realized, he'd been working on this all along. He had it figured. "You can quit your night job and go back to school if you want. Or open that flower shop. Whatever. I think that's what we should do."

"Really." Because her hand was unsteady, she set her coffee down. "Well that's very generous of you, Coop, but I don't have to get married to do any of those things. So thanks just the same."

He stared. "No? You're saying no? But you love me. You said it. Twice you said it."

"We can make it three," she said evenly. "Yes, I love you. No, I won't marry you. Now I really have to get ready for work."

"Just a damn minute." Hangover forgotten, he pushed back from the table and rose. "What kind of game is this? You love me, your kid's crazy about me, we're terrific in bed, I even know how to drive a damn car pool, but you won't marry me."

"You're such an idiot. You're such a fool. Do you think because I didn't put up a struggle before I fell into your bed that you can have everything your own way? When you want it, how you want it? Well, you're wrong. And you *are* a jackass."

He winced as she stormed from the room. Strike one, he thought. And he hadn't even seen the pitch.

But the game wasn't over, he thought grimly, until the fat lady sang.

Zoe was still steaming when she came home from work. Of all the arrogant, interfering, self-absorbed idiots she'd ever known, J. Cooper McKinnon took the gold medal. Imagine him telling her that marrying him was a good idea, then ticking off all the advantages she'd gain.

Oh, he thought he was a prize.

One day he's telling her to get any ideas of sneaking him into a relationship out of her head. As if she'd been baiting traps for him. The next he's taking pity on her and offering her a big male helping hand.

She should have bitten it off.

Not once, not once had he said what she would bring to him, what he felt for her, what he wanted. Not once had he brought up the fact that he could or would accept another man's child as his own.

She jerked open the front door, slammed it. He could take his half-baked proposal and sit on it.

"Mama! Hey, Mama!" Keenan zipped into the living room and grabbed her hand. "Come on, come on. We've got a surprise."

"What surprise? What are you doing home, Keenan? You're supposed to be at the Finklemans'."

"Coop's here." He tugged manfully on her hand. "We

have a surprise. And we have a secret. And you have to come *now!*"

"All right, I'm coming." She braced herself and let Keenan drag her into the kitchen.

There were flowers, banks of them, vases and baskets overflowing on the counters, on the floor, on the windowsills. There was music, some soft, dreamy classical sonata, on the radio. The table was set, crystal she'd never seen before glinting in the sunlight, a bottle of champagne chilling in a silver bucket. And Coop was standing there, in a neatly pressed shirt and slacks.

"It's a surprise," Keenan announced gleefully. "We made everything look nice so you'd like it. And Mrs. Finkleman said we could use the glasses and the plates. And Mr. Finkleman made his special chicken 'cause it's resistible."

"Irresistible," Coop said, his eyes on Zoe. "You, ah, said you didn't need flowers and candlelight, but I've never taken you out on a date. I thought this was the next-best thing."

"Do you like it, Mama? Do you?"

"Yes, it's very nice." She bent down to kiss Keenan. "Thank you."

"I get to go to the Finklemans' so you can have romance."

"Ah, come on, kid." Coop scooped Keenan up. "Let's get you started. You were supposed to keep quiet about it," he muttered when he carried the boy outside.

"What's romance?"

"I'll tell you later."

Satisfied with that, Keenan draped his arm around

Coop's neck. "Are you gonna tell Mama the secret about us all getting married?"

"That's the plan."

"And you'll live with us and you can be my daddy and that'll be okay?"

"That'll be great. It'll be perfect." He stopped by the fence to press a kiss to Keenan's mouth. "I love you, Keenan."

"Okay." He squeezed his arms hard around Coop's neck. "Bye."

"Bye."

"Yoo-hoo!" Mrs. Finkleman stood at the back door. She sent Coop a wink and an exaggerated thumbs-up sign before whisking Keenan inside.

She was standing pretty much where Coop had left her when he came back. He wasn't sure whether or not that was a good sign.

"So, ready for some champagne?"

"Coop, this is very nice of you, but—"

"Like the flowers?" Nervous as a cat, he popped the cork.

"Yes, they're wonderful, but—"

"I couldn't get them where you work, or I'd have spoiled the surprise. Keenan really gave me a hand setting things up." He handed her the glass, and when she was distracted, he leaned in for a slow, warm kiss. "Hi."

"Coop." She had to wait for her heart to finish its lazy somersault. "I know you must have gone to a lot of trouble—"

"I should have gone to it before. I didn't know I wanted to."

"Oh, Lord." She turned away and struggled to get

her emotions under control. "I've given you the wrong impression this time. I don't need the trappings. I don't have to have romantic evenings and—" she waved toward the tapers on the table, waiting to be lit "—candlelight."

"Sure you do. So do I, when they're with you."

"You're trying to charm me," she said unsteadily. "That's new."

"You know what I am. The way this house is set up, we've practically been living together for the past month or so. People get to know each other quicker that way than just by socializing. So you know what I am, and you fell for me anyway."

She took a drink. "You're awfully smug about it. I told you my feelings are my responsibility, and that holds true. A romantic dinner doesn't change it."

It looked like strike two, but Coop knew that if he was going to go down, he'd go down swinging. "So I want to give you a nice evening. Is something wrong with that? I want to do better than propose over scrambled eggs when I've got a hangover." His voice had risen, and he bit down on it. "Damn it, this is my first time, have a little tolerance. No, don't say anything, let me finish this. You don't need me." He took another long breath. "Not for taking care of things, for you or the kid, I mean, for mowing the grass or putting stupid barbecue grills together. What about what I need, Zoe?"

She blinked at him. "Well, that's just it. Don't you see? You made it clear that you don't need or want ties. I come with ties, Coop."

"I made it clear," he muttered. "I didn't make anything clear, because I didn't know. Didn't want to know.

I was scared. There. You feel better knowing that?" He glared at her. "I was scared, because I need you. Because I need to see your face and hear your voice and smell your hair. I just need you to be there. And I need to help you mow the grass and put the grill together. I need you to need me back."

"Oh." She shut her eyes. "I like hearing that."

"Then tell me you will." He took her arms until she opened her eyes again. "It's my last swing, Zoe. Marry me."

"I—" Yes. She wanted to say yes. "It's not just me, Coop."

"You think I don't want the kid? God, open your eyes. I'm crazy about him. I fell for him before I fell for you. I want to marry both of you, then maybe have another kid or two so I can start out on the ground floor. We already worked that out."

"You— Who did what?"

He swore, stepped back, shrugged. "I kind of ran it by the kid. I figured I should smooth the way a little, and find out where he stood." When she just stared, he jammed his hands in his pockets. "It didn't seem fair not to bring him into it, since he'd be mine."

"Yours," she murmured, staring blindly into her wine.

"Since you two are a team, it would be sort of like an expansion. Anyway, he's for it. So it's two against one."

"I see."

"Maybe I don't know a lot about the daddy stuff, but I love him. That's a good start."

She looked at him again, looked into his eyes. Her heart opened, flooded. "It's a good one, all right."

"I love you." His hands relaxed in his pockets. "That's the first time I've said that to any woman— except my mother. I love you, Zoe. So why don't you marry me and give me and the kid a break?"

"It looks like I'm outvoted." She lifted a hand to his cheek.

"Is that a yes?"

"That's definitely a yes." She laughed as he swung her into his arms. "Daddy."

"I like the sound of that." He crushed his lips down on hers. "I like it a lot."

* * * * *

IRISH REBEL

Chapter 1

As far as Brian Donnelly was concerned, a vindictive woman had invented the tie to choke the life out of man so that he would then be so weak she could just grab the tail of it and lead him wherever she wanted him to go. Wearing one made him feel stifled and edgy, and just a little awkward.

But strangling ties, polished shoes and a dignified attitude were required in fancy country clubs with their slick floors and crystal chandeliers and vases crowded with flowers that looked as if they'd been planted on Venus.

He'd have preferred to be in the stables, or on the track or in a good smoky pub where you could light up a cigar and speak your mind. That's where a man met a man for business, to Brian's thinking.

But Travis Grant was paying his freight, and a hefty price it was to bring him all the way from Kildare to America.

Training racehorses meant understanding them, working with them, all but living with them. People were necessary, of course, in a kind of sideways fashion. But country clubs were for owners, and those who played at being racetrackers as a hobby—or for the prestige and profit.

A glance around the room told Brian that most here in their glittery gowns and black ties had never spent any quality time shoveling manure.

Still, if Grant wanted to see if he could handle himself in posh surroundings, blend in with the gentry, he'd damn well do it. The job wasn't his yet. And Brian wanted it.

Travis Grant's Royal Meadows was one of the top thoroughbred farms in the country. Over the last decade, it had moved steadily toward becoming one of the best in the world. Brian had seen the American's horses run in Kildare at Curragh. Each one had been a beauty. The latest he'd seen only weeks before, when the colt Brian had trained had edged out the Maryland bred by half a neck.

But half a neck was more than enough to win the purse, and his own share of it as trainer. More, it seemed, it had been enough to bring Brian Donnelly to the eye and the consideration of the great Mr. Grant.

So here he was, at himself's invitation, Brian thought, in America at some posh gala in a fancy club where the women all smelled rich and the men looked it.

The music he found dull. It didn't stir him. But at

least he had a beer and a fine view of the goings-on. The food was plentiful and as polished and elegant as the people who nibbled on it. Those who danced did so with more dignity than enthusiasm, which he thought was a shame, but who could blame them when the band had as much life as a soggy sack of chips?

Still it was an experience watching the jewels glint and crystal wink. The head man in Kildare hadn't been the sort to invite his employees to parties.

Old Mahan had been fair enough, Brian mused. And God knew the man loved his horses—as long as they ended by prancing in the winner's circle. But Brian hadn't thought twice about flipping the job away at the chance for this one.

And, well, if he didn't get it, he'd get another. He had a mind to stay in America for a while. If Royal Meadows wasn't his ticket, he'd find another one.

Moving around pleased him, and by doing so, by knowing just when to pack his bag and take a new road, he'd hooked himself up with some of the best horse farms in Ireland.

There was no reason he could see why he couldn't do the same in America. More of the same, he thought. It was a big and wide country.

He sipped his beer, then lifted an eyebrow when Travis Grant came in. Brian recognized him easily, and his wife as well—the Irish woman, he imagined, was part of his edge in landing this position.

The man, Grant, was tall, powerfully built with hair a thick mixture of silver and black. He had a strong face, tanned and weathered by the outdoors. Beside him, his wife looked like a pixie with her small, slim build. Her hair was a sweep of chestnut, as glossy as the coat of a prize thoroughbred.

They were holding hands.

It was a surprising link. His parents had made four children between them, and worked together as a fine and comfortable team. But they'd never been much for public displays of affection, even as mild a one as hand-holding.

A young man came in behind them. He had the look of his father—and Brian recognized him from the track in Kildare. Brendon Grant, heir apparent. And he looked comfortable with it—as well as the sleek blonde on his arm.

There were five children, he knew—had made it his business to know. A daughter, another son and twins, one of each sort. He didn't expect those who had grown up with privilege to bother themselves overly about the day-to-day running of the farm. He didn't expect that they'd get in his way.

Then she rushed in, laughing.

Something jumped in his belly, in his chest. And for an instant he saw nothing and no one else. Her build was delicate, her face vibrant. Even from a distance he could see her eyes were as blue as the lakes of his homeland. Her hair was flame, a sizzling red that looked hot to the touch and fell, wave after wave, over her bare shoulders.

His heart hammered, three hard and violent strokes, then seemed simply to stop.

She wore something floaty and blue, paler, shades paler than her eyes. What must have been diamonds fired at her ears.

He'd never in his life seen anything so beautiful, so perfect. So unattainable.

Because his throat had gone burning dry, he lifted his beer and was disgusted to realize his hand wasn't quite steady.

Not for you, Donnelly, he reminded himself. Not for you to even dream of. That would be the master's oldest daughter. And the princess of the house.

Even as he thought it, a man with a well-cut suit and pampered tan went to her. The way she offered her hand to him was just cool enough, just aloof enough to have Brian sneering—which was a great deal more comfortable than goggling.

Ah yes, indeed, she was royalty. And knew it.

The other family came in—that would be the twins, Brian thought, Sarah and Patrick. And a pretty pair they were, both tall and slim with roasted chestnut hair. The girl, Sarah—Brian knew she was just eighteen—was laughing, gesturing widely.

The whole family turned toward her, effectively— perhaps purposely—cutting out the man who'd come to pay homage to the princess. But he was a persistent sort, and reaching her, laid his hand on her shoulder. She glanced over, smiled, nodded.

Off to do her bidding, Brian mused as the man slipped away. A woman like that would be accustomed to flicking a man off, Brian imagined, or reining him in. And making him as grateful as the family hound for the most casual of pats.

Because the conclusion steadied him, Brian took another sip of his beer, set his glass aside. Now, he decided, was as good a time as any to approach the grand and glorious Grants.

"Then she whacked him across the back of his knees with her cane," Sarah continued. "And he fell face first into the verbena."

"If she was my grandmother," Patrick put in, "I'd move to Australia."

"Sure Will Cunningham usually deserves a whack. More than once I've been tempted to give him one myself." Adelia Grant glanced over, her laughing eyes meeting Brian's. "Well then, you've made it, haven't you?"

To Brian's surprise, she held out both hands to him, clasped his warmly and drew him into the family center. "It appears I have. It's a pleasure to see you again, Mrs. Grant."

"I hope your trip over was pleasant."

"Uneventful, which is just as good." As small talk wasn't one of his strengths, he turned to Travis, nodded. "Mr. Grant."

"Brian. I hoped you'd make it tonight. You've met Brendon."

"I did, yes. Did you lay any down on the colt I told you of?"

"On the nose. And since it was at five-to-one, I owe you a drink, at least. What can I get you?"

"I'll have a beer, thanks."

"What part of Ireland are you from?" This was from Sarah. She had her mother's eyes, Brian thought. Warm green, and curious.

"I'm from Kerry. You'd be Sarah, wouldn't you?"

"That's right." She beamed at him. "This is my

brother Patrick, and my sister Keeley. Our Brady's already on campus, so we're one short tonight."

"Nice meeting you, Patrick." Deliberately he inclined his head in what was nearly a bow as he turned to Keeley. "Miss Grant."

She lifted one slim eyebrow, the gesture as deliberate as his own. "Mr. Donnelly. Oh, thank you, Chad." She accepted the glass of champagne, touched a hand briefly to the arm of the man who'd brought it to her. "Chad Stuart, Brian Donnelly, from Kerry. That's in Ireland," she added with an irony dry as dust.

"Oh. Are you one of Mrs. Grant's relatives?"

"I don't have that privilege, no. There are a few of us scattered through the country who are not, in fact, related."

Patrick snorted out a laugh and earned a warning look from his mother. "Well now, we're cluttering up the place as usual. We'll move this herd along to our table. I hope you'll join us, Brian."

"How about a dance, Keeley?" Chad asked, standing at her elbow in a proprietary manner.

"I'd love to," she said absently and stepped forward. "A little later."

"Have a care." Brian put a hand lightly on Keeley's elbow as they walked away. "Or you'll slip on the pieces of the heart you just broke."

She slid a glance over and up. "I'm very surefooted," she told him, then made a point of taking a seat between her two brothers.

Because he'd caught the scent of her—subtle sex, with an overlay of class—*he* made a point of sitting directly across from her. He sent her one quick grin, then settled in to be entertained by Sarah, who was already chattering to him about horses.

She didn't like the look of him, Keeley thought as she sipped her champagne. He was just a little too much of everything. His eyes were green, a sharper tone than her mother's. She imagined he could use them to slice his opponent in two with one glance. And she had a feeling he'd enjoy it. His hair was brown, but anything but a quiet shade, with all those gilded streaks rioting through it, and he wore it too long, so that it waved past his collar and around a face of planes and angles.

A sharp face, like his eyes, one with a faint shadow of a cleft in the chin and a well-defined mouth that struck her as being just a little too sensuous.

She thought he was built like a cowboy—long-legged and rangy, and looking entirely too rough-and-ready for his suit and tie.

She didn't care for the way he stared at her, either. Even when he wasn't looking at her it *felt* as if he were staring. And as if he'd read her thoughts, he shifted his eyes to hers again. His smile was slow, unmistakably insolent, and made her want to bare her teeth in a snarl.

Rather than give him the satisfaction, Keeley rose and walked unhurriedly to the ladies' lounge.

She hadn't gotten all the way through the door when Sarah bulleted in behind her. "God! Isn't he gorgeous?"

"Who?"

"Come on, Keel." Rolling her eyes, Sarah plopped down on one of the padded stools at the vanity counter and prepared to enjoy a chat. "Brian. I mean he is so *hot*. Did you see his eyes? Amazing. And that mouth—makes you just want to lap at it or something. Plus, he's got a terrific butt. I know because I made sure I walked behind him to check it out."

With a laugh, Keeley sat down beside her. "First, you're so predictable. Second, if Dad hears you talk that way, he'll shove the man on the first plane back to Ireland. And third, I didn't notice his butt, or anything else about him, particularly."

"Liar." Sarah propped her elbow on the counter as her sister took out a lipstick. "I saw you give him the Keeley Grant once-over."

Amused, Keeley passed the lipstick to Sarah. "Then let's say I didn't much like what I saw. The rough-edged and proud of it type just doesn't do it for me."

"It sure works for me. If I wasn't leaving for college next week, I'd—"

"But you are," Keeley interrupted, and part of her was torn at the upcoming separation. "Besides that, he's much too old for you."

"It never hurts to flirt."

"And you've made a career of it."

"That's just to balance your ice princess routine. 'Oh hello, Chad.'" Sarah put a distant look in her eye and gracefully lifted a hand.

Keeley's comment was short and rude and made Sarah giggle. "Dignity isn't a flaw," Keeley insisted, even as her own lips twitched. "You could use a little."

"You've got plenty for both of us." Sarah hopped up. "Now I'm going to go out and see if I can lure the Irish hunk onto the dance floor. I just bet he's got great moves."

"Oh, yeah," Keeley muttered when her sister swung out the door. "I bet he does."

Not, of course, that she was the least bit interested.

At the moment she wasn't particularly interested in men, period. She had her work, she had the farm, she had her family. The combination kept her busy, involved and happy. Socializing was fine, she mused. An interesting companion over dinner, great. An occasional date for the theater or a function, dandy.

Anything more, well, she was just too busy to bother. If that made her an ice princess, so what? She'd leave the heart melting to Sarah. But, she decided as she rose, if their father hired Donnelly, she was keeping an eye on him and her guileless sister over the next week.

She'd barely taken two steps out of the lounge when Chad appeared at her side again, asking for a dance. Because the ice princess crack was still on her mind, she offered him a smile warm enough to dazzle his eyes and let him draw her into his arms.

Brian didn't mind dancing with Sarah. It would be a pitiful man who couldn't enjoy a few moments of holding a pretty young girl in his arms and listening to her bubble over about whatever came into her head.

She was a sweetheart as far as he was concerned, miraculously unspoiled and friendly as a puppy. After ten minutes, he knew she intended to study equine medicine, loved Irish music, broke her arm falling out of a tree when she was eight, and that she was an innate and charming flirt.

It was a pure pleasure to dance with Adelia Grant, to hear his own country in her voice and feel the easy welcome of it.

He'd heard the stories, of course, of how she'd come to America, and Royal Meadows, to stay with her uncle

Patrick Cunnane, who was trainer in those days for Travis Grant. It was said she'd been hired on as a groom as she had her uncle's gift with horses.

But guiding the small, elegant woman around the dance floor, Brian dismissed the stories as so much pixie dust. He couldn't imagine this woman ever mucking out a stall—any more than he could picture her pretty daughters doing so.

The socializing hadn't been so bad, he acknowledged, and he couldn't say he minded the food, though a man would do better with a good beef sandwich. Still it was plentiful, even if you did have to pick your way through half of it to get to something recognizable.

But despite the evening not being quite the ordeal he'd imagined it would be, he was glad when Travis suggested they get some air.

"You've a lovely family, Mr. Grant."

"Yes, I do. And a loud one. I hope you still have your hearing left after dancing with Sarah."

Brian grinned, but he was cautious. "She's charming—and ambitious. Veterinary medicine's a challenging field, and especially when you specialize in horses."

"She's never wanted anything else. She went through stages, of course," Travis continued as they walked down a wide white stone path. "Ballerina, astronaut, rock star. But under it all, she always wanted to be a vet. I'm going to miss her, and Patrick, when they leave for college next week. Your family will miss you, I imagine, if you stay in America."

"I've been coming and going for some time. If I settle in America, it won't be a problem."

"My wife misses Ireland," Travis murmured. "A part

of her's still there, no matter how deep she's dug her roots here. I understand that. But..." He paused and in the backwash of light studied Brian's face. "When I take on a trainer, I expect his mind, and his heart, to be in Royal Meadows."

"That's understood, Mr. Grant."

"You've moved around quite a bit, Brian," Travis added. "Two years, occasionally three at one organization, then you switch."

"True enough." Eyes level, Brian nodded. "You could say I haven't found the place that wants to hold me longer than that. But while I'm where I am, that farm, those horses, have all my attention and loyalty."

"So I'm told. The boots I'm looking to fill are big. No one's managed to fill them to my satisfaction since Paddy Cunnane retired. He suggested I take a look at you."

"I'm flattered."

"You should be." Travis was pleased to see nothing more than mild interest on Brian's face. He appreciated a man who could hold his own thoughts. "I'd like you to come by the farm when you're settled."

"I'm settled enough. I prefer moving right along if it's all the same to you."

"It is."

"Fine. I'll come round tomorrow, for the morning workout, and have a look at how you do things, Mr. Grant. After I've seen what you have, and you've heard what I'd have in mind to do about it, we'll know if it works for both of us. Will that suit you?"

Cocky young son of a bitch, Travis thought, but

didn't smile. He, too, knew how to hold his thoughts. "It suits me fine. Come on back inside. I'll buy you a beer."

"Thanks just the same, but I think I'll go on back to my hotel. Dawn comes early."

"I'll see you tomorrow." Travis held out a hand, shook Brian's briskly. "I'll look forward to it."

"So will I."

Alone, Brian took out a slim cigar, lighted it, then blew out a long stream of smoke.

Paddy Cunnane had recommended him? The idea of it had both nerves and pleasure stirring in his gut. He'd told Travis he'd been flattered, but in truth, he'd been staggered. In the racing world, that was a name spoken of with reverence.

Paddy Cunnane trained champions the way others ate breakfast—with habitual regularity.

He'd seen the man a few times over the course of years, and had spoken to him once. But even with a well-fed ego, Brian had never thought that Paddy Cunnane had taken notice of him.

Travis Grant wanted someone to fill Paddy's boots. Well, Brian Donnelly couldn't and wouldn't do that. But he'd damn well make his mark with his own, and he'd make sure that would be good enough for anyone.

Tomorrow morning they would see what they would see.

He started down the path again when the light and shadows in front of him shifted briefly. Glancing over, he saw Keeley come out of the glass doors and walk across a flagstone terrace.

Look at her, Brian thought, so cool and solitary and perfect. She was made for moonlight, he decided. Or perhaps it was made for her. What breeze there was fluttered the layers of the filmy blue dress she wore as she crossed over to sniff at the flowers that grew out of a big stone urn in colors of rust and butter.

On impulse, he snapped off one of the late-blooming roses from its bush, and strode onto the terrace. She turned at the sound of his footsteps. Irritation flickered first in her eyes, so quickly here and gone he might have missed it if he hadn't been so focused on her. Then it was smoothed away, coated over with a thin sheen of cool politeness.

"Mr. Donnelly."

"Miss Grant," he said in the same formal tone, then held out the rose. "Those there are a bit too humble for the likes of you. This suits better."

"Really?" She took the rose because it would have been rude not to, but neither looked at it nor lifted it to sniff. "I like simple flowers. But thank you for the thought. Are you enjoying your evening?"

"I enjoyed meeting your family."

Because he sounded sincere she unbent enough to smile. "You haven't met them all yet."

"Your brother in college."

"Brady, yes, but there's my aunt and uncle. Erin and Burke Logan, and their three children, from the neighboring Three Aces farm."

"I've heard of the Logans, yes. Seen them round the tracks a time or two in Ireland. Don't they come to functions here?"

"Often, but they're away just now. If you stay in the area, you'll see quite a bit of them."

"And you? Do you still live at home?"

"Yes." She shifted, glanced back toward the light. "That's why it's home."

Which was where she wanted to be right now, she realized. Home. The thought of going back inside that overwarm and overcrowded room seemed unbearable.

"The music's better from a distance."

"Hmm?" She didn't bother to look at him, wished only that he would go away and give her back her moment of solitude.

"The music," Brian repeated. "It's better when you can barely hear it."

Because she agreed, wholeheartedly, she laughed. "Better yet when you can't hear it at all."

It was the laugh that did it. There'd been warmth then. The way smoke brought warmth even as it clogged your brain. He reached for her before he let himself think. "I don't know about that."

She went rigid. Not with a jerk as many women would, he noted, but by standing so absolutely still she stiffened every muscle.

"What are you doing?"

The words dripped ice, and left him no choice but to tighten his grip on her waist. Pride rammed against pride and the result was solid steel. "Dancing. You do dance, I saw you. And this is a better spot for it than in there, where you're jammed elbow to ass, don't you think?"

Perhaps she agreed. Perhaps she was even amused. Still, she was accustomed to being asked, not just grabbed. "I came out here to get away from the dancing."

"You didn't, no. You came out to get away from the crowd."

She moved with him because to do otherwise was too much like an embrace. And Sarah had been right, he had some lovely moves. Her heels brought her gaze level with his mouth. She'd been right, she decided. Entirely too sensuous. Deliberately she tilted her head back until their eyes met.

"How long have you been working with horses?" It was a safe topic, she thought, and an expected one.

"All my life, one way or another. And you? Are you one for riding, or just for looking from a distance?"

"I can ride." The question irritated her, and nearly had her tossing her collection of blue ribbons and medals in his face. "Relocating, if you do, would mean a big change for you. Job, country, culture."

"I like a challenge." Something about the way he said it, about the way his hand was spread over her back, had her eyes narrowing.

"Those that do often wander off looking for the next when the challenge is met. It's a game, lacking substance or commitment. I think more of people who build something worthwhile where they are."

Because it was no more than the truth, it shouldn't have stung. But it did. "As your parents have."

"Yes."

"It's easy, isn't it, to have that sensibility when you've never had to build something from the ground up with nothing but your own hands and wits?"

"That may be, but I respect someone who digs in for the long haul more than the one who jumps from opportunity to opportunity—or challenge."

"And that's what you think I'm doing here?"

"I couldn't say." She moved her shoulder, a graceful little shrug. "I don't know you."

"No, you don't. But you think you do. The rover with his eye on the prize, and stable dirt under his nails no matter how he scrubs at them. And less than beneath your notice."

Surprised, not just by the words but the heat under them, she started to step back, would have stepped back, but he held her in place. As if, she thought, he had the right to.

"That's ridiculous. Unfair and untrue."

"Doesn't matter, to either of us." He wouldn't let it matter to him. Wouldn't let her matter, though holding her had made him ache with ideas that couldn't take root.

"If your father offers me the job, and I take it, I doubt we'll be running in the same circles, or dancing the same dance, once I'm an employee."

There was anger there, she noted, just behind the vivid green of his eyes. "Mr. Donnelly, you're mistaken about me, my family, and how my parents run their farm. Mistaken, and insulting."

He raised his eyebrows. "Are you cold or just angry?"

"What do you mean?"

"You're trembling."

"It's chilly." She bit off the words, annoyed that he'd upset her enough to have it show. "I'm going back in."

"As you like." He eased away, but kept her hand in his, then angled his head when she tugged at it. "Even the stable boy learns manners," he murmured and walked her to the door. "Thank you for the dance, Miss Grant. I hope you enjoy the rest of your evening."

He knew it could cost him the offer of the job, but he couldn't resist seeing if there was any fire behind that wall of ice. So he lifted her hand, and with his eyes still on hers, brushed his lips over her knuckles. Back, forth, then back again.

The fire, one violent flash of it, sparked. And there it simmered while she yanked her hand free, turned her back on him and walked back into the polished crowd and perfumed air.

Chapter 2

Dawn at the shedrow was one of the magic times, when fog was eating its way along the ground and the light was a paler, purer gray. Music was in the jingle of harness, the dull thud of boot and hoof as grooms, handlers and horses went about their business. The perfume was horses, hay and summer.

Trailers had already been loaded, Brian imagined, and the horses picked by the man Grant had left in charge already gone to track for their workout or preparation for today's race. But here on the farm there was other work to be done.

Sprains to be checked, medication to be given, stalls to be mucked. Exercise boys would take mounts to the oval for a workout, or to pony them around. He imag-

ined Royal Meadows had someone to act as clocker
and mark the time.

He saw nothing that indicated anything other than
first-class here. There was a certain tidiness not all
owners insisted upon—or would pay for. Stables, barns,
sheds, all were neatly painted, rich, glossy white with
dark green trim. Fences were white too, and in perfect repair. Paddocks and pastures were all as neat as
a company parlor.

There was atmosphere as well. It was a clever man,
or a rich one, who could afford it. Trees in full leaf dotted the hillside pastures. Brian spotted one, a big beauty
of an oak, that rose from the center of a paddock and
was fenced around in white wood. In the center grass
of the brown oval was a colorful lake of flowers and
shrubs. Back away, curving between stables and track,
were trim green hedges.

He approved of such touches, for the horses. And for
the men. Both worked with more enthusiasm in attractive surroundings in his experience. He imagined the
Grants had glossy photos of their pretty farm published
in fancy magazines.

Of the house as well, he mused, for that had been an
impressive sight. Though it had still been more night
than day when he'd driven past it, he'd seen the elegant
shape of the stone house with its juts of balconies and
ornamental iron. Fine big windows, he thought now, for
standing and looking out at a kingdom.

There'd been a second structure, a kind of miniature
replica of the main house that had nestled atop a large
garage. He'd seen the shapes and silhouettes of flowers
and shrubberies there as well. And the big, shady trees.

But it was the horses that interested him. How they were housed, how they were handled. The shedrow—should he be offered this job and take it—would be his business. The owner was simply the owner.

"You'll want a look in the stables," Travis said, leading Brian toward the doors. "Paddy'll be along shortly. Between us we should be able to answer any questions you might have."

He got answers just from looking, from seeing, Brian mused. Inside was as tidy as out, with the sloped concrete floors scrubbed down, the doors of the box stalls of strong and sturdy wood each boasting a discreet brass plaque engraved with its tenant's name. Already stableboys were pitching out soiled hay into barrows or pitching in fresh. The scent of grain, liniment and horse was strong and sweet.

Travis stopped by a stall where a young woman carefully wrapped the foreleg of a bay. "How's she doing, Linda?"

"Coming along. She'll be out causing trouble again in a day or two."

"Sprain?" Brian stepped into the box to run his hands over the yearling's legs and chest. Linda flicked a glance up at him, then over at Travis, who nodded.

"This is Bad Betty," Linda told Brian. "She likes to incite riots. She's got a mild sprain, but it won't hold her back for long."

"Troublemaker, are you?" Brian put his hands on either side of Betty's head, looked her in the eye. A quick, hot thrill raced through him at what he saw. What he sensed. Here, he thought, was magic, ready to spring if only you could find the right incantation.

"It happens I like troublemakers," he murmured.

"She'll nip," Linda warned. "Especially if you turn your back on her."

"You don't want a bite of me, do you, darling?"

As if in challenge, Betty laid her ears back, and Brian grinned at her. "We'll get along, as long as I remember you're the boss." When he ran his fingertips down her neck, back again, she snorted at him. "You're too pretty for your own good."

He murmured to her, shifting without thought to Gaelic as Linda finished the bandage. Betty's ears pricked back up, and she watched him now with more interest than malice.

"She wants to run." Brian stepped back, scanning the filly's form. "Born for it. And more, born to win."

"One look tells you that?" Travis asked.

"It's in the eyes. You won't want to breed this one when she comes into season, Mr. Grant. She needs to fly first."

Deliberately he turned his back, and as Betty lifted her head, he glanced back over his shoulder. "I don't think so," he said quietly. They eyed each other another moment, then Betty tossed her head in the equine equivalent of a shrug.

Amused, Travis moved aside to let Brian out of the box. "She terrorizes the stableboys."

"Because she can, and is likely smarter than half of them." He gestured to the opposite box. "And who's this handsome old man here?"

"That's Prince, out of Majesty."

"Royal Meadows' Majesty?" There was reverence in Brian's voice as he crossed over. "And his Prince. You had your day, didn't you, sir?" Gently Brian stroked a hand down the dignified nose of the aged chestnut. "Like your sire. I saw him race, Mr. Grant, at the Curragh, when I was a lad, a stableboy. I'd never seen his like before, nor since for that matter. I worked with one of the stallions this one sired. He didn't embarrass his breeding."

"Yes, I know."

Travis showed him through the tack room, the breeding shed and birthing stalls, past a paddock where a yearling was going through his paces on a longe line, and then to the oval where a handsome stallion was being ponied around in the company of a well-behaved gelding.

A wiry little man with a blue cap over a white fringe of hair turned as they approached. He had a stopwatch dangling from his pocket and a merry grin on his weathered leprechaun's face.

"So you've had your tour then, have you? And what do you think of our little place here?"

"It's a lovely farm." Brian extended a hand. "I'm pleased to meet you again, Mr. Cunnane."

"Likewise, young Brian from Kerry." Paddy gave Brian's hand a firm shake. "I told them to hold Zeus until you got here, Travis. I thought you and the lad would like a look at his morning run."

"King Zeus, out of Prince," Travis explained. "He's running well for us."

"He took your Belmont Stakes last year," Brian remembered.

"That's right. Zeus likes a long run. Burke's colt snatched the Derby from him, but Zeus came back for the Breeder's Cup. He's a strong competitor, and he'll sire champions."

At Paddy's signal, an exercise boy trotted over mounted on a magnificent chestnut. The horse gleamed dark red in the strengthening sun, with a blaze like a lightning bolt down the center of his forehead. He pranced, sidestepping, head tossing.

Brian knew, at one glance, he was looking at poetry.

"What do you think of him?" Paddy asked.

"Beautiful form" was all Brian said.

Twelve hundred pounds of muscle atop impossibly long and graceful legs. A wide chest, sleek body, proud head. And eyes, Brian saw, that glinted with ferocious pride.

"Take him around, Bobbie," Paddy ordered. "Don't rate him. We'll let him show off a bit this morning." Whistling between his teeth, Paddy leaned on the fence, pulled out the stopwatch.

With his thumbs hooked in his pockets, Brian watched Zeus trot back onto the track, prance in place until the boy controlled him. Then the rider rose up in the stirrups, leaned over that long, powerful neck. Zeus shot forward, a bright arrow from a plucked bow. Those long legs lifted, stretched, fell, flew, shooting out clumps of dirt like bullets as he rounded the first curve.

The air roared with the thunder.

Inside Brian's chest, his heart beat the same way, at a hard and joyful gallop. The boy's hat flew off as they turned into the backstretch. When they streaked by, Paddy gave a grunt and flicked his timer.

"Not bad," Paddy said dryly and held out the watch.

Brian didn't need to see it. He had a clock in his head, and he knew he'd just watched a champion.

"I think I've seen the like of your Prince at last, Mr. Grant."

"And he knows it."

"You want your hands on that one, boy?" Paddy asked him.

There was a time, Brian thought, to hold your cards close, and a time to lay them out. "I do, yes." Struggling not to dance with eagerness, he turned to Travis again. "If the job's being offered, Mr. Grant, I'll take it."

Travis inclined his head, extended a hand. "Welcome to Royal Meadows. Let's go get some coffee."

Brian simply stared as Travis walked off. "Just like that?" he murmured.

"He'd already made up his mind," Paddy said, "or you wouldn't be here in the first place. Travis doesn't waste time—his or anyone else's. After you're done with your coffee and such, come over to my place—above the garage. You'll want a look at the condition book, and have a little conversation."

"Yes, I will. Thanks." A bit dazed, Brian headed off after Travis.

He caught up, surprised, and a little embarrassed, to find his palms were sweaty. A job was only a job, he reminded himself. "I'm grateful for the opportunity, Mr. Grant."

"Travis. You'll work for it. We have high standards at Royal Meadows. I expect you to meet them. I'd like you to start as soon as possible."

"I'll start today."

Travis glanced over. "Good."

Scanning the area, Brian gestured toward another small building, with the paddock set up with jumps. "Do you train jumpers, show horses, as well?"

"That's a separate enterprise." Travis smiled slightly. "You'll work the racehorses. You can move your things into the trainer's quarters when you're ready." Travis flicked a glance toward the garage house.

Brian opened his mouth—then shut it again. He hadn't expected housing to be part of the package, but wasn't about to argue it away. If it didn't suit him, they'd deal with it later.

"You have a beautiful home. Someone likes their flowers."

"My wife." Travis turned onto a slate path. "She's particularly fond of flowers."

And Brian imagined they had a staff of gardeners, landscapers, whatever it was, to deal with them. "The horses appreciate a pretty setting."

Travis stepped onto a patio, turned. "Do they?"

"They do."

"Did Betty tell you that when you were speaking to her?"

Brian met Travis's amused eyes levelly. "She indicated she was a queen and expected to be treated as such."

"And will you?"

"I will, until she abuses the privilege. Even royalty needs a bit of a yank now and again."

So saying, he stepped through the door Travis held open.

Brian didn't know what he'd been expecting. Something sleek and sophisticated. Something grand, certainly.

He hadn't been expecting to walk into the Grants' kitchen, nor to find it big and cluttered and despite the gleam of snazzy appliances and fancy tiles, homey.

Certainly the last thing he'd expected was to see the lady of the manor herself in an old pair of jeans, bare feet and a faded T-shirt standing at the stove with a skillet while she rang a peal over the head of her youngest son.

"And I'll tell you another thing, Patrick Michael Thomas Cunnane, if you think you can come and go at all hours as you damn please just because you're going off to college, you'd best get that thick head of yours examined in a hurry. I'll be happy to do it myself, with the skillet I have in my hand, just as soon as I'm done with it."

"Yes, ma'am." At the table Patrick sat with his shoulders hunched, wincing at his mother's back. "But since you're using it, maybe I could have some more French toast. Nobody makes it like you do."

"You won't get around me that way."

"Maybe I will."

She shot a look over her shoulder that Brian recognized as one only a mother could conjure to wither a child.

"And maybe I won't," Patrick muttered, then brightened when he saw Brian at the door. "Ma, we've got company. Have a seat, Brian. Had breakfast? My mother makes world-famous French toast."

"Witnesses won't save you," Adelia said mildly, but

turned to smile at Brian. "Come in and sit. Patrick, get Brian and your father plates."

"No, thank you. There's no need to trouble."

"Ma, I can't find my brown shoes." Sarah came bursting in. "Hello, Brian, morning, Dad."

"Sure I had my eyes right on them for weeks," Adelia said as she flipped sizzling bread in the pan. "I can't think how those shoes slipped out of my sight."

Sarah rolled her eyes and yanked open the refrigerator. "I'm going to be late."

"You could wear one of the other six thousand pairs of shoes jammed in your closet," her brother suggested.

Sarah rapped him on the back with the carton of juice she held and otherwise ignored him. "I don't have time for breakfast." She poured juice, glugged it down. "I'll be home by five."

"Take a muffin," Adelia ordered.

"We don't have any blueberry."

"Take what we do have."

"Okay, okay." She grabbed a muffin off a plate, gave her mother a smacking kiss on the cheek, rounded the table to give her father one in turn, crossed her eyes at her brother, then dashed out again.

"Sarah works at the vet's office during the summer," Adelia explained. "The pair of you wash up here now, and we'll get you something hot to eat."

Since the scent of that fried bread was impossible to resist, Brian started toward the sink. And saw the huge old dog stretched out by the stove. He resembled a long, black and outrageously shaggy floor mat.

"And who's this?" Automatically Brian crouched down.

"That's our Sheamus. He's an old man now, and likes to tuck himself at my feet while I'm cooking."

"My wife's fond of mutts," Travis said as he ran water in the sink.

"And they of me. He spends most of his time sleeping," she told Brian. "And isn't much for anyone but family now." Even as she said it her brows rose up. Brian had no more than stroked the old dog's head before Sheamus opened his eyes, thumped his ragged tail, and with a moan rolled over onto his back for a belly rub.

"Would you look at that? He's taken to you."

"Well mutts and I, we understand each other. You're a good old boy, aren't you? Fat and happy."

"Someone feeds him table scraps." Adelia slanted a look at her husband.

"I don't know what you're talking about." All innocence, Travis held out the soap when Brian stood up again.

"Hah" was all she said to that. "Would you have coffee, Brian, or tea?"

"Tea, thank you."

"Sit." She pointed to a chair, then shifted the finger to her son. "You, go. I'll finish with you later."

"I'll be at the stables, doing penance." With a heavy sigh, Patrick rose, then he wrapped his arms around his mother's waist, laid his chin on top of her head. "Sorry."

"Get."

But Brian saw her lay a hand over Patrick's, and squeeze. With a quick grin tossed to the room in general, he bolted.

"That boy's responsible for every other line on my face," Adelia muttered.

"What lines?" Travis asked, and made her laugh.

"That's the right answer. So, Brian, does Royal Meadows suit you?"

After drying his hands, he crossed to the table to sit. "Yes, ma'am."

"Oh, we're not so very formal around here. You don't have to ma'am me. Unless you're in trouble." She poured tea for him, and coffee for Travis, then stayed where she was, her free hand resting on her husband's shoulder.

"How did Zeus do this morning?"

"Took the oval in a minute-fifty flat."

"I'm sorry I missed it." She turned back to the stove to heap golden bread onto a platter.

"I'll offer you a one-year contract," Travis began.

"Can't you let the boy eat before you talk business?"

"The boy wants to know."

Brian took the platter, transferred three slices to his plate. "Yes, he does."

"You'll have a guaranteed annual salary." Travis named an amount that had Brian struggling not to bobble the syrup. "And, after two months, a two-percent share of each purse. In six months, we'll renegotiate that percentage."

"We'll negotiate it up." Steady again, Brian cut into his breakfast. "Because I promise you, I'll have earned it."

They discussed—haggled a bit for form sake—responsibilities, benefits, bonuses, duties.

Brian was on his second serving of toast, and Travis the last of his coffee, when Keeley came in.

She wore buff colored jodhpurs. Elegant and form-fitting. Her high black boots were shined like dark mirrors. Her white blouse draped soft with its wide collar buttoned high. She had tamed her hair into a sleek twist that left her face unframed. Small, complicated twists of gold glinted at her ears.

Her brow lifted at the sight of Brian eating breakfast in her kitchen, and her mouth thinned before it moved into a cool, practiced smile. "Good morning, Mr. Donnelly."

"Miss Grant."

"I'm pressed for time this morning." She walked to her father, bent down, rubbed her cheek against his.

"You should eat," her mother told her.

"I'll get something later." She went to the refrigerator, took out a soft drink. "I'll be done in a couple of hours." She went to her mother, bending first to scratch Sheamus on the top of the head, then in the same manner she'd used with her father, rubbed cheeks with Adelia before she headed out the back door.

"I'll come down in a bit," Adelia called after her. "I'd like to watch."

Twenty minutes later, Brian walked from the house toward the trainer's quarters. He saw Keeley in the paddock in front of the small building. She sat astride a black gelding. As she walked the horse, a man photographed her from various angles.

Brian paused to watch, hands on hips. She was getting her picture in some fancy magazine, he imagined. Royal Meadows Princess. No doubt she'd look fine and glossy in it.

She set the horse into a trot, then a canter, swinging in to sail over a jump. Brian's lips pursed. She had good form, he had to admit it. When she repeated that jump, then another, for the camera, he heard her laugh float out over the air.

He turned away, dismissing her. Trying to.

He climbed the stairs to the trainer's quarters, knocked.

"Come in, and welcome. In here," Paddy called out.

He sat at a desk in a room set up as an office. File cabinets lined one wall, and photographs of horses lined them all. The window was open, and on a shelf beside it sat a computer. If the dust on its cover was any indication, it was rarely, if ever, used.

Paddy's glasses balanced on the end of his nose as he gestured to a chair. "You and Travis worked out your details."

"We did. He's a fair man."

"Did you expect otherwise?"

"I don't expect anything from owners, and that way they don't often surprise me."

With a chuckle Paddy shoved up his glasses, scratched his nose. "This one might."

"I want to thank you for putting my name in so Mr. Grant would consider me."

"I've kept my eye and ear on things, though I've retired. Well, retired twice now, if the truth be known, and come out of it again as Travis and Dee haven't been satisfied with the trainers who've come along. This time I mean it to stick. I mean you to stick, boy."

When his glasses slid down again, Paddy grunted in annoyance and took them off. "We'll be bunking here together, if you have no objection, for the next week. After that, I'll be off, and the place is yours."

"Where are you going?"

"Home. Back to Ireland."

"After all these years?"

"I was born there. I've a mind to die there—though I've life left in me, no mistake. I've a yearning to spend the last years of it at home."

"What'll you do there?"

"Oh, go to the pub to tell lies," Paddy said with a twinkling grin. "Drink a pint of decent Guinness. You'll miss that here, I can tell you. It's just not the same built out of a Yank tap."

Brian had to laugh. "It's a long way to go for a pint, even for Guinness."

"Well now, there's a little farm in the south of Cork, not far from Skibbereen. Do you know Skibbereen, Brian?"

"Aye. It's a pretty town."

"Sloping streets and painted doorways," Paddy said, a bit dreamily. "Well, the farm's a bit of a ways from that pretty town. My Dee was raised there, by my sister after Dee's parents died. When my sister got sickly, the farm fell on hard times with Dee trying to run it and tend to her aunt Lettie. In the end, Lettie passed and the farm was lost, and Dee came here to me. A few years ago, the farm came up for sale, and though she told him not to, Travis bought it for her. The man knows her heart."

"So that's where you're going?" Brian asked, though he didn't have a clue why Paddy was telling him. "To be a farmer?"

"That's where I'm going, but I don't think I'll make much of a farmer. I'll have myself a few horses for company."

He shifted, turned his gaze to the window and the hills beyond where horses grazed in the late-morning sunshine.

"I'll miss my little Dee, and Travis, and the children. The friends I've made here. But I've a need to go. An itch, if you follow me."

"I do." There was little Brian understood more than an itch to be going.

"I imagine I'll be flying back and forth across the pond quite a bit—and they'll come to me as well. I've seen Dee married to a man I respect, and love like my own son. I've watched her children grow into fine young men and women. That's a rare thing. And I've had a hand in turning out champions. A man who has a thoroughbred put into his hands is a fortunate man."

"Have you no wish for your own place, your own champions?"

"I toyed with it—but in the end no, it wasn't for me." He turned his attention back to Brian. "Is that what you're after in the end?"

"No. Your own place means you're rooted, doesn't it? And there's no moving on if moving on strikes you. In any case, most owners leave the work and the decisions to the trainer, so you don't own, but you run."

"Travis Grant knows how to work." Paddy inclined his head. "He knows his horses. He loves them. If you earn his trust, he'll trust you, but he'll know every move you make. He's not one for strolling into the winner's circle after the day is done. Shedrow business will be his business, and Dee's, as much as it is yours. Whether you like it or not."

"His wife?"

Amused now, Paddy sat back. "You met her last night when she was done up fancy. I like seeing her looking fine that way. You're more like to see her down in the stables lancing an abscess or soothing a colicky mare. She's no delicate flower. My Dee's a thoroughbred. And she's bred true. Not one of her children would back away from a hard day's work when it's needed. You'll learn for yourself how things go around here, and you'll find it's not such a far distance from main house to shedrow as it is in some places."

"It's usually better all around if it is," Brian muttered, and Paddy cackled with laughter.

"Right you are, lad, in most cases. Owners can be a fly in your ointment without a doubt. You'll make up your own mind about this place, and these owners. And I hope you'll let me know what you think after a bit of time's passed. Now, let's take a look at the condition book to start off."

When Brian left Paddy, he was satisfied with the world in general. Or what, he thought as he trooped down the stairs, was soon to become his world in general. He'd make his mark at Royal Meadows, and live well doing it. His quarters were first-rate. The truth was, he'd have been willing to live in a hovel for the chance to work with Travis Grant's stable.

Everything he'd ever wanted was at his fingertips. He didn't intend to let it slip through.

He turned toward the stables where he'd parked his rental car. Paddy had told him to have a look at the little red lorry down that way, as he'd be selling it before leaving for Ireland. If the thing ran, it would do, Brian thought. He didn't require anything but the most elemental means of transportation. And time to get used to driving on the wrong damn side of the road.

As he rounded the garage he was scowling over that one sticking point, and nearly ran into Keeley.

She looked as fresh and perfect as she had that morning. Not a hair out of place, not a speck of dust on her boots. He wondered how the hell she managed it.

"Good day to you, Miss Grant. I saw you in the paddock earlier. That's a fine horse."

She was hot, irritable and very close to flash point since the photographer had hit on her. The photo shoot had been necessary. She needed the exposure, the publicity, but she damn well didn't need the hassle.

"Yes, he is." She made to move by, and Brian shifted to block her.

"Begging your pardon, princess. Did I neglect to pull my forelock?"

She held up a hand. Her temper was a vile thing when loose, and the drumming in her head warned her it was very close to springing free.

"I'm already annoyed. It won't take much to push me to furious." But she drew a deep breath. If the scene in the kitchen earlier meant anything, Brian Donnelly was now part of Royal Meadows. She didn't make a habit of sniping at a member of the team.

"Sam's a nine-year-old. Hunter. A thoroughbred, Irish Draught horse cross. I've had him since he was four." She lifted the bottle she carried and sipped her soft drink.

"Is that all you put in you?" He tapped a finger on the bottle. "Bubbles and chemicals?"

"You sound like my mother."

"Maybe that's why you have a headache."

Keeley dropped the hand she'd pressed to her temple. Those eyes of his, she thought, were entirely too keen. "I'm fine."

"Turn around."

"I beg your pardon."

Brian merely stepped around her, laid his hands on the nape of her neck. Her already stiff shoulders jerked in protest. "Relax. I'm not after grabbing you in a fit of passion when any member of your family might come along. I'd like to put in at least one day on the job before I get the boot."

As he spoke he was kneading, pressing, running those strong fingers over the knots. He hated seeing anything in pain. "Blow out a breath," he ordered when she stood rigid as stone. "Come on, *maverneen,* don't be so hardheaded. Blow out a nice long breath for me."

Out of curiosity she obeyed and tried not to think how marvelous his hands felt on her skin.

"Now another."

His voice had gone to croon, lulling her. As he worked, murmured, her eyes fluttered closed. Her muscles loosened, the knots untied. The threatening throbbing in her head faded away. She all but slid into a trance.

She arched against his hands, just a little. Moaned in pleasure. Just a little. He kept his hands firm, professional, even as he imagined skimming them down over her, slipping them under that soft white blouse. He wanted to touch his lips to her nape, just where his thumb was pressing. To taste her there.

And that, he knew, would end things before they'd

begun. Wanting a woman was natural. Taking one, where the taking held such risks, was suicide.

So he let his hands drop away, stepped back. She nearly swayed before she caught herself. When she turned toward him, it felt almost like floating. "Thank you. You're very good at that."

Magic hands, she thought. The man had magic in his hands.

"So I've been told." He shot her a cocky grin. "I've a feeling you need regular loosening up." He snatched the bottle out of her hand. "Go drink some water, and change. You're dressed too warmly for the heat of the day."

She angled her head and was just annoyed enough now to give him a long, thorough look. His hair, all that mass of gold streaked brown, was windblown. That wonderfully sculpted mouth just quirked at the corners.

"Any other orders?"

"No, but an observation."

"I'm fascinated."

"No, you're irritated again, but I'll tell you anyway. Your mouth's more appealing naked as it is now than when it's painted as it was this morning."

"So you don't approve of lipstick?"

"Not at all. Some women need it. You don't, so it's just a distraction."

Baffled, nearly amused, she shook her head. "Thanks so much for the advice." She started for the house— where she'd been going to change into something cooler in the first place.

"Keeley."

She stopped, but instead of turning merely glanced

over her shoulder to where he stood, thumbs in the pockets of ancient jeans. "Yes?"

"It's nothing. I just wanted to try out your name. I like it."

"So do I. Isn't that handy?"

This time he blew out a breath as she strode off— long legs in tight pants and tall boots. He lifted her soft drink, took a deep sip. Playing with fire with that one, Donnelly, he warned himself. Since he was damned sure singed fingers wouldn't be all he would get if he risked a touch, it was best to back away before the heat became too tempting to resist.

Chapter 3

"Heels down, Lynn. Good. Hands, Shelly. Willy, pay attention." Keeley scanned each one of her afternoon students' form. They were coming along.

Six horses mounted with six children circled the paddock at a sedate walk. Two months before three of those children had never seen a horse firsthand, much less ridden one. Royal Meadows Riding Academy had changed that. It was making a difference.

"All right. Trot. Heads up," she ordered, hands on hips as she watched her students change gaits with varying degrees of success. "Heels down. Knees, Joey. That's the way. You're a team, remember. Looking good. Much better."

She moved closer, tapped the heels of one of her two boys. He grinned and turned them down. Oh, yes, much better, she thought. A month before Willy had jerked like a puppet every time she'd touched him.

It was all about trust.

She had them change leads, reverse, then attempt a wide figure eight.

It was a little messy, but she let them giggle their way through it.

It was also all about fun.

Brian watched her from a distance. He hadn't seen her for a couple of days. Nearly all of his time had been spent at the stables, or at one of the tracks where the Grants' horses ran. Apparently Keeley didn't spend much time at any of those locations.

He'd looked for her.

And had assumed she whiled away her time having lunch in some trendy spot, or shopping. Having her hair done or her fingernails painted. Whatever it was rich daughters did with their days.

But here she was, circling the paddock with a bunch of kids, obviously instructing them. He supposed it was a kind of hobby, teaching the privileged children of country club parents how to ride in proper English style.

Hobby or not, she looked good doing it. She'd chosen an informal look of jeans and a cotton shirt the color of blueberries. She'd pulled her hair back in some sort of band so that it fell in a wildly curling ponytail. Her boots appeared old, scuffed and serviceable.

She seemed to be enjoying herself. He didn't believe he'd seen her smile like that before. Not so quick and open and warm. Unable to resist, he walked closer as she stopped one of her students, stroked a hand over the horse's neck as she and the little girl had what appeared to be an earnest conversation.

By the time he'd reached the fence, Keeley had lined up all but the girl. Teaching them to control their mounts, he decided, to keep them quiet while something was going on around them.

The single rider posted prettily around the paddock, while Keeley turned a circle to keep her in sight. And circling, she saw Brian leaning on the fence.

The smile vanished, and he thought that was a true shame. But there was something almost as appealing about that cool, suspicious look she often aimed in his direction. He answered it with a grin, and settled in to watch the rest of the lesson.

Keeley didn't mind an audience. Often her parents or one of her siblings or one of the hands stopped by to watch. She'd certainly carried on her lessons with a parent or two of a student looking on. But since she didn't care for this particular observer, she ignored him.

One by one she selected a student to go through the day's routine solo. She corrected form, encouraged, pushed a little when it was needed for more effort or concentration. When she called for dismount, every one of them groaned.

"Five more minutes, Miss Keeley. Can't we ride for five more minutes?"

"I already let you ride five more minutes." She patted Shelly's knee. "Next week we're going to try a canter."

"I'm getting a horse for Christmas," Lynn announced. "And next spring, my mother says we'll enter shows."

"Then you'll have to work very hard. Cool off your mounts."

"That's a fine-looking group you have there. Miss Keeley."

Ingrained manners had her acknowledging Brian, walking over to the fence as she kept her eye on her students. "I like to think so."

"That boy there?" He nodded toward the dark-eyed, thin-faced Willy. "He's in love with that horse. Dreams of him at night, of racing over fields and hills and adventuring."

It made her smile again. "Teddy loves him, too. Teddy Bear," she explained. "A big, gentle sweetheart."

"This lot's lucky to have the wherewithal for lessons with a good instructor, and smart mounts. You stable them here? I haven't seen any of these down in my area."

"They're mine. I stable them here." Her horses, her school, her responsibility. "Excuse me. The lesson's not over until the horses are groomed."

Here's your hat, what's your hurry? Brian thought. Well, he had a few things to see to. But that didn't mean he couldn't wander back this way in a bit.

He bothered her. There was no real explanation for it, Keeley thought. It just was. She didn't like the way he looked at her. And why was she the only one who seemed to notice that edge in his eyes when they landed on her?

She didn't like the way he talked to her. And again, she seemed to be the only one aware of that sly little lilt in his voice when he said her name.

Everyone else thought Brian Donnelly was just dandy, she mused as she ran her hands up a gelding's legs to check for heat. Her parents considered him the perfect man to replace Uncle Paddy—and Uncle Paddy had nothing but praise for him.

Sarah thought he was hot. Patrick thought he was cool. And Brendon thought he was smart.

"Outnumbered," she muttered, and lifted the horse's foreleg to check the hoof.

Maybe it was some chemical reaction. Something that caused her hackles to rise when he was in the vicinity. After all, he appeared to be perfectly competent in his work. More than, she admitted, from what she'd heard. And as they were both busy, they would rarely bump up against each other. So it shouldn't matter.

But she didn't like the fact that she was avoiding the stables and shedrow. That she was deliberately foregoing the pleasure of wandering down that way and watching the workouts, or lending a hand in grooming. She didn't like knowing that about herself.

She certainly didn't care for the fact that she suspected *he* knew it. Which gave him entirely too much importance.

Which, she admitted, she was doing even now just by thinking of him.

The horse wickered. Keeley's shoulders stiffened.

"You've a good eye for horses," Brian said.

It didn't surprise her that she hadn't heard him come in. And it didn't surprise her that despite not hearing she'd known he was there. The air changed, she thought, when he was in it.

"I come by it naturally."

"You do. Teddy Bear." He murmured it, causing her to look up as she lowered the gelding's leg. His eyes were on the horse's, his skilled and clever hands already moving over head and throat. Keeley heard the gelding blow out a soft breath. Pure pleasure.

"You've a kind and patient heart, don't you?" Brian moved into the box, those wide palmed hands still skimming, stroking, checking. "And a fine broad back for carrying small, dreamy boys. How long have you had him?"

She blinked, nearly flushed. There was something hypnotic about those hands, about that voice. "Nearly two years."

Brian ran his hands down the flank. Stopped. His eyes narrowed as he stepped closer and examined a crosshatch of scarring. "What's this?" But he knew, and turned on Keeley so quickly she backed up to the wall before she could stop herself. "This horse has been whipped, and whipped bloody."

"His previous owner," she said, icily as a defense against that first spurt of alarm, "had a heavy hand with a whip. He wanted to show Teddy, but Teddy shied at the jumps. This was his way of showing he was the boss."

"Bloody bastard." And though his eyes still glinted with heat, his voice went soft again. "You're in a better place now, aren't you, boy. A fine home with a pretty woman to rub you down. Rescued him, did you?" he said to Keeley.

"I wouldn't go that far. There are different methods of breaking a horse. I don't happen to—"

"I don't break horses." Brian ducked under Teddy's belly, then his eyes met Keeley's over the wide back. "I make them. Any idiot can use a bat or a whip and break both spirit and heart. It takes skill and patience and a gentle hand to make a champion, or even just a friend."

She waited a moment, surprised her knees wanted to shake.. "Why do you expect me to disagree with you?" she wondered aloud. She stepped out of the box, moved to the next.

The aging mare greeted her with a snort and a bump of head on shoulder. Keeley snatched up a body brush to finish off her student's sketchy grooming.

"I can't stand seeing anything mistreated." Brian spoke quietly from behind her. Keeley didn't turn, didn't answer. Now that the first spurt of anger had passed, he had just enough room for shame at the way he'd turned on her. "Especially something that has so little choice. It makes me sick, and angry."

"And you expect me to disagree, again?"

"I snapped at you. I'm sorry." He touched a hand to her shoulder, left it there even when she stiffened—as he would with a nervous horse. "You look into eyes like that one has over there, and you see inside them that huge, generous heart. Then the scars where someone beat him—because he could. It scrambles my brain."

With an effort she relaxed her shoulders. "It took me three months to get him to trust me enough not to shy every time I lifted my hand. One day, he stuck his head out when I came in and called to me the way they do when they're happy to see you. I fed him carrots and cried like a baby. Don't tell me about mistreatment and scrambled brains."

Shame wasn't something he felt often, but it was easy

to recognize. He took a deep breath and hoped to start again. "What's this pretty mare's story?"

"Why do you think there's a story? She's a horse. You ride her."

"Keeley." He laid a hand over hers on the brush. "I'm sorry."

She moved her hand, but gave in and rested her cheek on the mare's neck. Rubbing, Brian noted, as she did when she hugged her parents.

"Her crime was age. She's nearly twenty. She'd been left stabled, and neglected. She was covered with nettle rash and lice. Her people just got bored with her, I suppose."

He didn't think when he stroked her hair. His hands were as much a part of his way of communicating as his voice. "How many do you have?"

"Eight, counting Sam, but he's too much for the students at this point."

"And did you save them all?"

"Sam was a gift for my twenty-first birthday. The others...well, when you're in the center of the horse world, you hear about horses. Besides, I needed them for the school."

"Some would expect you to stock thoroughbreds."

"Yes." She shifted. "Some would. Sorry, I have to feed the horses, then I have paperwork."

"I'll give you a hand with the feeding."

"I don't need it."

"I'll give you one anyway."

Keeley moved out of the box, rested a hand on the door. Best, she decided, to deal with this clean and simple. "Brian, you're working for my family, in a vital and essential role, so I think I should be straight with you."

"By all means." The serious tone didn't match the glint in his eye as she leaned back.

"You bother me," she told him. "On some level, you just bother me. It's probably because I just don't care for cocky, intense men who smirk at me, but that's neither here nor there."

"No, that's here and it's there. What kind do you care for?"

"You see—that's just the sort of thing that annoys me."

"I know. It's interesting, isn't it, that I find myself compelled to do just the thing that gets a rise out of you? You bother me as well. Perhaps it's that I don't care for regal, cool-eyed women who look down their lovely noses at me. But here we are, so we should try getting on as best we can."

"I don't look down my nose at you, or anyone."

"Depends on your point of view, doesn't it?"

She turned on her heel and marched away, focusing intensely on measuring out grain.

"Why don't we talk of something safe?" he suggested. "Like what I think about Royal Meadows. I've worked on farms and around tracks since I was ten. Stableboy, exercise boy, groom. Working my way up, hustling my way through. Twenty years means I've seen all sides of training, racing and breeding. The bright and the dark. And in twenty years, I've never seen brighter than Royal Meadows."

She paused, and her gaze shifted to his face before she began to add supplements to the grain.

"To my way of thinking, there aren't many people as worthy as one good horse. Your parents are admirable people. Not just for what they have, but much more for what they've done, and what they do with it. I'm honored to work for them. And," he said when she turned to him again, "they're lucky to have me."

She laughed. "Apparently they agree with you." Shaking her head, she moved by to start the feeding, and as she passed him he breathed in the scent of her hair, of her skin.

"But you're not sure you do. Though you don't seem to have much interest in the workings of the farm itself."

"Don't I?"

He studied the neatly typed list on the wall that indicated which supplements in what amounts were added for each particular horse for the evening feed. "I see your sisters and your brothers on a daily basis," he commented as he began to fix Teddy's meal. "Everyone in your family, down at the shedrow, or at the track, but you."

She could have told him the time and placement of every horse they'd run that past week. Which were being medicated, which mares were breeding. Pride kept her silent. She preferred thinking of it as pride, and not sheer stubbornness.

"I suppose your little school keeps you busy."

Her teeth clamped together, wanted to grind, but she spoke through them. "Oh, yes, my little school keeps me busy."

"You're a good teacher." He moved to Teddy's box.

"Thank you so much."

"No need to be snotty about it. You are a good

teacher. And one of those rich kids might stick it out, rather than getting bored once horse fever's passed."

"One of my rich kids," she murmured.

"It takes skill, endurance, and money, doesn't it, to compete in horse shows. I don't follow show jumping myself, though I've found it pretty enough to watch. You might be training yourself a champion. The Royal International or Dublin Grand Prix. Maybe the Olympics."

"So, let's see if I get this. Rich kids compete in horse shows and win blue ribbons and those who aren't so privileged do what? Become grooms?"

"That's how the world works, doesn't it?"

"That's how it can work. You're a snob, Brian."

He looked up, flabbergasted. "What?"

"You're a snob, and the worst kind of snob—the kind who thinks he's broad-minded. Now that I know that, you don't bother me at all."

The stable phone rang, delighting her. Whoever was on the other end not only had perfect timing but they had her gratitude. It gave her great pleasure to see the absolute shock on Brian's face as she walked to the phone.

"Royal Meadows Riding Academy. Would you hold one moment, please." With a friendly smile, she laid a hand over the receiver. "Really, I can finish up here. I'm keeping you from your work."

"I'm not a snob," he finally managed to say.

"Of course you wouldn't see it that way. Can we discuss this another time? I need to take this call."

Irked, he shoved the scoop back in the grain. "I'm not the one wearing bloody diamonds in my ears," he muttered as he stalked out.

* * *

It put him out of humor for the rest of the day. It stuck in his craw and festered there. A nasty little canker sore on the ego.

Snob? Where did the woman get off calling him a snob? And after he'd made the effort to be friendly, even compliment her on her snooty little riding academy.

He did the evening check himself, as was his habit, and spent considerable time going over the prime filly who was to head down to Hialeah to race there. Travis wanted Brian to go along for this one, and he was more than happy to oblige.

It would do him a world of good to put a thousand miles or so between himself and Keeley.

"Shouldn't be looking in that direction, even for a blink," he muttered, then nuzzled the filly. "Especially when I've got a darling like you in hand. We'll have us a time in Florida, won't we, you and me?"

"Poker game tonight," one of the grooms called out as Brian left the stables. He added an eyebrow wiggle and a grin to the announcement.

"I'll be back then. And it'll be my pleasure to empty your pockets." But for now, he thought, he had paperwork of his own.

When he returned from Florida they'd separate the foals from their mothers. The weanlings would cause a commotion the first day or so. And the yearling training would begin in earnest. He had charts to make, schedules to outline, plans to ponder.

And he wanted to put a great deal of personal time into the forming of Bad Betty.

He had no business detouring toward Keeley's stable.

Still it would only take a minute, Brian told himself, to set the woman straight.

But instead of Keeley, he found her sister. Sarah stopped her dash past him and waved. "Hi. Wonderful evening, isn't it? I'm going to take advantage of it and sneak in a ride before sunset. Want to join me?"

It was tempting. She was good company, and he hadn't felt a horse under him in weeks. But there was work. "I'd love to, another time. You riding one of Keeley's?"

"Yeah. She's always up for someone to exercise one of her babies. The kids don't give them much of a workout, so they can get stale. Or bored. Her Saturday class is a little more advanced, but still."

He fell into step beside her. "I don't suppose an hour of posture and posting does much for the horses."

"Oh, she lets them out to pasture, and rides herself whenever she can fit it in. Which isn't as much as she'd like, but the kids are the priority. And that hour of posture and posting does a lot for them."

He made a noncommittal sound as they rounded the building. He hoped Keeley was still inside what he supposed was an office. He wanted a word with her. "I saw part of her class today."

"Did you? Aren't they cute? Today's what…oh, yeah, Willy. Did you notice the little guy, dark hair and eyes? He rides Teddy."

"Aye. He has good form, and he's cheerful about it."

"He is now. He was a scared little rabbit when Keeley took him on." Sarah swung into the stables, headed directly for the tack room.

"Afraid of horses?"

"Of everything. I don't know how people can do that to a child. I'll never understand it."

"Do what?"

She chose her tack, murmuring a thanks when Brian took the saddle from her. "Hurt them." She glanced back. "Oh, I thought since you'd seen the class, Keeley would have told you the whole deal about the school."

"No." He took the saddle blanket as well. "We didn't get to that. Why don't you tell me the whole deal?"

"Sure." She went to the old mare, cooed. "There's my girl. Want to go for a ride? Sure you do." She slipped the bridle on, fixed the bit, then led the mare out. "I don't know if it started with the horses or the kids. It all seemed to happen at the same time. She bought Eastern Star first. He was a thoroughbred, five years old, and he hadn't lived up to his potential. According to the owners. They pumped him up before a race."

"Drugged him."

"Amphetamines." Her pretty face went hard. "They got caught, but they'd damaged Star's heart and kidneys in the process. She bought him. We nursed him, did everything we could. He didn't last a year. It still gets me," Sarah murmured.

She shook her head and began to saddle her mount. "After that it was like a mission to Keeley. So I guess the horses came first. She put this place together, and got the word out that she was opening a small academy. The ones who can pay, pay a very stiff fee to have her teach their kids—and she's worth it. Those stiff fees help subsidize the other students."

"What other students?"

"Ones like Willy." Sarah cinched the saddle, checked

the stirrups. "Underprivileged, abused, circling the system kids. She takes them for nothing—no, she hunts them up, sponsors them, outfits them, works with a child psychologist. It's why she doesn't have as much time to ride as she used to. Our Keeley doesn't do anything halfway. She'd take more on, but she wants to keep the classes small so each kid gets plenty of attention. So she's campaigning for other academies, other owners to start similar programs."

Sarah patted the mare's neck. "I'm surprised she didn't mention it. She rarely misses an opportunity to talk someone into getting involved."

With a cheerful smile, she vaulted into the saddle. "Listen, would you like to come up for dinner? I hear Dad's grilling chicken."

"Thanks all the same, but I've plans. Enjoy your ride."

He had plans all right, he thought as Sarah trotted off. To eat crow. He wasn't sure what it tasted like, but he already knew he wasn't going to enjoy it.

He walked around to the office, knocked. He supposed if he'd been wearing a hat, he'd have held it in his hands. When she didn't answer, he opened the door, glanced in.

Neat, organized, as expected. The air smelled of her—just the faintest echo of scent.

But everything inside was designed for business. A desk—with a computer he imagined was a great deal more in use than Paddy's—a two-line telephone and a little fax machine. File cabinets, two trim chairs and a small fridge. Curious, he walked in and opened it. Then had to grin when he saw it was stocked with bottles of the soft drink she seemed to live on.

A scan of the walls had the grin turning to a wince. Blue ribbons, medals, awards were all neatly framed and displayed. There were photographs of her in formal riding gear flying over jumps, smiling from the back of a horse or standing with her cheek pressed to her mount's neck.

And in a thick frame was an Olympic medal. A silver.

"Well, hell. We'll make that two portions of crow," he murmured.

Chapter 4

It was his fault. She could put the blame for this entirely on Brian Donnelly's shoulders. If he hadn't been so insufferable, if he hadn't been there *being* insufferable when Chad had called, she wouldn't have agreed to go out to dinner. And she wouldn't have spent nearly four hours being bored brainless when she could've been doing something more useful.

Like watching paint dry.

There was nothing wrong with Chad, really. If you only had, say, half a brain, no real interest outside of the cut of this year's designer jacket and were thrilled by a rip-roaring debate over the proper way to serve a triple latte, he was the perfect companion.

Unfortunately, she didn't qualify on any of those levels.

Right now he was droning on about the painting he'd bought at a recent art show. No, not the painting, Keeley thought wearily. A discussion of the painting, of art, might have been the medical miracle that prevented her from slipping into a coma. But Chad was discoursing—no other word for it—on The Investment.

He had the windows up and the air conditioning blasting as they drove. It was a perfectly beautiful night, she mused, but putting the windows down meant Chad's hair would be mussed. Couldn't have that.

At least she didn't have to attempt conversation. Chad preferred monologues.

What he wanted was an attractive companion of the right family and tax bracket who dressed well and would sit quietly while he pontificated on the narrow areas of his interest.

Keeley was fully aware he'd decided she fit the bill, and now she'd only encouraged him by agreeing to this endlessly tedious date.

"The broker assured me that within three years the piece will be worth five times what I paid for it. Normally I would have hesitated as the artist is young and relatively unknown, but the show was quite successful. I noticed T.D. Giles considering two of the pieces personally. And you know how astute T.D. is about such things. Did I tell you I ran into his wife, Sissy, the other day? She looks absolutely marvelous. The eye tuck did wonders for her, and she tells me she's found the most amazing new stylist."

Oh God, was all Keeley could think. Oh God, get me out of here.

When they swung through the stone pillars at Royal Meadows, she had to fight the urge to cheer.

"I'm so glad our schedules finally clicked. Life gets much too demanding and complicated, doesn't it? There's nothing more relaxing than a quiet dinner for two."

Any more relaxed, Keeley thought, and unconsciousness would claim her. "It was nice of you to ask me, Chad." She wondered how rude it would be to spring out of the car before it stopped, race to the house and do a little dance of relief on the front porch.

Pretty rude, she decided. Okay, she'd skip the dance.

"Drake and Pamela—you know the Larkens of course—are having a little soirée next Saturday evening. Why don't I pick you up at eightish?"

It took her a minute to get over the fact he'd actually used the word *soirée* in a sentence. "I really can't, Chad. I have a full day of lessons on Saturday. By the time it's done I'm not fit for socializing. But thanks." She slid her hand to the door handle, anticipating escape.

"Keeley, you can't let your little school eclipse so much of your life."

Her hand stiffened, and though she could see the lights of home, she turned her head and studied his perfect profile. One day, someone was going to refer to the academy as *her little school,* and she was going to be very rude. And rip their throat out. "Can't I?"

"I'm sure it amuses you. Hobbies are very satisfying."

"Hobbies." She bared her teeth.

"Everyone needs an outlet, I suppose." He lifted a hand from the wheel and gracefully waved away over two years of hard work. "But you must take time for yourself. Just the other day Renny mentioned she hadn't seen you in ages. After all, when the novelty wears off, you'll wonder where all this time has gone."

"My school is not a hobby, an amusement, or a novelty. And it is completely my business."

"Naturally. Of course." He gave her a patronizing little pat on the knee as he stopped the car, shifted toward her. "But you must admit, it's taking up an inordinate amount of your time. Why it's taken us six months to have dinner together."

"Is that all?"

He misinterpreted the quiet response, and the gleam in her eyes. And leaned toward her.

She slapped a hand on his chest. "Don't even think about it. Let me tell you something, pal. I do more in one day with my school than you do in a week of pushing papers in that office your grandfather gave you between your manicures and amaretto lattes and soirées. Men like you hold no interest for me whatsoever, which is why it's taken six months for this tedious little date. And the next time I have dinner with you, we'll be slurping Popsicles in hell. So take your French tie and your Italian shoes and stuff them."

Utter shock had him speechless as she shoved open her door. As insult trickled in, his lips thinned. "Obviously spending so much time in the stables has eroded your manners, and your outlook."

"That's right, Chad." She leaned back in the door. "You're too good for me. I'm about to go up and weep into my pillow over it."

"Rumor is you're cold," he said in a quiet, stabbing voice. "But I had to find out for myself."

It stung, but she wasn't about to let it show. "Rumor is you're a moron. Now we've both confirmed the local gossip."

He gunned the engine once, and she would have sworn she saw him vibrate. "And it's a British tie."

She slammed the car door, then watched narrow-eyed as he drove away. "A British tie." A laugh gurgled up, deep from the belly and up into the throat so she had to stand, hugging herself, all but howling at the moon. "That sure told me."

Indulging herself in a long sigh, she tipped her head back, looked up at the sweep of stars. "Moron," she murmured. "And that goes for both of us."

She heard a faint *click,* spun around and saw Brian lighting a slim cigar. "Lover's spat?"

"Why yes." The temper Chad had roused stirred again. "He wants to take me to Antigua and I simply have my heart set on Mozambique. Antigua's been done to death."

Brian took a contemplative puff of his cigar. She looked so damn beautiful standing there in the moonlight in that little excuse of a black dress, her hair spilling down her back like fire on silk. Hearing her long, gorgeous roll of laughter had been like discovering a treasure. Now the temper was back in her eyes, and spitting at him.

It was almost as good.

He took another lazy puff, blew out a cloud of smoke. "You're winding me up, Keeley."

"I'd like to wind you up, then twist you into small pieces and ship them all back to Ireland."

"I figured as much." He disposed of the cigar and walked to her. Unlike Chad, he didn't misinterpret the glint in her eye. "You want to have a pop at someone." He closed his hand over the one she'd balled into a fist, lifted it to tap on his own chin. "Go ahead."

"As delightful as I find that invitation, I don't solve my disputes that way." When she started to walk away, he tightened his grip. "But," she said slowly, "I could make an exception."

"I don't like apologizing, and I wouldn't have to— again—if you'd set me straight right off."

She lifted an eyebrow. Trying to free herself from that big, hard hand would only be undignified. "And are you referring to my little school?"

"It's a fine thing you're doing. An admirable thing, and not a little one at all. I'd like to help you."

"Excuse me?"

"I'd like to give you a hand with it when I can. Give you some of my time."

Off balance, she shook her head. "I don't need any help."

"I don't imagine you do. But it couldn't hurt, could it?"

She studied him with equal parts suspicion and interest. "Why?"

"Why not. You'll admit I know horses. I have a strong back. And I believe in what you're doing."

It was the last that cut through her defenses. No one outside of family had understood what she wanted to do as easily. She flexed her hand in his, and when he released her, stepped back. "Are you offering because you feel guilty?"

"I'm offering because I'm interested. Feeling guilty made me apologize."

"You haven't apologized yet." But she smiled a little as she began to walk. "Never mind. I might be able to use a strong back from time to time." She glanced over as he fell into step beside her. It looked like he had one, she mused, skimming her gaze over the rough jeans and plain white T-shirt he wore.

A strong, healthy body, good hands and an innate understanding of horses. She could do a great deal worse, she supposed. "Do you ride?"

"Well, of course I ride," he began, then caught her smirky little smile. "Having me on again, are you?"

"That one was easy." She turned to wander along a path that meandered through late-blooming shrubs and an arbor of gleaming moonflowers. "I won't pay you."

"I've a job, thanks."

"The kids handle a lot of the chores," she told him. "It's part of the package. This isn't just about teaching them to post and change leads at a canter. It's about trust—in themselves, in their horse, in me. Making a connection with their horse. Shoveling manure makes quite a connection."

He grinned. "I can't argue with that."

"Still they're kids, so fun is a big part of the program. And they're learning so they don't always do the best job mucking out or grooming. And there isn't always enough time to have them deal properly with the tack."

"I started my illustrious career with a pitchfork in my hand and saddle soap in my pocket."

Idly he tugged a white blossom from the vine, tucked it into her hair. The gesture flustered her—the easy charm of it—and made her remember they were walking in the moonlight, among the flowers.

Not, she reminded herself, a good idea.

"All right then. If and when you've time to spare, I've got an extra pitchfork."

When she veered toward the house he took her hand again. "Don't go in yet. It's a pretty night and a shame to waste it with sleeping."

His voice was lovely, with a soothing lilt. There was no reason she could think of why it made her want to shiver. "We both have to be up early."

"True enough, but we're young, aren't we? I saw your medal."

Distracted, she forgot to pull her hand away. "My medal?"

"Your Olympic medal. I went looking for you in your office."

"The medal lures parents who can afford the tuition."

"It's something to be proud of."

"I am proud of it." With her free hand she brushed her hair as the breeze teased it. Her fingertips skimmed over the soft petals of the flower. "But it doesn't define me."

"Not like, what was it? A British tie?"

The laugh got away from her, and eased the odd tension that had been building inside her. "Here's a surprise. With a great deal of time and some effort, I might begin to like you."

"I've plenty of time." He released her hand to toy

with the ends of her hair. She jerked back. "You're a skittish one," he murmured.

"No, not particularly." Usually, she thought. With most people.

"The thing is, I like to touch," he told her and deliberately skimmed his fingers over her hair again. "It's that...connection. You learn by touching."

"I don't..." She trailed off when those fingers ran firmly down the back of her neck.

"I've learned you carry your worries right there, right at the base there. More worries than show on your face. It's a staggering face you have, Keeley. Throws a man off."

The tension was slipping away from under his fingers as he touched her, and building everywhere else. A kind of gathering inside her, a concentration of heat. The pressure in her chest was so sudden and strong it made her breath short. The muscles in her stomach began to twist, tighten. Ache.

"My face doesn't have anything to do with what I am."

"Maybe not, but that doesn't take away the pure pleasure of looking at it."

If she hadn't trembled, he might have resisted. It was a mistake. But he'd made them before, would make them again. There was moonlight, and the scent of the last of summer's roses in the air. Was a man supposed to walk away from a beautiful woman who trembled under his hand?

Not this man, he thought.

"Too pretty a night to waste it," he said again, and bent toward her.

She jerked back when his mouth was a whisper from hers, but his fingers continued to play over her neck, keeping her close. His gaze dropped to her lips, lingered, then came back to hers.

And he smiled. *"Cushla machree,"* he murmured, and as if it were an incantation, she slid under the spell.

His lips brushed hers, wing-soft. Everything inside her fluttered in response. He drew her closer, gradually luring her body to fit against his, curves to angles, as his hand played rhythmically up and down her spine.

A light scrape of teeth, and her lips parted for him.

Her head went light, her blood hot, and her body seemed balanced on the brink of something high and thin. It was lovely, lovely to feel this soft, this female, this open. She brought her hands to his shoulders, clung there while she let herself teeter on that delicious edge.

He knew how to be gentle, there had always been gentleness inside him for the fragile. But her sudden and utter surrender to him, to herself, had him forcing back the need to grab and plunder. Resistance was what he'd expected. Anything from cool disdain to impulsive passion he would have understood. But this…giving destroyed him.

"More," he murmured against her mouth. "Just a little more." And deepened the kiss.

She made a sound in her throat, a low purr that slipped into his system like silk. His heart shook, then it stumbled, then God help him, it fell.

The shock of it had him yanking her back, staring at her with the edgy caution of a man suddenly finding himself holding a tiger instead of a kitten.

Had he actually thought it a mistake? Nothing more than a simple mistake? He'd just put the power to crush him into her hands.

"Damn it."

She blinked at him, struggling to catch up with the abrupt change. His face was fierce, and the hands that had shifted to her arms no longer gentle. She wanted to shiver, but wouldn't permit another show of weakness.

"Let me go."

"I didn't force you."

"I didn't say you did."

Her lips still throbbed from the pressure of his, and her stomach quaked. Rumor was she was cold, she thought dimly. And she'd believed it herself. Finding out differently wasn't cause for celebration. But for panic.

"I don't want this." This vulnerability, this need.

"Neither do I." He released her to jam his hands into his pockets. "That makes this quite the situation."

"It's not a situation if we don't let it be one." She wanted to rub a hand over her heart, to hold it there. It amazed her that he couldn't hear it hammering. "We're both grown-ups, able to take responsibility for our own actions. That was a momentary lapse on both our parts. It won't happen again."

"And if it does?"

"It won't, because each of us have priorities and a…situation would complicate matters. We'll forget it. Good night."

She walked to the house. She didn't run, though part of her wanted to. And another part, a part that brought her no pride, simply wanted him to stop her.

* * *

He'd hoped the time away in Florida with work at the center of his world would help him do just what she'd said to do. Forget it.

But he hadn't, and couldn't, and finally decided it had been a ridiculous thing for her to expect. Since he was suffering, he saw no reason why he should let her off so damn easy.

He knew how to handle women, he reminded himself. And princess or not, Keeley was a woman under it all. She was going to discover she couldn't swat Brian Donnelly aside like a pesky fly.

He walked up from the stables, his bag slung over his shoulder. He'd yet to go to his quarters, and had slept very little on the drive back from Hialeah. He could have flown back, but the choice to stay with the horses and make the drive had been his.

His horses had done all he'd asked of them, made him proud at heart and plumper in the pocket. Seeing that they were delivered home and settled back again was the least he could do.

But right now he wanted nothing more than a hot shower, a shave and a decent cup of tea.

Though he'd have traded all of that for one more taste of Keeley.

Knowing it irritated him had him scowling in the direction of her paddock. The minute he was cleaned up, he promised himself, the two of them would have a little conversation. Very little, he decided, before he got his hands on her again. And when he did, he was going to—

The erotic image he conjured in his head burst like

a bubble when he rounded the house and saw Keeley's mother kneeling at the flower bed.

It was not the most comfortable thing to come across the mother when you'd been picturing the daughter naked. Then Adelia looked over at him, and he saw the tears on her cheeks. And his mind went blank.

"Ah... Mrs. Grant."

"Brian." Sniffling, she wiped her cheeks with the back of her hand. "I was doing some weeding. Just tidying up the beds here." She tugged at the cap on her head, then she lowered her hands, dropped back on her heels. "I'm sorry."

"Ah..." Said that already, he thought, panicked. Say something else. He was never so helpless as he was with female tears.

"I'm missing Uncle Paddy. He left yesterday." She didn't quite muffle a sob. "I thought if I came by here and fiddled, I'd feel some better, but it's knowing he's not down at the stables, or up there. I know he had to go. I know he wanted to go. But..."

"Ah..." Oh hell. Frantic, Brian dug in his back pocket for his bandanna. "Maybe you should..."

"Thanks." She took the cloth as he crouched beside her. "You'll know what it's like, I think, being away from family."

"Well, mine's not close, so to speak."

"Family's family." She dried her face, blew out a breath.

She looked so young, he thought, and not like a mother at all, with her cap crooked on her head and her eyes drenched. He did what came natural for him, and took her hand.

For a moment, she leaned her head on his shoulder, sighed. "He changed everything for me, Paddy did, when he brought me here. I was so nervous coming all this way. New place, new people. A new country. And I hadn't seen Paddy outside pictures for years, or even been face-to-face since I was a baby, but as soon as I saw him, it was all right again. I don't know what I'd have done without him."

It loosened the fist around her heart to talk. Soothed her that he gave her the quiet that was an offer to listen.

"I didn't want to blubber in front of Travis and the children because they're missing him, too. And I was holding on pretty well until I came down here. This is where I lived when I first came to Royal Meadows. In a pretty room with green walls and white curtains. I was so young."

"I guess you're old and decrepit now," Brian said and was relieved when she laughed.

"Well, perhaps not quite decrepit, but I was greener then. I'd never seen a place like this in all my life, and I was going to be living right in the middle of it thanks to Paddy. If it hadn't been for him, I don't think Travis would ever have taken the likes of me on as a groom."

"A groom." Brian's brows lifted. "I thought that was a made-up story."

"Indeed it's not," she said with some heat—and an unmistakable touch of pride. "I earned my keep around here, make no mistake. I was a damn fine groom in my time. Majesty was mine."

Brian lowered himself until he was sitting on the ground beside her. "You groomed Majesty?"

"That I did, and was there to watch him take the Derby. Oh, I loved that horse. You know what it's like."

"I do, yes."

"We lost him only last year. A fine long life he had. I think that was when Paddy decided it was time for him to go home again. He's there by now, and I know what he sees when he stands out in front of the house, and that's a comfort. As you've been just now, Brian. Thank you."

"I didn't do anything. I fumble with tears."

"You listened." She handed him back his bandanna.

"Mostly because tears render me speechless. You've a bit of garden dirt here."

Keeley came down the path just in time to see Brian gently wipe her mother's face with a blue bandanna. The tearstains had her leaping forward like a mama bear to her threatened cub.

"What is it? What did you do?" Hissing at Brian, she wrapped an arm around Adelia's shoulder.

"Nothing. I just knocked your mother down and kicked her a few times."

"Keeley." With a surprised laugh, Adelia patted her daughter's hand. "Brian's done nothing but lend me his hankie and his shoulder while I had a little cry over Uncle Paddy."

"Oh, Mama." Keeley pressed her cheek to Adelia's, rubbed. "Don't be sad."

"I have to be, a little. But I'm better now." She leaned over, surprising Brian with a kiss on the cheek. "You're a nice young man, and a patient one."

He got to his feet to help her up. "I don't have much of a reputation for either, Mrs. Grant."

"That's because not everyone looks close enough. You should be able to call me Dee easy enough now that I've cried on you. I'm going down to the stables, do some work."

"She never cries," Keeley murmured when her mother walked away. "Not unless she's very happy or very sad. I'm sorry I jumped at you that way, but when I saw she'd been crying, I stopped thinking."

"Tears affect me much the same way, so we'll let it be."

She nodded, then cast around for something to say that would help relieve the awkwardness. She'd been so sure she'd be controlled and composed when she saw him again. "So, I heard you did well at Hialeah."

"We did. Your Hero runs particularly well in a crowd."

"Yes, I've seen him. He lives to run." She noted the bag Brian had set down. "And here you are not even really back yet, and you've had one woman crying on your shoulder and another swiping at you. I really am sorry."

"Sorry enough to make me some tea while I clean up?"

"I…all right, but I've got less than an hour."

"Takes a good deal less to brew a pot of tea." Satisfied, he started up the steps. "You've a class this afternoon then?"

"Yes." Trapped, Keeley shrugged and followed him up and inside. He'd been kind to her mother, she reminded herself. She was obliged to repay that. "At three-thirty. I have some things to do before the students arrive."

"Well, I won't be long. You know where the kitchen is, I expect."

She frowned after him as he strolled off into the bedroom.

Making him cozy pots of tea wasn't how she'd expected to handle the situation, she thought. She'd given it a great deal of consideration and had decided the best thing all around would be to maintain a polite, marginally friendly distance. That business the other night had been nothing but a moment's foolishness. Harmless.

Incredible.

She gave herself a shake and got down the old teapot Paddy had favored. No, it was nothing to worry about. In fact, on one level she really should be grateful to Brian. He'd shown her she wasn't as indifferent to men as she'd believed. It had bothered her a little that she'd never felt that spark so many of her friends had spoken of.

Well, she'd certainly felt a whole firestorm of sparks when he'd put his hands on her. And that was good, that was healthy. Someone had finally caught her at the right time and the right place and the right mood. If it could happen once, it could happen again.

With someone else, of course. When she decided it was time.

She set the tea aside to steep, then opening a cupboard stretched high for a cup.

"I'll get that." He moved in behind her, handily trapping her between his body and the counter. Closed his hand over hers on the cup.

She could smell the shower on him, feel the heat of it. And her mouth went dry.

"I decided I don't care to forget it."

She had to concentrate on regulating her breathing. "I beg your pardon?"

"And that I'm not going to let you forget it, either."

She needed to swallow, but her throat wouldn't co-operate. "We agreed—"

"No, we didn't." He brought the cup down, set it aside. "We agreed we didn't want this." The ponytail she wore left a lovely curve of her neck bare. He nuzzled there. "And I'd say there's been an unspoken agreement that despite that, we want each other."

The firestorm was back, a burst at the base of her neck that showered heat down her spine. "We don't know each other."

"I know how you taste." He nipped lightly at flesh. "And feel, and smell. I see your face in my mind whether I want to or not." He spun her around, and his eyes were dark and restless. "Why should you have a choice when I don't?"

His mouth crushed down on hers, a hot and danger-ous thrill. With his hands gripped in her hair, he pressed his body to hers.

And this time she felt as much anger as passion in the embrace. Now, wrapped around the thrill, was a thin snake of fear. The combination was unbearably exciting.

"I'm not ready for this." She struggled back. "I'm not ready for this. Can you understand?"

"No." But he understood what he saw in her eyes. He'd frightened her, and he'd no right to do so. "But then again, I don't want to." So he backed away. "Your mother said I was a patient man. I can be, under some circumstances. I'll wait, because you'll come to me.

There's something alive between us, so when you're ready, you'll come to me."

"There's a thin line between confidence and arrogance, Brian. Watch your step," she suggested as she started for the door.

"I missed you."

Her hand closed over the knob, but she couldn't turn it. "You know all the angles," she murmured.

"That may be true. But still I missed you. Thanks for the tea."

She sighed. "You're welcome," she said, and left him.

Chapter 5

Bad Betty had more than earned her name. She didn't just make trouble, she looked for it. Nothing seemed to please her more than nipping at grooms. Unless it was kicking exercise boys. She chased other yearlings when out in pasture, then reared and kicked and snorted bad-temperedly when it was time to be stabled for the night.

For all those reasons, and more, Brian adored her.

There was a communal sigh of relief in the shedrow when he opted to deal with her personally. She tested him, and though she rarely got by Brian's guard he had an impressive rainbow of bruises with her name on them.

There were mutters that she was a man-eater, but Brian knew better. She was a rebel. And she was a win-

ner. It was only a matter of teaching her how to start
winning without damaging that wild spirit.

On the longe line he circled her into a walk while
she pretended to ignore him. Still, when he spoke to
her, her ears twitched, and now and then she sent him a
sidelong glance. And days of hard work were rewarded
when he lengthened the line and she broke into a canter.

"Ah, that's the way. What a beauty you are." He'd
liked to have captured that moment—the gorgeous filly
cantering gracefully in a circle, while green hills rolled
up to a blue sky.

It would make a picture, and look to some like a
frolic. But those who knew would see this moment—
a racehorse learning to take commands from signals
transmitted through her mouth—was another step toward the finish line.

He saw one more thing as he looked at her, as he
studied lines and form and that unmistakable gleam
in her eyes.

He saw his destiny.

"We'll go, you and I," he said quietly. "We were
meant to go together. Rebels we are, or so people say
who can't see where we're headed. We've races to win,
don't we?"

He shortened the line, and she dropped into a trot.
Shortened it still further and her gait changed to a walk.
Sweat gleamed on her coat, trickled down his back.
Summer wasn't just clinging to September. It was pum-
meling it.

They ignored the heat, and watched each other.

Again and again he used the line to signal her as she
circled, and all the while he praised her.

Watching was irresistible. She had work to do, chores piled up. But if she couldn't take a few moments out on a brilliant September day to watch a little magic, what was the point?

She leaned on the paddock fence, enjoying the view as Brian put Betty through her paces. Her father had been right in hiring him, she thought. There was a connection between man and horse that was stronger, and even more tangible than the line between them. She could feel it. Amusement, affection, challenge.

This wasn't something that could be taught. It simply was.

She knew Brian took time for every weanling on the farm when he wasn't out of town at a race. That wasn't an easy task in an operation as large as Royal Meadows. But it was the kind of touch that made a difference. A smart and caring horseman knew that the more a horse was handled, touched, communicated with during its youth, the better it would respond to later training.

"Looks good, doesn't she?" Brian said as he let out the line for one last canter.

"Very. You've made considerable progress with her."

"We've made progress with each other, haven't we *a ghra*. She's ready to feel a rider on her."

Knowing Betty's reputation, Keeley tucked her tongue in her cheek. "And who are you bribing—or threatening—to get up on her?"

Gradually Brian shortened the line, and Betty moved into an even trot. "Want the job?"

"I have a job, thanks." But it was tempting.

Brian knew when a seed planted needed to be left alone to sprout. "Well, she'll have her first weight on her tomorrow morning." He shortened the line again, moving Betty toward him, and both of them toward Keeley.

He liked the look of her there against the fence, with her hair as glossy as the filly's coat, and her eyes as cautious. "This one won't be placid and eager to please. But she'll come round, won't you, *maverneen?*"

He stroked the filly's neck, and she sniffed at the pouch on his belt, then turned her head away.

"She wants to let me know she doesn't care that I've apples in here. No, doesn't matter a bit to her." He looped the line around the fence and took an apple and his knife from his pocket. Idly he cut it in half. "Maybe I'll just offer this token to this other pretty lady here."

He held out the apple to Keeley, and Betty gave him a solid rap with her head that rammed him into the fence. "Now she wants my attention. Would you like some of this then?"

He shifted, held the apple out. Betty nipped it from his palm with dignified delicacy. "She loves me."

"She loves your apples," Keeley commented.

"Oh, it's not just that. See here." Before Keeley could evade—could think to—he cupped a hand at the back of her neck, pulled her close and rubbed his lips provocatively over hers.

Betty huffed out a breath and butted him.

"You see?" Brian let his teeth graze lightly before he released Keeley. "Jealous. She doesn't care to have me give my affection to another woman."

"Next time kiss her and save yourself a bruise."

"It was worth it. On both counts."

"Horses are more easily charmed than women, Donnelly." She plucked the apple out of his hand, bit in. "I just like your apples," she told him, and strolled away.

"That one's as contrary as you are." He nuzzled Betty's cheek as he watched Keeley walk to her stables. "What is it that makes me find contrary females so appealing?"

She hadn't meant to go down to the yearling stalls. Really. It was just that she was up early, her own morning chores were done. And she was curious. When she stepped inside the stables, out of the soft gray dawn, the first thing she heard was Brian's voice.

It made her smile. At least the exasperation in it made her smile.

"Come on now, Jim, you lost the draw. You can't be welshing on me."

"I'm not. I'm gearing up."

The young exercise boy was gritting his teeth and rolling his shoulders when Keeley stepped up to the box. "Good morning. I heard you drew the short straw, Jim."

"Yeah, just my luck." He shot a mournful look at Betty. "This one wants to eat me."

"Chew you up and spit you out more like," Brian said in disgust. "You're just giving her cause now by letting her know she intimidates you. You'll go down in history today—the first weight the next winner of the Triple Crown feels on her back."

As if reacting to the prediction, Betty snorted, tried to dance as Brian firmed his grip on the shortened reins. And Jim's eyes went big as moons in a pale face.

"I'll do it." Keeley wasn't sure if it was the challenge of it, or compassion for the terrified boy. "If it's an historic moment, it should be a Grant up on a Royal Meadows champion." She smiled at Jim as she said it. "Let me have the jacket and hat."

"You sure?" With more hope than shame, Jim looked from Keeley to Brian.

"She's the boss. In a manner of speaking," Brian told him. "Your loss here, Jim."

"I'll take the loss and save all my skin." A little too eagerly, he started out of the box. As if sensing her opening, Betty bunched, kicked out. Swearing, Brian shoved Jim aside with his shoulder and took the hoof in the ribs.

The air went blue, and every curse was in an undertone that only added impact. Without a second thought, Keeley moved into the box and laid her hand over his on the reins to help control the filly.

A thousand pounds of horse fought to plunge. Keeley felt the heat from her, and from Brian when their bodies bumped together. "How bad did she get you?"

"Not as bad as she'd like." But enough, he thought, to steal his breath and have the pain shooting up until he saw stars dancing.

He tossed the hair out of his eyes, blinked at the sweat stinging in them and muscled the filly down.

"Man, Bri, I'm sorry."

"You should have more sense than to turn your back on a skittish filly," Brian snapped out. "Next time I'll let her take a shot at your head. Go on out. She knows she's bested you. Stand back," he ordered Keeley in the same cold tone of command, then he jerked the reins just enough to bring Betty's head down.

"So this is how it's to be? You want all the temper

and none of the glory? Am I wasting my time with you? Maybe you don't want to run. We'll just wait until you come into season and bring a stallion in to mount you, and set you out to pasture to breed. Then you'll never know, will you, what it is to win."

Just outside the box, Keeley slipped on the padded jacket and hat. And waited. There was a line of damp down the back of his shirt, his hair was a wild tangle of brown and gold. Muscles rippled in his arms, and his boots were scarred and filthy.

He looked, she decided, exactly how a horseman should look. Powerful. Confident. And just arrogant enough to believe he could win over an animal more than five times his weight.

He kept talking, but he'd switched to Gaelic now. Slowly, the rhythm of the words smoothed out, and warmed. Almost like a song, they played in the air, rising, falling. Mesmerizing.

The filly stood quiet now, her dark brown eyes focused on Brian's green ones.

Seduced, Keeley thought. She was watching a kind of seduction. She'll do anything for him, Keeley realized. Who wouldn't if he touched you that way, looked at you that way, used his voice on you that way?

"Come in here," he told Keeley. "Let her get your scent. Touch her so she can feel you."

"I know how it's done," she murmured. Though she'd never seen it done quite like this.

She slipped into the stall, ran her hands gently over Betty's neck, her side. She felt the muscles quiver under her hand, but the filly looked at nothing and no one but Brian.

"I've seen countless people work in countless ways with countless horses." Keeley spoke quietly as she stroked Betty. But like the horse, her eyes were on Brian. "I've never seen anyone like you. You have a gift."

His eyes shifted, met hers, held for a moment. One timeless moment. "She has the gift. Talk to her."

"Betty. Not-so-bad Betty. You scared poor Jim, didn't you, but you don't scare me. I think you're beautiful." She saw the filly's ears lay back, felt the slight shift under her hands, but kept talking. "You want to race, don't you? Well, you can't do it alone. I'd tell you this isn't going to hurt, but you don't care about that anyway. It's all pride with you."

Once again she looked at Brian. "It's all pride," she repeated, understanding both horse and man. "But you can't have the pride of winning without this step."

When Brian tightened the saddle, everyone seemed to hold their breath. Then Keeley let hers out, and put her knee in Brian's hands for a leg up.

She bellied over the saddle, lay still as Betty shied. She knew just what could happen if the filly wasn't controlled. A wrong move on anyone's part and she could find herself under several hundred pounds of agitated horse.

But Brian's voice whispered, soft and dreamy, and the light began to go pale gold. Slowly Keeley eased herself up until she sat, her feet sliding into the stirrups.

The new sensation had Betty fighting to toss her head, dancing back and kicking out. Now Keeley leaned forward, stroking, and added her voice to Brian's.

"Get used to it," she ordered in a no-nonsense tone

directly opposed to his crooning. "You were born for this."

"There now, *cushla*." His lips twitched at the corners as he soothed Betty. "She's not so scary now, is she? She's hardly much of a thing at all up there on your big, beautiful back. She's only a princess, but you, you're a queen, aren't you?"

"So, I'm outranked?" Keeley wasn't sure if she was amused or insulted.

Gradually the restless movements stilled. Brian took a chunk of apple from his pocket, fed it to Betty with murmured praise and reassurance. "She's doing well."

"She'd like to bounce me off the ceiling."

"Oh aye, that she would, but she's not trying it at the moment. You're doing well, too." His gaze lifted until his eyes met Keeley's. "As natural at this as she is. Blue bloods, both of you."

"Are we making history, Brian?"

"Bet on it," he told her and kissed Betty just above the nose.

She gave him most of the morning. Dismounting, remounting, sitting quietly while he led them around the stall. Betty gave a couple of bucks, but everyone knew it was only for show.

"Will you try the walking ring with her?"

Keeley started to decline. She had work, and was already behind for the day. But the feel of the young, fresh horse under her was too much of a pleasure, too much of a challenge. She'd put in a few hours on paperwork that night.

"If you think she's ready."

"Oh, she's ready. It's the rest of us who have to catch up." He opened the box and led them out.

The walking ring was surrounded by a high wall, to give the student privacy and prevent distractions as she took her first steps under the control of a rider. As Brian led them toward it, several of the hands stopped work to watch. Money changed hands.

"Some of them bet we wouldn't manage her this morning," Brian said casually. "You just earned me fifty dollars."

"If I'd known there was a pool, I'd have bet myself."

He glanced up. "Which way?"

"I always bet to win."

He stopped inside the ring, handed Keeley the reins. "She's yours now."

Keeley angled her head. "In a manner of speaking," she said and nudged Betty into a walk.

They made a picture, Brian mused. A stunning one. The long-legged thoroughbred with her regal head and gleaming coat, and the delicate woman riding her.

If he'd ever wanted one horse for his own—and he didn't, hadn't—it would be this one.

If he'd ever wanted one woman for his own...

Well, that was the same. He'd never wanted the responsibilities that came from having. And neither of these could ever be his in any case. But he'd have something of each of them, and that was better all around.

For the horse, he'd have the knowledge that part of what he was went into the making of a champion. And the woman, before long he'd have the pleasure of knowing what it was to have her wrapped around him in the night. Maybe only once, but once would be enough.

Whatever the risks of that were, there was no stopping it. They came a bit closer to it every time they looked at each other. Today, he'd come to understand she knew it, too. Now it was only a matter of the time and place. And that would be up to her.

"They look good."

Brian didn't wince, but he wanted to. It was definitely inconvenient to have the father of the woman you were fantasizing about interrupt that particular image. Especially inconvenient when the man was also your employer.

"That they do. Betty needs a steady hand, and your daughter has one."

"Always has." Travis slapped a hand on Brian's shoulder and brought on instantaneous guilt. "I ran into Jim, who confessed all. You took a kick."

"It's nothing." He imagined his ribs would be sore for weeks.

"Have it looked at." The tone was casual, and carried command.

"I will shortly. Jim was spooked. I shouldn't have pushed him into it."

"He's young," Travis agreed. "But this is part of his job. At the moment, he feels bad enough that you could ask him to let Betty sit on him. I'd take advantage of it."

"And so I will. He's a good lad, Travis. Just a bit green yet. I'm thinking of taking him with me to the track more, letting him get some seasoning."

"That's a good idea. You have a number of them. Good ideas," Travis added.

"That's what you pay me for." Brian hesitated, then plunged. "Betty's not just your best shot at your Derby, she's the one who'll do it for you. And I'll wager my full year's contract pay she'll wear the Triple Crown."

"That's a leap, Brian."

"Not for her. I say she'll break records, smash them to bits. And when it comes time to breed her, it should be Zeus. I've done the charts," Brian continued. "I know you and Brendon manage the breeding end of the farm yourselves, but—"

"I'll look at your charts, Brian."

Brian nodded, shifted to watch Betty. "It's not the charts so much, though they'll bear me out. It's that I know her. Sometimes…" Despite himself, he found himself staring at Keeley. "You just recognize it all."

"I know it." Eyes narrowed in consideration, Travis scanned Betty's form. "Work out the race schedule you think will work for her—once she's ready. We'll talk about it."

Keeley walked Betty toward them, pulling her up with a tug of the reins and a quiet vocal command. "She's decided to tolerate me."

"What do you think?" Travis stroked the filly's neck, ignoring her first instinctive feint at nipping.

"She's not common," Keeley began, "though she has some behavioral problems that would make her so if they aren't corrected. She's smart. A fast learner. Which means you have to stay a step ahead of her. It's early days yet, of course, but I'd say this isn't a horse that's going to loaf. She'll work hard, and she'll race hard, under the right hand. If I were still competing, I'd want her."

"She's not meant for the show ring." Brian took out another chunk of apple. "She's for the oval."

Betty took the reward, then as if to show he was the only one of the three humans who mattered, bumped her head lightly against his shoulder.

"She still has to prove she can run in a crowd," Keeley pointed out. "You might want to put blinders on her."

"Not with this one, I'm thinking. The other horses won't be distractions to her. They'll be competitors."

"We'll see." Keeley dismounted, started to hand Brian the reins, but her father took them.

"I'll walk her back."

And that, Brian thought, absurdly bereft, was the difference between training and owning.

"No need to look so annoyed." Keeley cocked her head as Brian scowled after Betty. "She did very well. Better than I'd expected."

"Hmm? Oh, so she did, yes. I was thinking of something else."

"Ribs hurting?" When he only shrugged, she shook her head. "Let me take a look."

"She barely caught me."

"Oh, for heaven's sake." Impatient, Keeley did what she would have done with one of her brothers: She tugged Brian's T-shirt out of his jeans.

"Well, darling, if I'd known you were so anxious to get me undressed, I'd have cooperated fully, and in private."

"Shut up. God, Brian, you said it was nothing."

"It's not much."

His definition of not much was a softball-size bruise over the ribs in a burst of ugly red and black. "Macho is tedious, so just shut up."

He started to grin, then yelped when she pressed her fingers to the bruise. "Hell, woman, if that's your idea of tender mercies, keep them."

"You could have a cracked rib. You need an X ray."

"I don't need a damned—ouch! Bollocks and bloody hell, stop poking." He tried to pull his shirt down, but she simply yanked it up again.

"Stand still, and don't be a baby."

"A minute ago it was don't be macho, now it's don't be a baby. What do you want?"

"For you to behave sensibly."

"It's difficult for a man to behave sensibly when a woman's taking his clothes off in broad daylight. If you're going to kiss it and make it better, I've several other bruises. I've a dandy one on my ass as it happens."

"I'm sure that's terribly amusing. One of the men can drive you to the emergency room."

"No one's driving me anywhere. I'd know if my ribs are cracked as I've had a few in my time. It's a bruise, and it's throbbing like a bitch now that you've been playing with it."

She spotted another, riding high on his hip, and gave that a poke. This time he groaned.

"Keeley, you're torturing me here."

"I'm just trying…" She trailed off as she lifted her head and saw his eyes. It wasn't pain or annoyance in them now. It was heat, and it was frustration. And it was surprisingly gratifying. "Really?"

It was wrong, and it was foolish, but a sip of power was a heady thing. She trailed her fingers along his hip, up his ribs and down again, and felt his muscles quiver. "Why don't you stop me?"

His throat hurt. "You make my head swim. And you know it."

"Maybe I do. Now. Maybe I like it." She'd never been deliberately provocative before. Had never wanted to be. And she'd never known the thrill of having a strong man turn to putty under her hands. "Maybe I've thought about you, Brian, the way you said I would."

"You pick a fine time to tell me when there's people everywhere, and your father one of them."

"Yeah, maybe that's true, too. I need that buffer, I guess."

"You're a killer, Keeley. You'd tease a man to death."

He didn't mean it as a compliment, but to her it was a revelation. "I've never tried it before. No one's ever attracted me enough. You do, and I don't even know why."

When she dropped her hand, he took her wrist. It surprised him to feel the gallop of her pulse there, when her eyes, her voice had been so cool, so steady. "Then you're a quick learner."

"I'd like to think so. If I come to you, you'd be the first."

"The first what?" Temper wanted to stir, especially when she laughed. Then his mind cleared and the meaning flashed through like a thunderbolt. His hand tightened on her wrist, then dropped it as though she had turned to fire.

"That scared you enough to shut you up," she observed. "I'm surprised anything could render you speechless."

"I've…" But he couldn't think.

"No, don't fumble around for words. You'll spoil your image." She couldn't think just why his dazed expression struck her as so funny, or why the shock in his eyes was endearing somehow.

"We'll just say that, under these circumstances, we both have a lot to consider. And now, I'm way behind in my work, and have to get ready for my afternoon class."

She walked away, as easily, as casually, Brian thought numbly, as she might have if they'd just finished discussing the proper treatment for windgalls. She left him reeling.

He'd gone and fallen in love with the gentry, and the gentry was his boss's daughter. And his boss's daughter was innocent.

He'd have to be mad to lay a hand on her after this.

He began to wish Betty had just kicked him in the head and gotten it all over with.

Served her right, Keeley decided. Spend the morning indulging herself, spend half the night doing the books. And she hated doing the books.

Sighing, she tipped back in her chair and rubbed her eyes. In another year, maybe two, the school would generate enough income to justify hiring a bookkeeper. But for now, she just couldn't toss the money away for something she could do herself. Not when she could use it to subsidize another student, or buy one of them a pair of riding boots.

It was tempting, particularly at times like these, to dip into her own bank account. But it was a matter of pride to keep the school going on its own merit, as much as she possibly could.

Ledgers and forms and bills and accounts, she

thought, were her responsibility. You didn't have to like your responsibilities, you just had to deal with them.

She had two full-tuition students on her waiting list. One more, she calculated—two would be better—but one more and she could justify opening another class. Sunday afternoons.

That would give her eighteen full tuitions. Two years before, she'd had only three. It was working. And so, now, should she.

She swiveled back to the computer and focused on her spreadsheet program. Her eyes were starting to blur again when the door behind her opened.

She caught the scent of hot tea before she turned and saw her mother.

"Ma, what are you doing out here? It's midnight."

"Well, I was up, and I saw your light. I thought to myself, that girl needs some fuel if she's going to run half the night." Adelia set a thermos and a bag on the desk. "Tea and cookies."

"I love you."

"So you'd better. Darling, your eyes are half shut. Why don't you turn this off and come to bed?"

"I'm nearly done, but I can use the break—and the fuel." She ate a cookie before she poured the tea. "I'm only behind because I played this morning."

"From what your father tells me you weren't play-ing." Adelia took a chair, nudged it closer to the desk. "He's awfully pleased with how Brian's bringing Betty along. Well, he's pleased with Brian altogether, and so am I from what I've seen. But Betty's quite the chal-lenge."

"Hmm." So was Brian, Keeley thought. "He has his

own way of doing things, but it seems to work." Considering, she drummed her fingers on the desk. She'd always been able to discuss anything with her mother. Why should that change now?

"I'm attracted to him."

"I'd worry about you if you weren't. He's a fine-looking young man."

"Ma." Keeley laid a hand over her mother's. "I'm very attracted to him."

The amusement faded from Adelia's eyes. "Oh. Well."

"And he's very attracted to me."

"I see."

"I don't want to mention this to Dad. Men don't look at this sort of thing the way we do."

"Darling." At a loss, Adelia sighed out a breath. "Mothers aren't likely to look at this sort of thing the same way their daughters do. You're grown up, and you're a woman who answers to herself first. But you're still my little girl, aren't you?"

"I haven't been with a man before."

"I know it." Adelia's smile was soft, almost wistful. "Do you think I wouldn't know if that had changed for you? You think too much of yourself to give what you are to something unless it matters. No one's mattered before."

Here the ground was boggy, Keeley thought. "I don't know if Brian matters in the way you mean. But I feel different with him. I want him. I haven't wanted anyone before. It's exciting, and a little scary."

Adelia rose, wandered around the little office looking at the ribbons, the medals. The steps and the stages.

"We've talked about such matters before, you and I. About the meaning and the precautions, the responsibilities."

"I know about being responsible and sensible."

"Keeley, while it is true that all that is important, it doesn't tell you—it can't tell you—what it is to be with a man. There's such heat." She turned back. "There's such a force you make between you. It's not just an act, though I know it can be for some. But even then it's more than just that. I won't tell you that giving your innocence is a loss, for it shouldn't be, it doesn't need to be. For me it was an opening. Your father was my first," she murmured. "And my only."

"Mama." Moved, Keeley reached for her hands. Her mother's hands were so strong, she thought. Everything about her mother was strong. "That's so lovely."

"I only ask you to be sure, so that if you give yourself to him, you take away a memory that's warm and has heart, not just heat. Heat can chill after time passes."

"I am sure." Smiling now, Keeley brought her mother's hand to her cheek. "But he's not. And, Ma, it's so odd, but the way he backed off when I told him he'd be the first is why I'm sure. You see, I matter to him, too."

Chapter 6

It was amazing, really, how two people could live and work in basically the same place, and one could completely avoid the other. It just took setting your mind to it.

Brian set his mind to it for several days. There was plenty of work to keep him occupied and more than enough reason for him to spend time away from the farm and on the tracks. But he found avoidance scraped his pride. It was too close a kin to cowardice.

Added to that, he'd told Keeley he wanted to help her at the school and had done nothing about it. He wasn't a man to break his word, no matter what it cost him. And, he reminded himself as he walked to Keeley's stables, he was also a man of some self-control. He had no intention of seducing or taking advantage of innocence.

He'd made up his mind on it.

Then he stepped into the stables and saw her. He wouldn't have said his mouth watered, but it was a very close thing.

She was wearing one of those fancy rigs again—jodhpurs the color of dark chocolate and a cream sort of blouse that looked somehow fluid. Her hair was down, all tumbled and wild as if she'd just pulled the pins from it. And indeed, as he watched she flipped it back and looped it through a wide elastic band.

He decided the best place in the universe for his hands to be were in his pockets.

"Lessons over?"

She glanced back, her hands still up in her hair. Ah, she thought. She'd wondered how long it would take him to wander her way again. "Why? Did you want one?"

He frowned, but caught himself before he shifted his feet. "I said I'd give you a hand over here."

"So you did. As it happens I could use one. You did say you could ride, didn't you?"

"I did, and I do."

"Good." Perfect. She gestured toward a big bay. "Mule really needs a workout. If you take him, I'll be able to give Sam some exercise, too. Neither of them has had enough the last couple of days. I'm sure I have tack that'll suit you." She opened a box door and led out the already saddled Sam. "We'll wait in the paddock."

As they clipped out, Brian eyed Mule, Mule eyed Brian. "She's a bossy one, isn't she now?" Then with a shrug, Brian headed to the tack room to find a saddle that suited him.

She was cantering around the paddock when he came

out, her body so tuned to the horse they might have been one figure. With the slightest shift in rhythm and angle, she took her mount over three jumps. Cantering still, she started the next circle, then spotted Brian. She slowed, stopped.

"Ready?"

For an answer, he swung into the saddle. "Why are you all done up today?"

"It was picture day. We take photographs of the classes. The kids and the parents like it. Mule's up for a good run, if you are."

"Then let's have at it." With a tap of his heels he sent the horse out of the open gate at an easy trot.

"How are the ribs?" she asked as she came up beside him.

"They're all right." They were driving him mad, because every time he felt a twinge he remembered her hands on him.

"I'm told the yearling training's coming along well, and Betty's one of the star pupils—as predicted."

"She has the thirst. All the training in the world can't give a horse the thirst to race. We'll be giving her a taste of the starting gate shortly, see how she does with it."

Keeley headed up a gentle slope where trees were still lush and green despite the encroaching fall. "I'd use Foxfire with her," she said casually. "He's a sturdy one, with lots of experience. He loves to charge out of the gate. She sees him do it a couple of times, she won't want to be left behind."

He'd already decided on Foxfire as Betty's gate tutor, but shrugged. "I'm thinking about it. So...have I passed the audition here, Miss Grant?"

Keeley lifted a brow, and a smile ghosted around her mouth as she looked Brian over. She'd been checking his form, naturally. "Well, you're competent enough at a trot." With a light tap, she sent Sam into a canter. The minute Brian matched her pace, she headed into a gallop.

Oh, she missed this. Every day she couldn't fly out across the fields, over the hills, was a sacrifice. There was nothing to match it—the thrill of speed, the power soaring under her, through her, the thunder of hooves and the whip of wind.

She laughed as Brian edged by her. She'd seen the quick grin of challenge, and answered it by letting Sam have his head.

It was like watching magic take wing, Brian thought. The muscular black horse soared over the ground with the woman on his back. They streaked over another rise, moving west, into the dying sun. The sky was a riot of color, a painting slashed with reds and golds. It seemed to him she would ride straight into it, through it.

And he'd have no choice but to follow her.

When she pulled up, turned to wait for him, her face flushed with pleasure, her eyes gleaming with it, he knew he'd never seen the like.

And wanting her was apt to kill him.

"I should've given you a handicap," she called out. "Mule runs like a demon, but he's no match for this one." She leaned over the saddle to pat Sam's neck. She straightened, shook her hair back. "Gorgeous out, isn't it?"

"Hot as blazes," Brian corrected. "How long does summer last around here?"

"As long as it likes. Mornings are getting chilly, though, and once the sun dips down behind the hills, it'll cool off quickly enough. I like the heat. Your Irish blood's not used to it yet."

She turned Sam so she could look down at Royal Meadows. "It's beautiful from up here, isn't it?"

The buildings spread out, neat, elegant, with the white fences of the paddocks, the brown oval, the horses being led to the stable. A trio of weanlings, all legs and energy, raced in the near pasture.

"From down there, too. It's the best I've ever seen."

That made her smile. "Wait till you see it in winter, with snow on the hills and the sky thick and gray with more—or so blue it hurts your eyes to look at it. And the foalings start and there are babies trying out their legs. When I was little, I couldn't wait to run down and see them in the morning."

They began to walk again, companionably now, as the light edged toward dusk. She hadn't expected to be so comfortable with him. Aware, yes, she always seemed aware of him now. But this simple connection, a quiet evening ride, was a pleasure.

"Did you have horses when you were a boy?"

"No, we never owned them. But it wasn't so far to the track, and my father's a wagering man."

"And are you?"

He tilted his face toward her. "I like playing the odds, and fortunately, have a better feel for them than my father. He loved the look of them, and the rush of a race, but never did he gain any understanding of horses."

"You didn't gain any, either," Keeley said and had him frowning at her. "What you've got you were born with. Just like them," she added, gesturing toward the weanlings.

"I think that's a compliment."

"I don't mind giving them when they're fact."

"Well, fact or fiction, horses have been the biggest part of my life. I remember going along with my da and seeing the horses. When he could manage it, he liked to go early, check out the field, talk with the clockers and the grooms, get himself a feel for things—or so he said. He lost his money more often as not. It was the process that appealed to him."

That, and the flask in his pocket, Brian thought, but with tolerance. His father had loved the horses and the whiskey. And his mother had understood neither.

"One of the first times I went along, I saw an exercise boy, very young lad, ponying a sorrel around the track. And I thought, there, that's it. That's what I want to do, for there can't be anything better than doing that for your life and your living. And while I was still young enough, and small enough, I slid out of going to school as often as it could be managed and hitched rides to the track to hustle myself. Walk hots, muck stalls, whatever."

"It's romantic."

He caught himself. He hadn't meant to ramble on that way, but the ride, the evening, the whole of it made him sentimental. When he started to laugh at her statement, she shook her head.

"No, it is. People who aren't a part of the world of it don't understand, really. The hard work, the disappointments, the sweat and blood. Freezing predawn workouts, bruises and pulled muscles."

"And that's romantic."

"You know it is."

This time he did laugh, because she'd pegged him. "As a boy, when I hung around the shedrow, I'd see the horses come back through the mist of morning, steam rising off their backs, the sound of them growing louder, coming at you before ever you could see them. They'd slip out of the fog like something out of a dream. Then, I thought it the most romantic thing in the world."

"And now?"

"Now, I know it is."

He broke into a canter, riding with her until the lights of Royal Meadows began to flicker on and glow. He hadn't expected to spend a comfortable, contented hour in her company, and found it odd that underlying all the rest that buzzed between them they'd seemed to have formed a kind of friendship.

He'd been friends with women before, and was well on the way to being convinced he'd do just fine keeping it all on a friendly level with Keeley. He was the one who'd initiated the sexual charge, so it seemed reasonable and right that he be the one to dampen it again.

The logic of it, and the ride, relaxed him. By the time they reached the stables to cool down the horses, he was in an easy mood and thinking about his supper.

Since she was interested, he told her of the yearling training, the progress, the five-year-old mare with colic, and the weanling with ringbone.

Together they watered the horses, and while Brian took the saddles and bridles to the tack room, Keeley set up the small hay nets and set out the grooming kits.

They worked across from each other, in opposite boxes.

"I heard you and Brendon are heading off to Saratoga next week," she commented.

"Zeus is running. And I think Red Duke is a contender, and your brother agrees. Though I've only seen that track on paper and in pictures. We're off to Louisville as well. I want to be well familiar with that course before the first Saturday in May."

"You want Betty to run the Derby."

"She will run it. And win it." He picked up the curry comb to scrape out the body brush. "We've conversed about it."

"You've talked to Brendon about the Derby?"

"No, Betty. And your father as well. I expect Brendon and I will talk it through while we're away."

"What does Betty have to say?"

"Let's get on with it." He glanced over, saw she was running her fingers over Sam's coat, checking for lumps or irregularities. "Why aren't you still competing? With that one under you you'd need a vault for all your medals."

"I'm not interested in medals."

"Why not? Don't you like to win?"

"I love to win." She leaned gently against Sam, lifted his leg and sent Brian a long look that had his stomach jittering before she gave her attention to picking out the hoof. "But I've done it, enjoyed it, finished with it. Competing can take over your life. I wanted the Olympics, and I got it."

She shifted to clean out the next hoof. "Once I had, I realized that so much of what I was, what I felt and thought had been focused on that single goal. And then it was over. So I wanted to see what else there was out there, and what else I had in me. I like to compete, but I found out it doesn't always have to be done, and won, in the show ring."

"With the kind of school you've got going here, you should have someone working with you."

She shrugged and began to rub in hoof oil. "Up until now I'd been able to draft Sarah or Patrick into giving me a hand. Ma helps out when she can, and so does Dad. Brendon and Uncle Paddy put in hours with each one of my horses as I got them. And the cousins—Burke and Erin's kids from Three Aces—they're always willing to pitch in if I need extra hands."

"I haven't seen anyone working here but you."

"Well, that's very simple. Patrick and Sarah are off to college—and Brady, who's another I can browbeat into shoveling boxes when he's here. Brendon's doing a lot more traveling now than he used to. Uncle Paddy's in Ireland, and the cousins are just back from a holiday and in school. Either my mother or father, sometimes both, show up here at dawn half the time. Whether I ask them or not."

She got to her feet. "And now that I've got you interested, I've come up with a part-time groom/exercise boy/stablehand. That's a pretty good deal for a small riding academy."

She strolled out to start the evening feeding.

"You could get an eager young boy or girl to come in before and after school—pay them in lessons."

"Before school, eager young boys and girls should

be eating breakfast, and after they should be playing with friends and doing homework."

"That's very strict."

She chuckled and mixed some sliced carrots into the feed as an extra treat. "That's what all my students say. I want them well-rounded. My family saw to it that I had interests and friendships outside the stable, that I got an education, that I saw something of the world besides the track and the barn. It matters."

They divvied up the horses, and the stables filled with the sounds of whickers and whinnies as the meal was served.

"If you don't mind my saying so, you don't seem to be getting out and about much now."

"I'm compulsive. Goal oriented. I see what I want and well, it's like putting on blinders and heading down the backstretch. All I see is the finish line."

She leaned in to rub a gelding's neck as if he were a pet dog. "Which is why my parents wouldn't let me spend my entire childhood around or on a horse. I took piano lessons, and as soon as I started I was determined to be the best student at the recital. If it was my job to clean the kitchen after dinner, then that damn kitchen was going to sparkle so bright you'd need sunglasses for your midnight snack."

"That's frightening."

Responding to the humor in his eyes, she nodded. "It can be. Focusing on the school means, even though it's still a single goal, that my compulsion to succeed is spread out to encompass so many elements—the kids, the horses as well as the academy itself. Once it's firmly established, I can delegate a bit more, but I need to learn from the ground up. I don't like to make mistakes. Which is why I haven't been with a man before now."

He was thrown off balance so quickly and completely, he could hear his own brain stumble. "Well, that's…that's wise."

He took one definite step back, like a chessman going from square to square.

"It's interesting that makes you nervous," she said, countering his move.

"I'm not nervous, I'm…finished up here, it seems." He tried another tactic, stepped to the side.

"Interesting," she continued, mirroring his move, "that it would make you nervous, or uneasy if you prefer, when you've been… I think it's safe to use the term 'hitting on me' since we met."

"I don't think that's the proper term at all." Since he seemed to be boxed into a corner, he decided he was really only standing his ground. "I acted in a natural way regarding a physical attraction. But—"

"And now that I've reacted in a natural way, you've felt the reins slip out of your hands and you're panicked."

"I'm certainly not panicked." He ignored the terror gripping claws into his belly and concentrated on annoyance. "Back off, Keeley."

"No." With her eyes locked on his, she stepped in. Checkmate.

His back was hard up against a stall door and he'd been maneuvered there by a woman half his weight. It was mortifying. "This isn't doing either of us any credit." It took a lot of effort when the blood was rapidly draining out of his head, but he made his voice cool and firm. "The fact is I've rethought the matter."

"Have you?"

"I have, yes, and—stop it," he ordered when she ran the palms of her hands up over his chest.

"Your heart's pounding," she murmured. "So's mine. Should I tell you what goes on inside my head, inside my body when you kiss me?"

"No." He barely managed a croak this time. "And it's not going to happen again."

"Bet?" She laughed, rising up just enough to nip his chin. How could she have known how much *fun* it was to twist a man into aroused knots? "Why don't you tell me about this rethinking?"

"I'm not going to take advantage of your—of the situation."

That, she thought, was wonderfully sweet. "At the moment, I seem to have the advantage. This time you're trembling, Brian."

The hell he was. How could he be trembling when he couldn't feel his own legs? "I won't be responsible. I won't use your inexperience. I *won't* do this." The last was said on a note of desperation and he pushed her aside.

"I'm responsible for myself. And I think I've just proven to both of us, that if and when I decide you'll be the one, you won't have a prayer." She drew a deep, satisfied breath. "Knowing that's incredibly flattering."

"Arousing a man doesn't take much skill, Keeley. We're cooperative creatures in that area."

If he'd expected that to scratch at her pride and cut into her power, he was mistaken. She only smiled, and the smile was full of secret female knowledge. "If that was true between us, if that were all that's between us, we'd be naked on the tack room floor right now."

She saw the change in his eyes and laughed delightedly. "Already thought of that one, have you? We'll just hold that thought for another time."

He swore, raked his hands through his hair and tried to pinpoint the moment she'd so neatly turned the tables on him, when the pursued had become the pursuer. "I don't like forward women."

The sound she made was something between a snort and a giggle, and was girlish and full of fun. It made him want to grin. "Now that's a lie, and you don't do it well. I've noticed you're an honest sort of man, Brian. When you don't want to speak your mind, you say nothing—and that's not often. I like that about you, even if it did irritate me initially. I even like your slightly overwide streak of confidence. I admire your patience and dedication to the horses, your understanding and affection for them. I've never been involved with a man who's shared that interest with me."

"You've never been involved with a man at all."

"Exactly. That's just one reason why. And to continue, I appreciate the kindness you showed my mother when she was sad, and I appreciate the part of you that's struggling to back away right now instead of taking what I've never offered anyone before."

She laid a hand on his arm as he stared at her with baffled frustration. "If I didn't have that respect and that liking for you, Brian, we wouldn't be having this conversation no matter how attracted I might be to you."

"Sex complicates things, Keeley."

"I know."

"How would you know? You've never had any."

She gave his arm a quick squeeze. "Good point. So, you want to try the tack room?" When his mouth fell open, she laughed and threw her arms around him for a noisy kiss on his cheek. "Just kidding. Let's go up to the main house and have some dinner instead."

"I've work yet."

She drew back. She couldn't read his eyes now. "Brian, neither of us have eaten. We can have a simple meal in the kitchen—and if you're worried, we won't be alone in the house so I'll have to keep my hands off you. Temporarily."

"There's that." He couldn't stand it. How could he be expected to? She'd thrown her arms around him with such easy affection. And his heart was balanced on a very thin wire. Trying to keep the movement casual, he set her aside. "Well, I could eat."

"Good."

She would have taken his hand, but his were already in his pockets. It amused and touched her how restrained he was determined to be. And if it made her naturally competitive spirit kick in, well, she couldn't help it, now could she?

"I'm hoping to get down to Charles Town and watch some of the workouts once you take Betty and some of the other yearlings to the track."

"She'll be ready for it soon enough." Relief was like a cool wave through his blood. Talking of horses would make it all easier. "I'd say she'll surprise you, but you've been up on her. You know what she's made of."

"Yeah, good stock, good breeding, a hard head and

a hunger to win." She flashed him a smile as they approached the kitchen door. "I've been told that describes me. I'm half Irish, Brian, I was born stubborn."

"No arguing with that. A person might make the world a calmer place for others by being passive, but you don't get very far in it yourself, do you?"

"Look at that. We have a foundation of agreement. Now tell me you like spaghetti and meatballs."

"It happens to be a favorite of mine."

"That's handy. Mine, too. And I heard a rumor that's what's for dinner." She reached for the doorknob, then caught him off guard by brushing a light kiss over his lips. "And since we'll be joining my parents, it would probably be best if you didn't imagine me naked for the next couple of hours."

She sailed in ahead of him, leaving Brian helplessly and utterly aroused.

There was nothing like an extra helping of guilt to cool a man's blood. And it was guilt as much as the hot food and the glass of good wine that got Brian through the evening in the Grant kitchen. The size of it left little room for lust, considering.

There was Adelia Grant giving him a warm greeting as if he was welcome to swing in for dinner anytime he had the whim, and Travis getting out an extra plate himself—as if he waited on employees five days a week—and saying that there was plenty to go around as Brendon had other plans for dinner.

Before he knew it, he was sitting down, having food heaped in front of him and being asked how his day had been. And not in a way that expected a report.

He didn't know what to do about it. He liked these people, genuinely liked them. And there he was lusting after their daughter. An alley mutt after a registered purebred.

And the hell of it was, he liked her as well. It had been so simple at first, when there'd been only heat. Or he'd been able to tell himself that's all there was. For a time it had been possible to tolerate being in love with her—or at least talking himself out of believing it. But *caring* for her made it all a study in frustration.

He could certainly convince himself that he was in love with the *idea* of her rather than the woman. The physical beauty, the class, the sheer inaccessibility of her. That was all a kind of challenge, a risk he enjoyed taking. But she'd gone and opened herself up to him, so every time he was around her, she showed him more of herself.

The kindness, the humor, the strength of purpose and sense of self he admired.

And now this teasing, this sexual flirt in an innocent's body was driving him mad. And God help him, he liked it.

"Have some more, Brian."

"I'll be sorry if I do." But he took the big bowl Adelia offered him. "Sorrier if I don't. You're a rare cook, Mrs. Grant."

"Dee, I told you. And rare was just what I was for a number of years. Before Hannah retired—that was our housekeeper. She was with Travis longer than I've been with him. When she retired a few years back I just didn't want another woman, a stranger, you know, in the house day and night and so on. I figured I'd better learn to cook something more than fish and chips or we'd all starve to death."

"Nearly did the first six months," Travis commented and earned a narrow-eyed stare from his wife.

"Well, sure and the experience made you get a handle on that fancy grill outside, didn't it? The man was spoiled rotten. I wager you could even put a meal together for yourself, Brian."

Idly he rubbed Sheamus—who was snoring under the table—with the side of his boot. "If I've no choice in the matter."

Brian caught the lazy look Keeley sent him as she sipped her wine. Heat balled in his belly. In defense he turned to Travis. "I'm told you enjoy a hand or two of poker from time to time."

"I've been known to."

"The lads're talking about a game tomorrow night."

"I might come down—I've heard you're a hard man to beat."

"If you're going to play cards, you should ask Burke to join you," Adelia put in. "Then maybe Keeley, Erin and I can find something equally foolish to do with our evening."

"Good idea. More wine, Brian?" Keeley lifted the bottle, cocked a brow. The purr in her voice was subtle, but he heard it. And suffered.

"No, thanks. I've work yet."

"I'll walk down with you when you're ready," Travis told him. "I'd like a look at that colicky mare."

"The two of you go ahead. We'll see to the dishes."

Travis grinned like a boy. "No KP?"

"There's not that much to be done, and you can make

up for it tomorrow." She got up to clear, and kissed his temple. "Go on, I know you've been worrying about her."

"Thank you for the fine meal, Dee," Brian added when she angled her head.

"And you're very welcome."

"Good night, Keeley."

"Good night, Brian. Thanks for the ride."

Adelia waited until the men were out, then turned to her daughter. "Keeley, I never would've thought it of you. You're tormenting the poor man."

"There's nothing poor about that man." Delighted with herself, Keeley broke off a piece of bread and crunched down on it. "And tormenting him is so rewarding."

"Well, there's not a woman with blood in her could argue with that. Mind you don't hurt him, darling."

"Hurt him?" Seriously shocked, Keeley rose to help with the dishes. "Of course I won't. I couldn't."

"You never know what you will or you can do." Adelia patted her daughter's cheek. "You've a lot to learn yet. And however much you learn you'll never really understand everything that goes on inside a man."

"I've good a pretty good idea about this one."

Adelia opened her mouth, then shut it again. Some things, she knew, couldn't be explained. They had to be lived.

Chapter 7

Brian came to know the roads leading from Maryland into West Virginia as well as he knew those in the county of Kerry. The highways where cars flashed by like little rockets, and the curving back roads where everything meandered were all part of his life now, and what some people would say led to a feeling of home.

There were times the green of the hills, the rise of them, reminded him of Ireland. The pang he felt at those moments surprised him as he didn't consider himself a sentimental man. At others, he'd drive along a winding road that followed a winding creek and the land was all so very different with its thick woods and walls of rock. Almost exotic. Then he'd feel a sense of contentment that surprised him nearly as much.

He didn't mind contentment. It just wasn't what he was looking for.

He liked to move. To travel from place to place. It was all to the good that his position at Royal Meadows gave him that opportunity. He figured in a couple of years, he'd have seen a great deal of America—even if the oval was in the foreground of each view.

He told himself he didn't think of Ireland as home— or Maryland as home, either. Home was the shedrow, wherever it might be.

Still, he felt a sense of welcome and ease when he drove between the stone pillars at Royal Meadows. And he felt pleasure when he saw Keeley in her paddock with one of her classes. He stopped to watch as she took her group from trot to canter.

It was a pretty sight, not despite the clumsiness and caution of some of the children, but because of it. This was no slick and choreographed competition but the first steps of a new adventure. Fun, she'd said, he remembered. They would learn, take responsibility, but she didn't forget they were children.

And some of them had been hurt.

Seeing her with them, looking at what she'd built herself when she could have spent her days exactly as he'd once imagined she did, brought him more than respect for what she was. It brought admiration that was a little too bright for comfort.

He could hear the squeals, and Keeley's calm, firm voice—a pretty sight and a pretty sound. He climbed out of the truck and walked over for a closer view.

There were grins miles wide, and eyes big as platters. There were giggles and there were gasps. As far as

Brian could see, the mood ran from screaming nerves
to wild delight. Through it all, Keeley gave orders, instruction, encouragement, and used each child's name.

Her long fire-fall of hair was roped back again. Her
jeans were faded to a soft blue-gray like the many-
pocketed vest she topped over it. Under that she wore
a slim sweater the color of spring daffodils. She liked
her bright tones, Keeley did, Brian mused. And her glit-
ters as well, he mused as the light caught the dangle of
little stones at her ears.

She'd be wearing perfume. She always had some
cagey female scent about her. Sometimes just a drift
that you had to get right up beside her to catch. And
other times it was a siren call that beckoned you from
a distance.

Never knowing which it would be was enough to
drive a man mad.

He should stay away from her, Brian told himself.
God knew he should stay away from her. And he figured he had as much chance of doing so as one of her
riding hacks had of winning the Breeder's Cup.

She knew he was there. The ripple of heat over her
skin told her so. She couldn't afford to be distracted
with six children depending on her full attention. But
oh, the awareness of him, of herself and that quick trip
of the pulse, was a glorious sensation.

She began to understand why women so often made
fools of themselves for men.

When she ordered the class to switch back to a trot,
there were a few groans of disappointment. She had
them change directions, then took them through all their

paces, and back down to walk. Brian waited until she instructed them to stop, then applauded.

"Nicely done," he said. "Anyone here looking for a job, you just come see me."

"We have an audience today. This is Mr. Donnelly. He's head trainer at Royal Meadows. He's in charge of the racehorses."

"Indeed I am, and I've always got my eyes open for a new jockey."

"He talks pretty," one of the girls whispered, but Brian's ears were keen. He shot her a grin and had her blushing like a rosebud.

"Do you think so?"

"Mr. Donnelly's from Ireland," Keeley explained. Amazing, she thought, he even makes ten-year-old girls moon.

"Miss Keeley's mother's from Ireland. She talks pretty, too."

Brian glanced up and saw the boy he remembered as Willy studying him. "No one talks prettier than those from Ireland, lad. It's because we've all been kissed by the fairies."

"You're supposed to get money from the Tooth Fairy when you lose a tooth, but I never did."

"That's just your mother." The girl behind Willy rolled her eyes. "There aren't real fairies."

"Maybe they don't live here in America, but we've plenty where I come from. I'll put a word in for you, Willy, next time you lose a tooth."

His eyes rounded. "How did you know my name?"

"A fairy must've told me."

Keeley struggled to compose her features as Willy goggled. "Class. Dismount. Cool and water your mounts."

There was a great deal of chatter and movement now. Though Willy dismounted, he stood, holding the reins and studying Brian. Too cautious a look for one so young, Brian thought. And it tugged at his heart.

Willy took a breath, seemed to hold it. "I have one that's loose. A tooth."

"Do you?" Unable to resist, Brian climbed over the fence, hunched down. "Let's have a look."

Willy obliged by baring his teeth and poking his tongue against a wobbly incisor. "That's a good one. You'll be able to spit through where that was in a day or two."

"You're not supposed to spit." Willy slanted a look up at Brian as he began to walk.

"Who says?"

"Ladies." Bobby added a shrug. "They don't like you to burp, either."

"Ladies can be fussy about certain things. It's best to spit and burp among the men, I suppose."

"You're not supposed to run like a wild animal, either." Peeking around to make certain Keeley wasn't frowning in his direction, Willy shoved up the sleeve of his shirt. "This is from running like a wild animal on the playground at school. I skidded for*ever* and scraped lots of skin right off so it got really bloody."

Understanding his role, Brian pursed his lips, nodded. "That's very impressive, that is."

"I've got an even better one on my knee. Have you got any?"

"I've got a pretty good bruise." To play the game properly, Brian glanced around first, then tugged his shirt up to display the yellowing bruise on his ribs.

"Wow! That musta really hurt. Did you cry?"

"I couldn't. Miss Keeley was watching. Here she comes," he added in a conspirator's whisper and pulled his shirt down, whistled idly.

"Willy, you need to water Teddy."

"Yes, ma'am. I had a dream about Teddy last night."

"You tell me about it when we're grooming him, okay?"

"Okay. Bye, mister."

"Now that's a taking little creature," Brian murmured as Willy led his horse out to the water trough.

"Yes, he is. What were you talking about?"

"Man business." Brian hooked his thumbs in his pockets. "I've got to get down to the shedrow or I'd help you with the grooming. I could send you up a hand if you like."

"Thanks, but it's not necessary."

"Just ring down if you change your mind." He needed to go, let them both get on with work. But it was so nice to stand here and smell her. Today, the scent was subtle, just a hint of heat. "They looked good at the canter."

"They'll look better in a few weeks." It was time to get the horses inside, start the grooming session. But... What would another minute hurt? "I heard you took a few pots in the poker game last night."

"I came away about fifty ahead. Your cousin Burke's a slick one. I'd say he whistled home with double that."

"And my father?"

Brian's grin flashed. "I like thinking that's where

I got the fifty. I told him he's better off sticking with the horses."

Keeley's brow rose. "And his response to that?"

"Isn't something I can repeat in polite company."

She laughed. "That's what I thought. I've got to get the horses inside. Parents will be trickling along soon."

"Don't they ever come to watch?"

"Sometimes. Actually I've asked them to give us a few weeks so the kids aren't distracted or tempted to show off. You were a good test audience."

"Keeley." He touched her arm as she turned away. "The little boy. Willy. He's got a tooth he'll be losing in a couple of days. It'd be nice if someone remembered to put a coin under his pillow."

Her heart, which had leaped at his touch, quieted. Melted. "He's with a very good foster family right now. Very nice and caring people. They won't forget."

"All right then."

"Brian." This time it was her hand on his arm. Despite the curious eyes of her students, she rose to her toes to brush her lips over his cheek. "I have a soft spot for a man who believes in fairies," she murmured, then walked away to gather her students.

A very soft spot, she thought, for a man with a cocky grin and a kind heart. She opened the terrace doors of her room, stepped out into the night. There was a chill in the air, and a sky so clear the stars flamed like torches. She could smell the flowers, the spice of the first mums, the poignancy of the last of the roses.

A breeze had the leaves whispering.

The three-quarter moon was pale gold, shedding

light that gilded the gardens and shimmered over the fields. It seemed she could cup her hands, let that light pour into them and drink it like wine.

How could anyone sleep on so perfect a night?

Slowly she shifted and looked toward Brian's quarters. Light gleamed in his windows. And her pulse fluttered in her throat.

She told herself if his lights were off, she would close the doors again and try to sleep. But there they were, bright against dark, beckoning.

She closed her eyes on a shiver of anticipation and nerves. She'd prepared herself for this step, this change in her life, in her body. It wasn't an impulse, it wasn't reckless. But she felt impulsive. She felt reckless.

She was a grown woman, and the decision was hers.

Quietly she stepped back and closed the doors.

Brian closed the condition book, pressed his fingers to his tired eyes. Like Paddy, he wasn't quite sure he trusted the computer, but he was willing to fiddle with it a bit. Three times a week he spent an hour trying to figure the damn thing out with the notion that eventually he could use it to generate his charts.

Graphics, they called it, he thought, shifting to give the machine a suspicious glare. Timesaving and efficient, if you believed all the hype. Well, tonight he was too damn tired to spend an hour trying to be timesaving and efficient.

He hadn't had a decent night's sleep in a week. Which had nothing to do with his job, he admitted. And everything to do with his boss's daughter.

It was a good thing he had that trip to Saratoga coming up, he decided as he pushed away from his desk and rose. A little distance was just what was needed. He didn't care for this unsteady sensation or this worrying ache around the heart.

He wasn't the type to fret over a woman, he thought. He enjoyed them, and was happy for them to enjoy him, then each moved on without regrets.

Moving on was always the end plan.

New York, he remembered, was a fair distance away. It should be far enough. As for tonight, he was going to have a shot of whiskey in his tea to help smooth out the edges. Then by God, he was going to sleep if he had to bash himself over the head to accomplish it.

And he wasn't going to give Keeley another thought.

The knock on the door had him cursing under his breath. Though she'd been doing well, his first worry was that the mare with bronchitis had taken a bad turn. He was already reaching for the boots he'd shed when he called out.

"Come in, it's open. Is it Lucy then?"

"No, it's Keeley." One brow lifted, she stood framed in the door. "But if you're expecting Lucy, I can go."

The boots dangled from his fingertips, and those fingertips had gone numb. "Lucy's a horse," he managed to say. "She doesn't often come knocking on my door."

"Ah, the bronchitis. I thought she was better."

"She is. Considerably." She'd gone and let her hair loose, he thought. Why did she have to do that? It made his hands hurt, actually hurt with wanting to slide into it.

"That's good." She stepped in, shut the door. And because it seemed too perfect not to, audibly flipped the lock. Seeing a muscle twitch in his jaw was incredibly satisfying.

He was a drowning man, and had just gone under the first time. "Keeley, I've had a long day here. I was just about to—"

"Have a nightcap," she finished. She'd spotted the teapot and the bottle of whiskey on the kitchen counter. "I wouldn't mind one myself." She breezed past him to flip off the burner under the now sputtering kettle.

She'd put on different perfume, he thought viciously. Put it on fresh, too, just to torment him. He was damn sure of it. It snagged his libido like a fishhook.

"I'm not really fixed for company just now."

"I don't think I qualify as company." Competently she warmed the pot, measured out the tea and poured the boiling water in. "I certainly won't be after we're lovers."

He went under the second time without even the chance to gulp in air. "We're not lovers."

"That's about to change." She set the lid on the pot, turned. "How long do you like it to steep?"

"I like it strong, so it'll take some time. You should go on home now."

"I like it strong, too." Amazing, she thought, she didn't feel nervous at all. "And if it's going to take some time, we can have it afterward."

"This isn't the way for this." He said it more to himself than her. "This is backward, or twisted. I can't get my mind around it. No, just stay back over there and let me think a minute."

But she was already moving toward him, a siren's smile on her lips. "If you'd rather seduce me, go ahead."

"That's exactly what I'm not going to do." Though the night was cool and his windows were open to it, he felt sweat slither down his back. "If I'd known the way things were, I'd never have started this."

That mouth of his, she thought. She really had to have that mouth. "Now we both know the way things are, and I intend to finish it. It's my choice."

His blood was already swimming. Hot and fast. "You don't know anything, which is the whole flaming problem."

"Are you afraid of innocence?"

"Damn right."

"It doesn't stop you from wanting me. Put your hands on me, Brian." She took his wrist, pressed his hand to her breast. "I want your hands on me."

The boots clattered to the floor as he went under for the third time. "It's a mistake."

"I don't think so. Touch me."

His hand closed over her. She was small, delicate, and through some momentary miracle, his. "Doesn't matter if it's a mistake," he said, giving up entirely.

"We won't let it be one." Her head fell back as his hands began to move.

"Doesn't matter. But I'll be careful with you."

Her eyes were blue and brilliant as she lifted her arms, slid her hands into his wildly waving hair. "Not too careful, I hope."

When he swept her up in his arms she let out a shuddering sigh. "Oh, I was hoping you'd do that." Thrilled, she pressed her lips to the side of his neck. "I was really hoping you'd do that."

He turned his face into her hair, drew in the scent,

held it inside him. "You've only to tell me what you like."

She tipped her head back to look at him as he carried her into the bedroom. "Show me what I like."

With moonlight and cool breezes shimmering through the open windows, he laid her on the bed. There had been moonlight the first time he'd kissed her, soft fingers of it then, as there were now. He'd never forget the look of it, or of her.

There had been few gifts in his life that had mattered, that had stayed in him, in his heart and memory. She would, he knew. She was a gift he would cherish.

"This," he murmured, nibbling at her lips till they parted for him.

She opened, willing, wanting to be touched and tasted and taken. Even as he sensed her eagerness he led her slowly, patiently, thoroughly through the layers of sensations.

He caressed, his fingertips, palms, light as the air, then lingering at some secret place that had her breath catching on little jolts of pleasure. His mouth cruised lazily over her skin, sliding her into warmth, then it would come back to hers again, with a hungry bite that shot her into the heat.

Instinctively, avidly, she arched against him.

He was murmuring to her, lovely, stirring words in the old tongue, each like a tender kiss on the soul. Her heart fluttered, wings spreading wide for flight.

There were no nerves, no doubts as she raised herself to him, wrapped herself around him. When he slipped off her shirt, the breeze and his fingertips whispered over her. She felt beautiful.

Her skin was white silk, her hair rich flame. Every tremble was a gift, every sigh a treasure. In his life he'd never held anything as lovely as Keeley discovering herself.

She never shied when he undressed her, but embraced each new moment, welcomed each fresh sensation. Her curious hands moved over him, undressing him in turn. He'd never known how arousing it could be to be someone's first.

Her heart hammered under his mouth, and the scent she'd dabbed on that fragile flesh swirled into his senses until they were as clouded as hers. He took more, just a little more, and she began to move under him in mindless invitation.

So much. There was so much, was all she could think. Her body was flooded with sensations, her flesh quivering from them. She could hear her own moans, her own ragged breaths but could do nothing to control them. The very loss of control was thrilling.

Everything inside her was tangled and straining. And desperate. Her nails bit into his back, her teeth found his shoulder. Then his hand closed over her.

She cried out from the shock of it, all that pulsing, pumping pleasure, the sheer heat of it that washed in one huge wave that crashed over her, inside her, and left her shuddering. She reared up, eyes blind, her fingers diving into his hair.

Then his mouth was on hers again, hotter now, hungrier, giving her no chance to catch her breath or her sanity.

"Give yourself to me," he whispered, the blood

pounding in his head as her eyes, heavy, stunned, looked into his. "Take me in."

With her eyes on his, she opened and arched, and gave.

It was like rising into the air, each stroke another beat of wings. Pleasure climbed higher and higher still, lifting through her body, sweeping through her mind. All she could see were his eyes, dark and green and focused on her, even as his body was focused on hers. Mated and matched and moving with her.

Staggered by the beauty of it, she lifted a hand to his cheek, murmured his name.

And he was lost. Love and passion, dreams and desire stabbed through his heart. Helpless, he buried his face in her hair and let himself go.

With her eyes closed she absorbed the delights of being a well-loved woman. Her body felt gloriously heavy, her mind wonderfully muffled. There was no need to wonder or worry if she had given Brian the same pleasure. She had seen it in his face, and felt it as he lay over her with his heart still thundering.

There was a change inside her, she thought. Awareness, understanding. And a soaring kind of triumph.

Smiling to herself, she traced a finger down his back. "How are the ribs?"

"What?"

And didn't it feel grand to hear that sleepy slur in his voice? "Your ribs. That's still a nasty bruise you have there."

"I can't feel anything." His head was still spinning. "What's this scent you've put on? It's devious."

"Just one of my many secrets."

He lifted his head, started to grin at her, then it swamped him again. The look of her, the love of her. Lowering his head he brought his lips to hers in a long, dreamy kiss that came out of his soul and stirred hers.

Her hand slid limply to the mattress. "Brian."

"I'm crushing you." He said it briskly. He'd terrified himself.

He shifted away and shattered the moment. "There's not really very much of you." Suddenly aware that the breeze fluttering in the windows he left open was cold, he tugged at the bedspread until he could wrap it around her. "Are you all right then?"

"I'm fabulous, thank you." Laughing, she sat up, without a shrug for modesty as the spread slid to her waist. She caught his face in her hands and gave him a quick, affectionate kiss. "Are you all right then?" she said, mimicking his brogue.

"That I am, but I've had a bit of practice."

"I'll bet. But let's not bring up all your conquests just now. I'd hate to be obliged to punch you when I'm feeling so friendly."

"I wouldn't say they were conquests precisely. But we'll let that be."

"Wise choice."

"Let me close the windows. You're cold."

She angled her head as he rose. "There's nurturing in that bruised body of yours, Donnelly."

"I beg your pardon?"

"I'd say it comes from the horses." She pursed her lips, considered while he *thunked* a window down and scowled. "You look after them, worry about them, make plans for them, see to their needs and their comfort—oh and their training, of course. Then if you don't watch yourself you start to do it with people, too."

"I don't nurture people." He found the idea mildly insulting. "People can look after themselves. I don't even like people very much." He stalked over and shut the other window. "Present company excepted, as you're sitting naked in my bed and it would be rude to say otherwise."

"You didn't phrase that quite right. You don't like very many people. Do you have a robe?"

"No." He wasn't sure if it was the truth in what she said, or her understanding of him that irked him.

"Figures." She spied one of his work shirts tossed over a chair, and though it smelled of horses, slipped it on. "I'd say that tea's probably strong enough to hammer nails by now. Do you still want it?"

She looked…interesting in his shirt. Interesting enough that his blood began to churn again. "What are my options?"

"On my schedule, we have a cup of tea, a little conversation, then you get to seduce me back into bed and make love to me again before I go home."

"That's not bad, but I think it bears improving."

"Oh, and how's that?"

"We cut out the tea and conversation."

She ran her tongue over her top lip—his taste was still there—as he walked toward her. "That would take us straight to you seducing me? Correct?"

"That's my plan."

"I can be flexible."

His grin flashed. "I'd like to test that out."

They never got around to the tea.

And when she'd left him, he stood at the door and watched her run along the path. Love-struck idiot, he told himself. You can't keep her. You've never kept anything in your life that you couldn't fit in the bag you toss over your shoulder.

It was a bad turn of luck, that was all, that he would slip up and fall in love. It was bound to hurt like blazes before it was done. He'd get over it, of course. Over her and over this slippery feeling inside his heart. He wasn't so far gone as to believe this sort of madness lasted.

So best to enjoy it, he decided, and turned away when Keeley disappeared in the dark.

When he climbed into bed, her scent was on his pillow. For the first time in a week he slept deep and slept well.

Chapter 8

She missed him. It was the oddest thing to find herself thinking about Brian off and on during the day, and thinking of a dozen things she wanted to tell him, or show him when he got back from Saratoga.

She wasn't the only one.

During his next lesson Willy asked if Mr. Donnelly was coming so he could show off the fresh gap in his teeth. The man, Keeley mused, made an impression and made it fast.

It wasn't as if she didn't have enough to occupy her mind or her time. She'd found enough tuition students to add another class and was even now snaking her way through the maze of bureaucracy to arrange for three additional subsidized students.

She'd had meetings with the psychologist, the social

worker, the parents and the children. The paperwork alone was enough to, well, choke a horse, she admitted. But it would be worth it in the end.

With some amusement, she flipped through the article in *Washingtonian Magazine*. She knew the exposure was responsible for netting her the new full tuition students. The photographs were gorgeous and the text made full use of her background, her Olympic medal and her social standing.

No problem there, she decided, particularly since the academy was mentioned several times.

She glanced at the phone with a little sigh as it rang. It hadn't stopped since the article had been published. The time was coming, Keeley thought, when she was going to have to break down and hire an assistant.

But for now, the school was all hers.

"Good morning, Royal Meadows Riding Academy." Her coolly professional tone warmed when she heard her cousin Maureen's voice.

Fifteen minutes later, she was hanging up and shaking her head. It appeared she was going to dinner and the races that evening. She'd said no—at least Keeley was fairly certain she'd said no five or six times. But nobody held out against Mo for long. She just rolled over you.

Keeley eyed the piles of paperwork on her desk, huffed out a breath when the phone rang again. Just do the first thing, she reminded herself, then do the second, and keep going until it was done.

She'd done the first, the second and the third, when her father came in.

He stopped in the doorway, held up a hand. "Wait,

don't tell me. I know you. The face is very familiar." He narrowed his eyes as she rolled hers. "I'm sure I've seen you before, somewhere. Tibet? Mazetlan? At the dinner table a year or two ago."

"It hasn't been more than a week." She reached up as he bent to kiss her. "But I've missed you, too. I've been swamped here."

"So I've heard." He flipped open the magazine to her article. "Pretty girl. I bet her parents are proud of her."

"I hope so." When the phone rang, she muffled a shriek, waved her hands. "Let the machine get it. It's been ringing off the hook since Sunday. Half the parents who call in to inquire about lessons haven't even asked their kids if they want to ride."

She scooted her chair to the little fridge and took out two bottles of soda. "So thanks."

"For?" Travis prompted as he took the soft drink.

"For always asking."

"Then you're welcome. I hear I'm escorting two lovely women to dinner tonight."

"Mo caught you?"

He chuckled before he tipped back the bottle to drink. "'We haven't had an inter-family gathering in weeks,'" he mimicked. "'Don't you love me anymore?'"

"She always pushes the right button." Keeley studied the toe of her oldest boots. "So…have you heard from Brendon?"

"Late yesterday. They should be home tonight."

"That's good." You'd think the man could have called her once, she thought, scowling at her boots. Sent a telegram, a damn smoke signal.

"I imagine Brian's anxious to get back."

Her head jerked up. "Really?"

"Betty's making progress—as are several of the other yearlings. She's doing particularly well on the practice oval. She's ready for Brian to take her over full-time."

"I caught one of her morning workouts. She looks strong."

"We breed true at Royal Meadows." There was something wistful in his tone that had Keeley lifting her brows.

"What's the matter?"

"Nothing." Travis shrugged it off and rose. "Getting old."

"Don't be ridiculous."

"Yesterday you were riding on my shoulders," he murmured. "The house was full of noise. Clomping up and down the steps, doors slamming. Scattered toys. I don't know how many times I stepped on one of those damned little cars of Brady's."

Turning back, he ran a hand over her hair. "I miss that. I miss all of you."

"Daddy." In one fluid movement she rose and slid her arms around him.

"It's the way it's supposed to work. Three of you off at college, Brendon moving around to get a handle on the business of things. It's what he wants. And you, building your own. But… I miss the crowd of you."

"I promise to slam the door the very first chance I get."

"That might help."

"Sentimental softie. I love that about you."

"Lucky for me." He gave her a quick, hard squeeze, then glanced over as the phone rang again. "Actually I didn't stop in for sentiment, but to give you some business advice." He drew her back. "You need help around here."

"I'm thinking about it. Really," she added when he angled his head. "As soon as I straighten things out I'll look into it."

"I seem to recall you saying the same thing six months ago."

"It just hasn't been the right time. I've got it all under control." Even as she said it, the phone rang again.

"Keeley, getting help doesn't mean you won't be in charge, doesn't mean it won't be your school."

"I know, but...it won't be the same."

"I'm here to tell you nothing stays the same. The farm's more than it was when it passed to me, and less than it will be when it passes to you and your brothers and sisters. But I've put my mark on it. Nothing can change that."

"I guess I just don't want it to get away from me."

"You've already proven you can do it."

"You're right. Of course, you're right. But it isn't easy to find the right person. It would have to be someone good with kids and horses, and who'd be able to pitch in with the administrating to some extent and wouldn't quibble about shoveling manure. Plus I'd have to be able to depend on them, and get along with them. And they'd have to be diplomatic with parents, which is often the trickiest part."

Travis picked up his soft drink again. "I might be able to point you in the right direction there."

"Oh? Listen, Dad, I appreciate it, but you know, a friend of a friend or the son or daughter of an acquaintance. That kind of thing gets very sticky if it doesn't work out."

"Actually, I was thinking of someone a little closer to home. Your mother."

"Ma?" With a half laugh Keeley sat again. "Ma doesn't want this headache, even if she had time for it."

"Shows what you know." Smug now, he drank. "Just mention it to her, casually. I won't say a word about it."

By the time the day's lesson was over, and the last horse groomed and fed, Keeley dragged herself into the house. She wanted nothing more than a long bath and a quiet night. And if she ducked the evening plans, her cousin Mo would dog her like a hound. Better to face an evening out than weeks of nagging.

She moved through the kitchen, into the hall. Her father was right, she realized. How would any of them get used to the quiet? No one was shouting down the stairs or rushing in the door or playing music so loud it vibrated the eardrums.

She paused at the top of the steps, looking right. There was the room Brady and Patrick shared. She still remembered that during one spat Brady had run a line of black tape from the ceiling, down the wall, across the floor, and up again, cutting the room in half.

One had been marked Brady's Territory. The other he'd dubbed No Man's Land.

And how many times had she heard Brendon pound

a fist on the wall between his room and theirs ordering them to keep it down before he came in and knocked their heads together?

When she passed Sarah's room, she saw her mother sitting on the bed, stroking a red sweater.

"Ma?"

"Oh." Adelia looked up. Her eyes were damp, but she shook her head and smiled. "You startled me. It's so bloody quiet in this house."

Keeley stepped in. The room had bright blue walls. The curtains and spread picked up that bold hue and matched it with an equally vivid green in wide stripes. It should have been horrible, Keeley mused, as she often did. But it worked.

And it was completely Sarah.

"Do you and Dad share the same brain?" Keeping her voice light, Keeley sat on the bed. "He was feeling sad this morning over the same thing."

"I suppose after all these years together, you pick up the same vibrations or whatever. And Sarah called just a bit ago. She's desperately in need for this particular red sweater, which she can't think how she forgot to take with her. She sounds so happy and busy and grown up."

"They'll all be home next month for Thanksgiving, then again for Christmas."

"I know. Still, if I could think of a way to get away with it, I'd deliver this sweater myself instead of shipping it. Lord, look at the time. I've got to get myself cleaned up and changed for dinner. And so do you."

"Yeah." Keeley pursed her lips in thought while her mother smoothed the sweater one more time and rose.

"I'm running behind today," she began. "I seem to be running behind a lot lately."

"That's what happens to successful people."

"I suppose so. And adding on this class is going to crowd my time and energy even more."

"You know I'll give you a hand when you need it, and so will your father." Adelia walked out of the room and into her own to lay Sarah's sweater aside.

"Yes, I appreciate that. I guess I'm going to have to seriously consider something more formal and permanent, though. I really hate to. I mean, taking on an outsider, it's difficult for me. But…"

Keeley let the word hang, surprised when her mother—who usually had something to say—remained silent.

"I don't suppose you'd be interested in working part-time at the school?"

Adelia turned her head, met Keeley's eyes in the mirror over the bureau. "Are you offering me a job?"

"It sounds awfully strange when you put it that way, but yes. But don't do it because you feel obliged. Only if you think you'd have the time or the inclination."

Adelia spun around, her face brilliant. "What the devil's taken you so long? I'll start tomorrow."

"Really? You really want to?"

"I've been *dying* to. Oh, it's taken every bit of my willpower not to come down there every day until you just got so used to me being around you didn't realize I *was* working there. This is exciting!" She rushed over to give Keeley a hug. "I can't wait to tell your father."

Keeping her arms tight around her daughter, Adelia did a quick dance. "I'm a groom again."

* * *

"If I'd known you were available, Dee, and looking for work, I'd've hired you." Burke Logan settled back in his chair and winked at his wife's cousin.

"We like to keep the best on at Royal Meadows." Adelia twinkled at him across the table in the track's dining room. He was as handsome and as dangerous to look at as he'd been nearly twenty years before when she'd first met him.

"Oh, I don't know." Burke trailed a hand over his wife's shoulder. "We have the best bookkeeper around at Three Aces."

"In that case, I want a raise." Erin picked up her wine and sent Burke a challenging look. "A big one. Trevor?" Her voice was smooth, shimmering with Ireland as she addressed her son. "Do you have in mind to eat that pork chop or just use it for decoration?"

"I'm reading the *Racing Form,* Ma."

"His father's son," Erin muttered and snagged the paper from him. "Eat your dinner."

He heaved a sigh as only a twelve-year-old boy could. "I think Topeka in the third, with Lonesome in the fifth and Hennessy in the sixth for the trifecta. Dad says Topeka's generous and a cinch tip."

At his wife's long stare, Burke cleared his throat. "Stuff that pork chop in your mouth, Trev. Where's Jena?"

"She's fussing with her hair," Mo announced, and snatched a French fry from Travis's plate. "As usual," she added with the worldly air only an older sister could achieve, "the minute she turned fourteen she decided her hair was the bane of her existence. Huh. Like having long, thick, straight-as-a-pin black hair is a problem. This—" she tugged on one of the hundreds of wild red curls that spiraled around her face "—is a problem. If you're going to worry about something as stupid as hair, which I don't. Anyway, you guys have to come over and see this weanling I have my eye on. He's going to be amazing. And if Dad lets me train him..."

She trailed off, slanting a look at her father across the table.

"You'll be in college this time next year," Burke reminded her.

"Not if I can help it," Mo said under her breath.

Recognizing the mutinous look, Erin changed the subject. "Keeley, Burke tells me your new trainer is a natural with the horses, with Travis and with cards as well."

"And I hear he's gorgeous, too," Mo added.

"Where'd you hear that?" Keeley demanded before she could bite her tongue in two.

"Oh, word gets around in our snug little world," Mo said grandly. "And Shelley Mason—one of your kids? Her sister Lorna's in my World History class, a *huge* bore by the way. The class, that is, not Lorna, who's only a small bore. Anyway, she picked Shelley up last week from your place and got a load of the Irish hunk, so I heard all about it. Which is why I'm planning on coming over as soon as I can and getting a load of him myself."

"Trevor, give your sister your pork chop so she can stuff it in her mouth."

"Dad." Giggling, Mo snatched another fry. "I'm just going to look. So, Keeley, is he gorgeous? I respect your opinion more than Lorna Mason's."

"He's too old for you," Keeley said, a bit more sharply than she intended and had Mo rolling her eyes.

"Jeez. I don't want to marry him and have his children."

Travis's laugh prevented Keeley from snapping back with something foolish. "Good thing. Now that I've found someone who comes close to replacing Paddy, I don't intend to lose him to Three Aces."

"Okay." Mo licked salt from her fingertip. "I'll just ogle him."

Annoyed, and feeling ridiculous at the reaction, Keeley pushed back her chair. "I think I'll go down and take a look at the field, and check on Lonesome. He's always a little sulky before a race."

"Cool." Mo sprang up. "I'll go down with you."

Mo rushed out of the dining room, heading out past the betting windows at a fast clip, so that Keeley was forced to step lively to keep pace. "It's going to be so much fun for you, having your mom work at the school. There's nothing like a family operation, you know. Which is all I want. I mean, come on, I don't have to go to college to be a trainer. If I already know what I want to do, and I'm learning how to do it every day right at home, what's college going to do for me?"

"Expand your brain?" Keeley suggested.

Ignoring that, Mo hurried outside where the air had turned crisp. "I know horses, Keeley. You understand what it's like. It's instinct and experience and it's *doing*." She gestured widely. "Well, I've got time to nag my parents into submission."

"No one does it better."

With a laugh, Mo hooked her arm through her cousin's. "I'm so glad to see you. The summer just winged by, you know, with all of us so busy with stuff."

"I know."

They made the turn for the shedrow and the world was suddenly horses.

Some were being prepped for the next race. In the boxes, grooms wrapped long, thin legs that would carry those huge bodies in a blur of speed and power. Trainers with keen eyes and gentle hands moved among the horses to pamper a skittish ride or rev up another.

The hot walkers cooled down horses who'd already run. Legs were examined, iced down. Through the sharp air came the hoofbeats that signaled another field was coming back from the race. Steam rose off the horses' backs, turning into a fine and magical mist.

"Of all the shedrows in all the world." Brendon came out of the stables, grinning.

"You're back."

"Just." He strolled over to rub a hand over Mo's hair. "I talked to Ma a couple of hours ago from the road and she said you were all coming here tonight. So we swung by on the way home."

"We?"

"Yeah, Bri's taking a look at Lonesome, giving him a pep talk. Moodiest damn horse. Figured we might as well catch the race, then I can hook a ride back with you guys and Brian can trailer Zeus back home."

"Sounds like a plan." It pleased her to hear the calm of her own voice while her heart was galloping. "Actually I came down to take a look at Lonesome myself."

"He's all yours—and Bri's. Hey, I've got time to get some dinner. See you up there."

"Now you can introduce me to the hunk." Mo fell into step beside Keeley.

"I will if you can behave like you have a brain as well as glands."

"It has nothing to do with glands, I'm just curious. Don't worry, I'm taking a page out of your book there when it comes to men."

Keeley stopped at the door to the stables. "Excuse me?"

"You know, guys are fine to look at, or to hang around with occasionally. But there are lots more important things. I'm not going to get involved with one until I'm thirty, soonest."

Keeley wasn't certain whether to be amused or appalled. Then she heard Brian's voice, the lilt of it. And she forgot everything else.

He was in the box with Lonesome, a temperamental roan gelding. The horse moped, as was his habit before a race.

"They ask too much of you, there's no doubt about it," Brian was saying as he checked the wrappings on Lonesome's legs. "It's a terrible cross you have to bear, and you show great courage and fortitude day after day. Perhaps if you win this one I can put a word in for you. You know, extra carrots and that sort of thing, a bit of molasses in the evening. A bigger brass plaque for your box at home."

"That's bribery," Keeley murmured.

Brian turned, his eyes going warm. "That's bargaining," he corrected. "But if I can interest you in a bribe," he began and opened the box door intending to snatch Keeley inside for a much anticipated welcome back kiss.

He nearly stepped over Mo. "Sorry. Didn't see you there."

"I'm short. That's my cross to bear. I'm Mo Logan." She stuck out a friendly hand. "Keeley's cousin from Three Aces."

"Pleased to meet you. You've a horse running tonight, Ms. Logan?"

"Mo. Hennessy. Sixth race. My money says he'll win laughing."

"I'll keep that in mind if I get up to the betting window."

"I want to take a look at Hennessy before his race. Come up to the dining room if you have time, Brian, for food or a drink. The family's all there."

"Thank you for that. Pretty thing," Brian murmured when Mo dashed off.

"She wanted to take a look at you, too. She heard you were a hunk."

"Is that so?" Amused, Brian shifted. "Did you tell her that?"

"I certainly did not. I have more respect for you than to speak of you in such a sexist way."

"Respect's a good thing." He yanked her into the box, crushing his mouth to hers before she could laugh. "But I'm banking on passion just at the moment. Have you passion for me, Keeley?" he murmured against her mouth.

"Apparently." Her ears were ringing. "Oh, Brian, I want—" She strained against him until they bumped into the horse. "You. Now. Somewhere. Can't we…it's been days."

"Four." He wanted to tear off the long slim dress she

wore and mount her like a stallion, all blinding heat and primitive need.

He'd thought, convinced himself, that he'd be sensible about her, kept his wants and wishes under control. And all it had taken was seeing her. Just seeing her. It was exactly as it had been that first time he'd laid his eyes on her. A lightning strike in heart and blood.

"Keeley." He ran kisses over her face, buried his in her hair, then started all over again. "I've such a need for you. It's like burning from the inside out. Come with me, out to the lorry."

"Yes." At that moment, she'd have gone anywhere. It seemed he would swallow her whole. "Hurry. Let's hurry."

She took his hand, fumbled with the door herself. Breathless, she would have stumbled if he hadn't caught her. "Teach me to wear heels in the damn stable," she muttered. "My legs are shaking."

With a nervous laugh she turned back to him. Her legs stopped trembling. At least she couldn't feel them. All she could feel now was the unsteady skipping of her heart.

He was staring at her, his eyes intense. When she'd turned his hands had reached up to frame her face. "You're so beautiful."

She'd never believed words like that mattered. They were so easily, and so often carelessly, said. But they didn't seem easy from him. And there was nothing careless about the tone of his voice. Before she could speak, before she could think of what could be said, there was a shout and the sound of running feet.

"Keeley, hurry, come with me." Oblivious to the intimacy of the scene she'd burst in on, Mo grabbed her hand. "I need backup. The bastard."

"What? What's happened?"

"If he thinks he's going to get away with it, he's got another think coming." Dragging Keeley, Mo barreled through the stables, turned and charged toward a stall.

Keeley could already hear the voices raised in argument. She saw the man first. She recognized him. Peter Tarmack with his oiled hair and cheap pinkie ring made a habit of picking up horses in claiming races, then running them into the ground.

The jockey was a familiar face as well. He was past his prime and, like Tarmack, was known to enjoy a few too many nips from the bottle at the track. Still, he picked up rides now and again when a regular jockey was sick or injured.

"I tell you, Tarmack, I won't ride him. And you won't get anyone else to. He's not fit to run."

"Don't you tell me what's fit. You'll get up and you'll ride, and you'll damn well place. You've been paid."

"Not to ride a sick and injured horse. You'll get your money back."

"What you haven't already put in a bottle."

Because Mo was quivering and had sucked in a breath to speak, Keeley squeezed her hand hard enough to grind bone. "Is there a problem, Larry?"

"Miss Keeley." The jockey yanked off his cap and turned his wrinkled, flustered face to hers. "I'm trying to tell Mr. Tarmack here that his horse isn't fit to race tonight. He's not fit."

"It's not your place to tell me anything. And I don't

need one of the almighty Grant's damn whelps interfering in my business."

Before Keeley could respond, Brian had moved in.
She blinked and he had hauled Tarmack up to his toes.
"That's no way to be speaking to a lady." His voice
was quiet, the eye of a storm. And the storm, with all
its vengeance, was in his eyes. "You'll want to apologize for that, while you still have teeth to help you form
the words."

"Brian, I can handle this."

"You'll handle what you like." He kept his eyes on
Tarmack's now bulging ones. "But he'll by God apologize with his very next breath."

"I beg your pardon." Tarmack choked it out, wheezed
in air as Brian relaxed his grip a little. "I'm simply trying to deal with a washed-up jockey—and one I've paid
in advance."

"You'll get your money back," the jockey replied,
then turned to Keeley. "Miss Keeley, I'm not getting
up on this ride. He's half lame from a knee spavin, and
anybody with eyes can see he's hidebound. He ain't fit
to race."

"Excuse me." Her voice viciously cold, she pushed
past Tarmack and moved into the box to examine the
horse for herself. Within moments, her hands were
shaking with rage.

"Mr. Tarmack, if you try to put a jockey on this
horse, I'll have you up on charges. In fact, I'm damn
well having you up on charges regardless. This gelding's sick, injured and neglected."

"Don't hang that on me. I've only had him a couple
weeks."

"And in a couple weeks you haven't noticed his condition? You've been working him despite it?"

"Now you look." He started to take a step forward and found himself looking eye to eye with Brian again. "Listen," he said, his tone shifting to a whine. "Maybe you can be sentimental when you've got money. Me, I make my living moving horses. They don't run, I go in the red."

"How much?" Keeley laid a hand on the gelding's cheek. In her heart, he was already hers. "How much did he cost you?"

"Ah...ten grand."

Brian merely shoved a finger into Tarmack's breastbone. "Pull the other one. It has bells on it."

Tarmack shifted his shoulders. "Maybe it was five thousand. I'd have to check my books."

"You'll have a check for five thousand tomorrow. I'm taking the horse tonight. Brian, would you take a look at him, please?"

"Wait just a minute."

This time it was Keeley who turned and she who shoved Tarmack aside. "Be smart. Take the money. Because whether you do or don't I'm taking this horse with me."

"The knee needs treatment," Brian said after a quick look. It burned his blood to see how the injury had been neglected. "We can deal with that. From the look of him, I'd say he has a good case of bots. He needs tending."

"He'll get tending."

Keeley merely glanced over her shoulder at Tarmack. "You can go." Her voice held the regal ring of dismissal—princess to peasant. "Someone will deliver the check to you in the morning."

The tone burned in Tarmack's gut. She wouldn't be so hoity-toity without her damn bodyguard, he thought. He'd have taught her a little respect if the Irish bastard hadn't been around.

He bunched a fist impotently in his pocket and tried to save face. "I'm not just letting you take the horse and leave me with nothing but your say-so. I don't give a damn who you are."

Brian straightened again, blood in his eye, but Keeley merely held up a hand. "Mo, would you please take Mr. Tarmack to the dining room. If you'd ask my father to write him a check for the five thousand, and I'll straighten it out later."

"Happy to." She grabbed Keeley by the shoulders, kissed her. "I knew you'd do it." Then with a sniff she turned away. "Come with me, Tarmack. You'll get your money."

"I'm sorry, Miss Keeley." Larry ran his cap through his hands. "I didn't know how bad it was till I saw the ride here. I couldn't get up on him seeing how he was."

"You did the right thing. Don't worry."

"He did pay me ahead, like he said."

She nodded, stepped out of the box again, gesturing to him. "How much do you have left?"

"'Bout twenty."

"Come and see me tomorrow. We'll take care of it."

"'Preciate it, Miss Keeley. That horse there, he ain't worth no five, you know."

She studied the gelding. His color was muddy, his face too square for elegance and made homelier still by an off-center blaze of dirty white. And his eyes were unbearably sad.

"Sure he is, Larry. He's worth it to me."

Chapter 9

"You don't have to help with this."

Brian said nothing, simply continued to clip the gelding's legs. Bots were a common enough problem, especially with horses at grass. But this one had been sadly neglected. He had no doubt the eggs the botfly had laid on the gelding's legs had been transferred to the stomach.

"Brian, really." Keeley continued to mix the blister for the knee spavin. "You've had a really long day. I can handle this."

"Sure you can. You can handle this, morons like Tarmack, washed-up jockeys and everything else that comes along before breakfast. Nobody's saying different."

Since the statement wasn't delivered in what could

be mistaken for a complimentary tone, Keeley turned to frown at him. "What's wrong with you?"

"There's not a bloody thing wrong with me. But you could use some work. Do you have to do everything yourself, every flaming step and stage of it? Can't you just take help when help's offered and shut the hell up?"

She did shut the hell up, for ten shocked seconds. "I simply assumed that you'd be tired after your trip."

"I'll let you know when I'm tired."

"The gelding here doesn't seem to be the only one with something nasty in his system."

"Well, it's you in my system, princess, and it feels a bit nasty at the moment."

Hurt came first, a quick short-armed jab. Pride sprang in to defend. "I'll be happy to purge you, just like I'll purge this horse tomorrow."

"If I thought it would work," he muttered, "I'd purge myself. You'll want to wait until at least midday," Brian told her. "You can't be sure the last time he was fed."

"I know how to treat stomach-bots, thank you." Gently she began to apply the blister to the injured knee.

"Here, you'll get that all over your clothes."

Keeley jerked away bad-temperedly when Brian reached for the pot of blister. "They're my clothes."

"So you should have more respect for them. You've no business treating a horse in clothes like that. Silk dresses for God's sake."

"I've got a closetful. We princesses tend to."

"Nevertheless." He curled his fingers around the lip of the pot, and under the sick gelding they began a vicious little tug-of-war. He would have laughed, was on the point of it, when he looked at her face and saw that her eyes were wet.

He let go of the pot so abruptly, Keeley fell back on her butt. "What are you doing?" he demanded.

"I'm applying a non-irritating blister to a knee spavin. Now go away and let me get on with it."

"There's no reason to start that up. None at all." Panic jingled straight to his head, nearly made him dizzy. "This is no place for crying."

"I'm upset. It's my stable. I can cry when and where I choose."

"All right, all right, all right." Desperately he dug into his pocket for a bandanna. "Here, just blow your nose or something."

"Just go to hell or something." Rather grandly, she turned her shoulder on him and continued to apply the blister.

"Keeley, I'm sorry." He wasn't sure for exactly what, but that wasn't here nor there. "Dry your eyes now, *a grha,* and we'll make this lad comfortable for the night."

"Don't take that placating tone with me. I'm not a child or a sick horse."

Brian dragged his hands through his hair, gave it one good yank. "Which tone would you prefer?"

"An honest one." Satisfied the blister was properly applied, she rose. "But I'm afraid the derisive one you've used since we got here fits that category. In your opinion, I'm spoiled, stubborn and too proud to accept help."

Though the tears appeared to have passed, he thought it wise to be cautious. "That's pretty close to the truth," he agreed, getting to his feet. "But it's an interesting mixture, and I've grown fond of it."

"I'm not spoiled."

Brian raised his eyebrows, cocked his head. "Perhaps the word means something different to you Yanks. Seems to me it's not everyone who could casually ask their father to write a check for five thousand dollars for a sick horse."

"I'll pay him back in the morning."

"I've no doubt of it."

Baffled now, she threw up her hands. "Should I have just left him there, walked away so that idiot Tarmack could find a jockey who would go up on him?"

"No, you did exactly right. But the fact's the same that you could toss around that kind of money without blinking an eye."

Brian walked to the gelding's head to examine his eyes and teeth. It grated on him. He wished it didn't, as it said little for him that her easy dismissal of money scored his pride.

But it had, at that heated moment at the track, slammed the distance between them right in his face.

"You're a generous woman, Keeley."

"But I can afford to be," she finished.

"True enough." He ran his hands down the horse's neck, soothing. "But that doesn't take away from the fact that you are." Slowly he continued to work his way over the horse. "You'll have to forgive me—Irish of my class are generally a bit resentful of the gentry. It's in the blood."

"The class system's in your head, Brian."

That, he thought, wasn't even worth commenting on. What was, was. His fingers found a small knot.

"He's a bit of an abscess here. We'll want to bring this to a head."

They'd bring something else to a head, she decided and moved in so they faced each other over the gelding's back. "So tell me, how do men of your class deal with taking women of mine to bed?"

His eyes flashed to hers, held. "I'd keep my hands off you if I could."

"Is that supposed to flatter me?"

"No. It just is, and doesn't flatter either of us." He moved out of the box to get flannel to heat for a hot fermentation.

No, she thought. She'd be damned if she'd leave it at that. "Is that all there is to it, Brian?" she demanded as she followed him out. "Just sex?"

He ran water, hot as his hand could bear, and soaked a large section of flannel in it. "No." He spoke without turning around. "I care about you. That just makes it more difficult."

"It should make it easier."

"It doesn't."

"I don't understand you. Would you be happier if we just jumped each other, without any connection, any understanding or feelings?"

He hauled up the bucket. "Infinitely. But it's too late for that, isn't it?"

Baffled, she walked back into the box behind him. "You're angry with me because you care about me. This water's too hot," she said when she tested it.

"No, it isn't. And I'm not angry with you at t'all." Murmuring to the gelding, he lay the heated flannel over the abscess. "A bit with myself, maybe, but it's more satisfying to take it out on you."

"That, at least, I can understand. Brian, why are we fighting?" She laid a hand over the one he held pressed to the flannel. "We're doing the right thing here tonight. The method of how we got the gelding here isn't as important as what happens to him now."

"You're right, of course." He studied the contrast of their hands. His big, rough from work and hers small and elegant.

"And why we care for each other isn't as important as what we do about it."

About that he wasn't as sure, so he said nothing while she lifted another square of flannel and wrung it out.

Morning dawned misty and cool. As she'd slept poorly, Keeley's mind refused to click into gear. Her usual rush of morning adrenaline deserted her so that she began her daily chores with her body dragging and her brain fogged.

Brian's doing, she thought sulkily. This inconsistency of his, this off-and-on insistence to keep a distance between them was baffling. She'd never run into a problem she couldn't solve, an obstacle she couldn't overcome. But this one, this one man, might just be the exception.

He hurt her, and she hadn't been prepared for it. Could they have spent so much time together, been so intimate, and not understand each other? He cared about her, and that made it a problem. What kind of logic was that? she asked herself. Where was the sense in that kind of thinking?

Caring about someone made all the difference. She'd seen that constant well of compassion in him. It was, she admitted, as attractive, as appealing to her as that long, tough body, that thick, unkempt mane of sun-streaked hair.

The look of him, the face of planes and angles, the bold green eyes, might have stirred her blood—and had, though she'd been more annoyed than pleased initially. But it was the heart, the patience, the nurturing side he refused to acknowledge that had won her interest and respect.

Rather than being a problem, it had been, and was, the solution for her.

How could he look at her now, after all they'd shared, and see only the pampered daughter of a privileged home?

How could he, believing that, have feelings for her?

It was baffling, irritating and very close to infuriating. Or would be, she thought with a yawn, if she wasn't so damned tired.

The lack of energy struck unfairly keen when Mo bounced into the stables. "Just had to come by before I headed off to the eternal hell of school." She popped right into the box where Keeley was examining the injured knee. "How's he doing?"

"He's more comfortable." Testing, Keeley lifted the gelding's foot, bending the knee. He snorted, shied. "But you can see there's still pain."

"Poor guy. Poor big guy." Clucking, Mo patted his flank. "You were such a hero last night, Keel. I mean just stepping in and taking right over. I knew you would."

Keeley's brows drew together. "I didn't take over. I don't take over."

"Sure you did—you always do. The original take-charge gal. Very cool to watch. And this guy's grateful, aren't you, boy? Oh, and the hunk wasn't hard on the eyes, either." Grinning, she gave an obvious and deliberate shudder. "The real physical type. I thought he was going to punch that idiot Tarmack right in the face. Was kinda hoping he would. Anyway, the pair of you made a great team."

"I suppose."

"So, what about those smoldering looks?"

"What smoldering looks?"

"Get out." Mo cheerfully wiggled her eyebrows. "I got singed and I was only an innocent bystander. The guy looks at you like you were the last candy bar on the shelf and he'd die without a chocolate fix."

"That's a ridiculous analogy, and you're imagining things."

"He was going to pound Tarmack into dust for dissing you. Man, I just wanted to melt when he hauled the guy up by the collar. Too romantic."

"There's nothing romantic about a fight. And though I certainly could have handled Tarmack myself, I appreciated Brian's help."

Damn it, she thought. She hadn't even thanked him. Scowling, she stomped out of the box for a pitchfork.

"Yeah, you could have handled him. You handle everything. But not really needing to be rescued sort of makes *being* rescued more exciting, you know."

"No, I don't know," Keeley snapped. "Go to school, Mo. I've got mucking out to do."

"I'm going, I'm going. Sheesh. You must be low on the caffeine intake this morning. I'll come by later to see how the gelding's doing. I've got a kind of vested interest, you know? See you."

"Yeah, fine. Whatever." Keeley muttered to herself as she went to work on the stalls. There was nothing wrong with being able to handle things herself. Nothing wrong with wanting to. And she did appreciate Brian's help.

And she didn't need caffeine.

"I like caffeine," she grumbled. "I enjoy it, and that's entirely different from needing it. Entirely. I could give it up anytime I wanted, and I'd barely miss it."

Annoyed, she snagged the soft drink she'd left on a shelf and guzzled.

All right, so maybe she would miss it. But only because she liked the taste. It wasn't like a craving or an addiction or...

She couldn't say why Brian popped into her head just then. She was certain if he'd seen her staring in a kind of horror at a soft drink bottle, he'd have been amused. It was debatable what his reaction would be if he'd realized she wasn't actually seeing the bottle, but his face.

No, that wasn't a need, either, she thought quickly. She did not *need* Brian Donnelly. It was attraction. Affection—a cautious kind of affection. He was a man who interested her, and whom she admired in many ways. But it wasn't as if she needed...

"Oh God."

It had to be overreaction, she decided, and set the bottle aside as carefully as she would have a container of nitro. What she was going through was something as simple as overromanticizing an affair. That would be natural enough, she told herself, particularly since this was her first.

She didn't want to be in love with him. She began wielding the pitchfork vigorously now, as if to sweat out a fever. She didn't *choose* to be in love with him. That was even more important. When her hands trembled she ignored them and worked harder still.

By the time her mother joined her, Keeley had herself under control enough to casually ask Adelia to work in the office while she exercised Sam.

Keeley Grant had never run from a problem in her life, and she wasn't about to start now. She saddled her mount, then rode off to clear her head before she dealt with the problem at hand.

The portable starting gate was in place on the practice oval. The air was soft and cool. Brian had seen the blush of color coming onto the leaves, the hints of change. Though he imagined it would all be a sight in another week or two, his attention was narrowed onto the horses.

He was working in fields of five, using two yearlings and three experienced racers at a go. This last phase of schooling just prior to public racing would teach him every bit as much as it taught the yearlings.

He needed to watch their style, learn their preferences, their quirks, their strengths. Much of it would be guesses—educated ones to be sure, but guesses nonetheless, at least until they had a few solid races under their belts.

But Brian was very good at guessing.

"I want Tempest on the rail." He chewed on a cigar as it helped him think. "Then The Brooder, then Betty, Caramel and Giant on the outside."

He glanced around at the sound of hoofbeats, then lost his train of thought as Keeley trotted toward the oval. Irritated, he looked deliberately away and slammed the door on that increasingly wide area of his mind she insisted on occupying.

"I don't want the yearlings rated," he ordered, telling the exercise boys not to hold them back. "Nor punished, either. No more than a tap of the bat to signal. My horses don't need to be whipped to run."

Despite his concentration, he was aware when Keeley dismounted behind him. He took out his stopwatch, turning it over and over in his hand as the field was led to the gate.

"I don't know the yearling at the rail," Keeley said conversationally as she looped her reins around the top rung of the fence.

"Your father named him Tempest in a Teacup, as he's got a small build, but he's full of spirit. You don't often ride this way in the morning."

"No, but I wanted to see the progress. And my new assistant is handling things at the office."

He glanced over. She'd taken the band out of her hair. It flowed wild over her shoulders, but her face was cool and very serious. "Assistant is it? When did this happen?"

"Yesterday. My mother's working with me at the school now. Contrary to some beliefs, I don't insist on handling all the steps and stages by myself, when help is offered."

"Touchy still, are you?"

"Apparently."

"Well, you'll have to snarl at me later. I'm busy. Jim! Hold him steady now," Brian called out as Tempest shied a bit at the gate. "That one still objects a bit to being penned in. There, that's it," he murmured as the horses were loaded and the back gate shut. He held a finger over the timer, plunging when the gates sprang open.

The horses flew out.

He wondered if there was anything that gave his heart more of a knock than that instant, that first rush of speed, that blur of great bodies surging forward on the track.

But through the thrill of it, his eyes missed nothing. The stretch of legs, the clouds of dirt, the figures riding low over the necks.

"She wants the lead, right from the start," he murmured. "Wants the rest tasting her dust."

Caught up, Keeley leaned over the rail as the horses made the first turn. The thunder of hoofbeats drummed in her blood. "She runs well in a crowd. You were right about that. Tempest is a little nervy."

"We might try a shadow roll on him. He wants the outside. He's about endurance. The longer the race, the better he'll like it. There's Betty now. She wants the rail. Aye, she'll hug it like a lover."

Without thinking, he laid his hand over Keeley's on the rail. "Just look at her, will you? That's a champion. She doesn't need any of us. She knows it."

With his hand warm and firm over hers, Keeley watched the horses streak down the backstretch with

Betty nearly a length in the lead. Pride and pleasure tangled inside her.

When Brian let out a shout, clicked his watch again, she started to turn, to indulge the giddy thrill by throwing her arms around him. But he was already drawing away.

"That's good time, damn good time. And she'll do better yet." He nodded, his eyes tracking as the riders rose high in their stirrups and slowed their mounts. "I'll find the right race for her, give her a taste of the real thing."

Giving Keeley an absent pat on the shoulder, he vaulted the fence.

She watched him go to the horses, to stroke and compliment Tempest, give the rider a few words before moving on to Betty.

The filly pranced flirtatiously, then lowered her head to nibble delicately on Brian's shoulder.

You're wrong, Keeley thought. Whatever she knows, whatever she is, she needs you.

And so, damn it, do I.

After he'd stroked, nuzzled, praised, and the horses were led away to be cooled down, Brian jumped over the fence again to pick up his clipboard.

"I'd hoped your father would be down to see her first run with a field."

"I'm sure he would have. He must be tied up with something."

With a grunt in response, Brian continued to scribble notes. "Well, I'm running more of the yearlings this morning, so he'll see plenty. How's the gelding?"

"Comfortable. The swelling's down a little. I want

to wait until after my class today to drench him. It's a messy business and I don't need a half dozen kids coming around once it starts to work on him."

"Best to wait till late in the day anyway. You want a good twenty-four hours between his last feeding and the drenching. I can do that for you if you're busy."

The automatic refusal was on the tip of her tongue. She nipped it off, took a breath. "Actually, I was hoping you'd find time to take a look at him later."

"I can do that." He glanced up, saw how set and serious her face was. "What is it? Are you that worried?"

"No." She took another breath, ordered herself to relax. "I'm sure everything will be fine." She'd make sure of it, she told herself. One way or the other. "I'll feel better when things are under control, that's all."

She worked it out. She felt better when she had a situation defined and a goal in mind. This one wasn't really so complicated, after all. She wanted Brian. She was fairly certain she was in love with him. Being certain of that would take a little more time, she imagined, a little more consideration.

After all this was new territory and needed to be approached with caution and preparation.

But her feelings for him were strong, and not as one-dimensional as simple attraction.

If it was love, then she needed to make him fall in love with her. She was perfectly willing to work toward what she wanted, as long as she got it in the end.

Pleasantly tired after a long day's work, she gave her horses their evening meal. There was no question about it, she decided. Having her mother help had taken a huge burden of time and effort off her shoulders.

Was it stubbornness, she wondered, that caused her to pull back from a helping hand so often? She didn't think so. But it was something nearly as mulish. She wanted the people she loved and who loved her to be proud of her. And she equated that, foolishly, she admitted, with the need to be perfect.

But she preferred thinking of it as taking responsibility.

Just as she was doing now with Brian, she mused. If she was in love with him, she was responsible for her own feelings. And it was up to her to try to generate those same feelings in him.

If she failed… No, she wouldn't consider that. Once you considered failure you were one step farther away from success.

Moving into the gelding's box, she hung his hay bag and measured out his feed. "It's better tonight, isn't it?" Gently she checked the swelling on his knee. When she heard the footsteps heading down on concrete, she smiled to herself.

"You're feeding him?" Brian stepped into the box. "I couldn't get up here any sooner."

"That's all right. He took the drenching without a quibble. And you can take my word for it, it worked." She straightened up, smiled. "You can see by the way he's eating, he's feeling better."

"Knows he's fallen into roses, he does." Brian examined the injury himself, nodded. "We have a stallion with the strangles, which is what held me up."

"Delicate creatures, aren't they?" She ran her hand

over the gelding's withers. "Deceptive. The size of them, the speed and strength. It all shouts power. But under it all, there's the delicacy. You can be fooled by looking at something—at the face, at the form—and judging it without knowing what's inside."

"True enough."

"I'm not delicate, Brian. I have iron bred in me."

He looked at her. "I know you're strong, Keeley. And still, you've skin like a rosebud." Gently he ran his thumb over her cheek. "I have big hands, and they're hard, so I need to take care. It doesn't mean I think you're weak."

"All right."

He turned back to the horse. "Have you named him?"

"As a matter of fact, I have. We had a dog when I was a girl. My mother found him, a very homely stray who started sneaking up to the house. She fed him, gained his confidence. And before my father knew it, he had a big, sloppy mutt on his hands. His name was Finnegan." She laid her cheek on the gelding's, rubbed. "And so now is his."

"You've a sentimental streak along with that iron, Keeley."

"Yes, I do. And a latent romantic one."

"Is that so?" he murmured, a little surprised when she turned and ran her hands up his chest.

"Apparently. I didn't thank you for riding to my rescue last night."

"I don't recall riding anywhere." His lips twitched as she backed him out of the box.

"In a manner of speaking. You cut a bully down to size for me. I was upset and worried about the gelding, so I didn't really think about it at the time. But I did later, and I wanted to thank you."

"Well, you're welcome."

"I haven't finished thanking you." She bit lightly on his bottom lip, heard his quick indrawn breath.

"If that's what you have in mind, you could finish thanking me up in my bedroom."

"Why don't I just show you what I have in mind? Right here."

She had his shirt unbuttoned before he realized they were standing in an empty stall, freshly bedded with hay. "Here?" He laughed, taking both her hands to tug her out again. "I don't think so."

"Here." She countered his move by ramming his back against the side wall. "I know so."

"Don't be ridiculous." His lungs were clogged, and his mind insisted on following suit. "Anyone could come along."

"Live dangerously." She pulled the stall door shut behind them.

"I have been, since I first set eyes on you."

The thrum of the heart in her throat turned her voice husky. "Why stop now? Seduce me, Brian. I dare you."

"I've always found it hard to turn aside a dare." He reached out, tugged the band from her hair. "You cloud my senses, Keeley, like perfume. Before I know it, there's nothing there but you." He slid his hand around to cup the back of her neck, to draw her toward him. "And nothing that needs to be."

His mouth covered hers, soft, smooth in a kiss silky enough to have her gliding down on that alone. She'd asked for seduction knowing seduction wasn't needed.

"I want you, Brian. I wake up wanting you. Kiss me again."

And the way her body simply melted into his, the way her lips warmed and parted, inviting him in had every pulse in his body throbbing like a wound.

"I don't want to be gentle this time." He reversed their position until her back was against the wall, and his eyes, so suddenly dark, burned into hers. "I don't want to be so careful, just this once."

The thrill of it was a bolt through the heart. "Then don't. I'm not fragile like your horses, Brian. Don't be fooled."

"I'll frighten you." He couldn't have said if it was a threat or warning, but her answer was just another dare.

"Try it."

He tore her shirt open, sending buttons flying. He watched her eyes widen in shock even as he crushed his mouth to hers to swallow her gasp. Then his hands were on her, a rough scrape of callus over sensitive skin. Part of him expected her to object, to struggle away, but she only moaned against his savaging mouth, and held on.

When her knees gave like heated butter, he dragged her down to the mound of hay.

He used his mouth on her, his teeth, his tongue. A kind of wild fury. His hands raced over her, rough and possessive in their impatience to have more. To take all.

Her choked cries had the horses moving restlessly in their boxes. As he propelled her over that first breathless edge, she fisted her hands in his hair as if to anchor herself. Or to drag him with her.

He'd given her tenderness, shown her the beauty of lovemaking with patience and care. Now he showed her the dark glory of it with reckless demands and bruising hands.

Still she gave. Even with the whirlwind rushing inside him, he felt her give. Flesh dampened until it was slick, hearts pounded until the beat of them seemed to slap the air, but she rolled with him, accepting. Offering.

Even when her eyes were blind, the blue of them blurred as dark as midnight, she stayed with him. The sound of his name rushing through her lips seemed to sing in his blood.

She cried out, arching against his busy mouth when her world shattered into shards bright as glass. There was nothing to cling to, no thread to tie her to sanity, and still he drove her harder until the breath tearing from her lungs turned to harsh, primitive pants.

"It's me who has you." Wild to mate, he gripped her hips, jerked them high. "It's me who's in you." And plunged into her as if his life depended on it.

She heard a scream, high, thin, helpless. But it wasn't helplessness she felt. She felt power, outrageous power that pumped through her blood like a drug. Drunk on it, she reared up, her eyes locked on his as she fisted her hands in his hair once more.

She fixed her mouth on his, savaging it as he rode her, hard and fast. And she held on, held on, matching him beat for beat though she thought her body would burst, until she felt him fall.

"It's me," she said on a sob, "who has you." And still holding fast, let herself leap after him.

Chapter 10

As far as Keeley was concerned it was perfect. She'd fallen in love with a man who suited her. They had a strong foundation of common interests, enjoyed each other's company, respected each other's opinions.

He wasn't without flaws, of course. He tended to be moody and his confidence very often crossed the line into arrogance. But those qualities made him who he was.

The problem, as she saw it, was nudging him along from affair to commitment and commitment to marriage. She'd been raised to believe in permanency, in family, in the promise two people made to love for a lifetime.

She really had no choice but to marry Brian and make a life with him. And she was going to see to it he had no choice, either.

It was a bit like training a horse, she supposed. There was a lot of repetition, rewards, patience and affection. And a firm hand under it all.

She thought it would be most sensible for them to become engaged at Christmas, and marry the following summer. Certainly it would be most convenient for them to build their life near Royal Meadows as both of them worked there. Nothing could be simpler.

All she had to do was lead Brian to the same conclusions.

Being the kind of man he was, she imagined he'd want to make the moves. It was a little galling, but she loved him enough to wait until he made his declaration. It wouldn't be with hearts and flowers, she mused as she walked Finnegan around the paddock. Knowing Brian there would be passion, and challenge and just a hint of temper.

She was looking forward to it.

She stopped to check the gelding's leg for any heat or swelling. Gently she picked up his foot to bend the knee. When he showed no signs of discomfort, she gave him a brisk rub on the neck.

"Yeah," she said when he blew affectionately on her shoulder, "feeling pretty good these days, aren't you? I think you're ready for some exercise."

His coat looked healthy again, she noted as she saddled him. Time, care and attention had turned the tide for him. Perhaps he'd never be a beauty, and certainly he was no champion, but he had a sweet nature and a willing spirit.

That was more than enough.

When she swung into the saddle, Finnegan tossed

his head, then at her signal started out of the paddock in a dignified walk.

She went cautiously for a time, tuning herself to him, checking for any hitch in his gait that would indicate he was favoring his leg. It pleased her so much to feel him slide into a smooth rhythm that after a few moments she relaxed enough to enjoy the quiet ride.

Fall had used a rich and varied palette this year to paint the trees in bold tones of golds and reds and orange. They swept over the hard blue canvas of sky and flamed under the strong slant of sunlight.

The fields held onto the deep green of high summer. Weanlings danced over the pastures, long legs reaching for speed as they charged their own shadows. Mares, their bellies swollen with the foals they carried, cropped lazily.

On the brown oval, colts and fillies raced in the majestic blur of power that brought thunder to the air.

This painting, Keeley thought, had been hers the whole of her life. The images that came back, repeating season after season. The beauty and strength of it, and the settled knowledge that it would go on year into year.

This she could, and would, pass on to her own children when the time came. The solidity of it, and the responsibilities, the joys and the sweat.

Sitting aside the healing gelding, she felt her throat ache with love. It wasn't just a place, it was a gift. One that had been treasured and tended by her parents. Her part in it, of it, would never be taken for granted.

When she saw Brian leaning on the fence, his attention riveted on the horses pounding down the backstretch, her aching throat seemed to snap shut.

For a moment she could only blink, stunned by the sudden, vicious pressure in her chest. Her skin tingled. There was no other word to describe how nerves swarmed over her in a wash of chills and heat.

As she fought to catch her breath, her heart pounded, a hammer on an anvil. The gelding shied under her, and had danced in a fretful half circle before she thought to control him.

And her hands trembled.

No, this was wrong. This wasn't acceptable at all. Where did this come from—how did she get this ball of terror in her stomach? She'd already accepted that she loved him, hadn't she? And it had been easy, a simple process of steps and study. Her mind was made up, her goals set. Damn it, she'd been pleased by the whole business.

So what was this shaky, dizzy, *painful* sensation, this clutch of panic that made her want to turn her mount sharply around and ride as far away as possible?

She'd been wrong, Keeley realized as she pressed an unsteady hand to her jumpy heart. She'd only been falling in love up to now. How foolish of her to be lulled by the smooth slide of it. This was the moment, she understood that now. This was the moment the bottom dropped away and sent her crashing.

Now the wind was knocked out of her, that same shock of sensation that came from losing your seat over a jump and finding yourself flipping through space until the ground reached up and smacked into you. Jolting bones and head and heart.

Love was an outrageous shock to the system, she thought. It was a wonder anyone survived it.

She was a Grant, Keeley reminded herself and straightened in the saddle. She knew how to take a tumble, just as she knew how to pick herself back up and focus mind and energy on the goal. She wouldn't just survive this knock to the heart. She'd thrive on it. And when she was done with Brian Donnelly, he wouldn't know what had hit him.

She steadied herself much as she had done before competitions. She took slow and deliberate breaths until her pulse rate slowed, focused her mind until it was calm as lake water, then she rode down to face her goal.

Brian turned when he heard her approach. The vague irritation at the interruption vanished when he saw Finnegan. He felt a keen interest there, and passing his clipboard and some instructions to the assistant trainer, moved toward the gelding.

"Well now, you're looking fit and fine, aren't you?" Automatically he bent down to check the injured leg. "No heat. That's good. How long have you had him out?"

"About fifteen minutes, at a walk."

"He could probably take a canter. He's looking good as new, no signs of swelling." Brian straightened, narrowing his eyes against the sun as he looked up at Keeley. "But you? Are you all right? You're a bit pale."

"Am I?" Small wonder, she thought, but smiled as she enjoyed the sensation of holding a secret inside her. "I don't feel pale. But you..." Swimming in the river of discovery, she leaned down. "You look wonderful. Rough and windblown and sexy."

His narrowed eyes flickered, and he stepped back, a little uneasy when she rubbed a hand over his cheek.

There were a half a dozen men milling around, he thought. And every one of them had eyes.

"I was called down to the stables early this morning, didn't take time to shave."

She decided to take his evasive move as a challenge rather than an insult. "I like it. Just a little dangerous. If you've got time later, I thought you might help me out."

"With what?"

"Take a ride with me."

"I could do that."

"Good. About five?" She leaned down again and this time took a fistful of his shirt to yank him a step closer. "And, Brian? Don't shave."

The woman threw him off balance, and he didn't care for it. Giving him those hot looks and intimate little strokes in the middle of the damn morning so he went through the whole of the day itchy.

Worse yet the man who was paying him to work through the day, not to be distracted by his glands, was the woman's father.

It was a situation, Brian thought, and he'd done a great deal to bring it on himself. Still how could he have known in the beginning that he'd become so involved with her on so many levels inside himself? Falling in love had been a hard knock, but he'd taken knocks before. You got bruised and you went on. A bit of attraction was all right, a little flirtation was harmless enough. And the truth was, he'd enjoyed the risk of it. To a point.

But he was well past that point now. Now he was all wrapped up in her and at the same time had become fond of her family. Travis wasn't just a good and fair boss, but was on the way to becoming a kind of friend.

And here he was finding ways to make love to his friend's daughter as often as humanly possible.

Worse than that, he admitted as he strode toward her stables, he was—from time to time—catching himself dreaming. These little fantasies would sneak into his head when he was busy doing something else. He'd find himself wondering how it would all be between Keeley and him if things were different, if they were on the same level, so to speak. And he thought—well, that is if he were the settling down sort—that she might be just the one to settle down with.

If he were interested in rooting in one place with one person, that is. Which of course, wasn't in his plans at all. Even if it was—which it wasn't—it wouldn't work.

She was clubhouse and he was shedrow, and that was that.

Keeley was just kicking up her heels a bit. He understood about that, couldn't hold it against her. For all the privilege, she'd had a sheltered life and now was taking a few whacks at the boundaries of it. He'd rebelled himself against the borders of his own upbringing by sliding his way out of school and into the stables when he'd still been a boy. Nothing had stopped him, not the arguments, the threats, the punishments.

As soon as he'd been able, he'd left home, moving from stable to stable, track to track. He'd kept loose, he'd kept free and unfettered. And had never looked back. His brothers and sisters married, raised children, planted gardens, worked in steady jobs. They owned things, he thought now, while he owned nothing that couldn't easily fit in his traveling bag or be disposed of when he took to the next road.

When you owned things you had to tend them. Before you knew it, you owned more. Then the weight of them kept your feet planted in one spot.

He flicked a glance up at the pretty stone building that was his quarters, and admired the way it stood out against the evening sky. Flowers in colors of rust and scarlet and gold ran along the foundation, and the truck he'd bought from Paddy was parked like it belonged.

He stopped and, much as Keeley had that morning, turned to survey the land. It was a place, he realized, that could hold a man if he wasn't careful. The openness of it could fool you into believing it wasn't confining, then it would tempt you to plant things—yourself included—until it had you, heart and soul.

It was smart to remember it wasn't his land, any more than the horses were his horses. Or Keeley was his woman.

But when he stepped over toward her paddock, that fantasy snuck up on him again. In the long, soft shadows and quiet light of evening she saddled the big buff-colored gelding he knew she called Honey. Her hair was pinned on top of her head in an absentminded, messy knot that was ridiculously sexy. She wore jeans and a sweater of Kelly green.

She looked…reachable, Brian realized. Like the kind of woman a man wanted with him after a long day's work. There'd be a lot to talk about with this woman, over dinner, in the privacy of bed. Shared loves, shared jokes.

A man could wake up in the morning with a woman like that and not feel trapped, or worry that she did.

Catching himself, Brian shook his head. That was foolish thinking.

"Look at this." Brian walked up to the fence, leaned on it. "You've done all the work already."

"You've caught me on a good day." Keeley checked the cinch, stepped back. She knew his stirrup length now, and his favored bit and bridle. "I had no idea how much time I'd free up by having Ma help out on a regular basis."

"And what do you intend to do with it?"

"Enjoy it." When he opened the gate she led both horses through. "I've been so focused on the work the last couple of years, I haven't stepped back often enough to appreciate the results." She handed him the reins. "I like results."

"Then maybe you'll use some of that free time to come by the track." He vaulted into the saddle once she was mounted. "I'm looking for results there. I have Betty entered in a baby race tomorrow."

"Her maiden race? I wouldn't want to miss that."

"Charles Town. Two o'clock."

"I'll ask my mother to take my afternoon class. I'll be there."

They kept it to a walk, skirting the paddock and heading toward the rise of land swept with trees gone brilliant in the softening slants of sunlight. Overhead a flock of Canada geese arrowed across the evening sky sending out their deep calls.

"Twice daily," Brian said, watching the flight. "Off they go on their travels, honking away, dawn and dusk."

"I've always liked the sound of them. I guess it's something else that says home this time of year." She kept her eyes on the sky until the last call echoed away.

"Uncle Paddy phoned today."

"And how's he doing?"

"More than well. He'd bought himself a pair of young mares. He's decided to try his hand at some breeding."

"Once a horseman," Brian said. "I didn't figure he could keep out of the game."

"You'd miss it, wouldn't you? The smell and the sound of them. Have you ever thought of starting your own place, your own line?"

"No, that's not for me. I'm happy making another man's horses. Once you own, it's a business, isn't it? An enterprise. I've no yearning to be a businessman."

"Some own for the love of it," Keeley pointed out. "And even the business doesn't shadow the feelings."

"In the rare case." Brian looked over, scanning the outbuildings. Yes, this was a place, he thought, built on feelings. "Your father's one, and I knew another once in Cork. But ownership can get in the blood as well, until you lose touch with that feeling. Before you know it, it's all facts and figures and a thirst for profit. That sounds like bars to me."

Interesting, she thought. "Making a living is a prison?"

"The need to make one, and still a better one, first and foremost. That's a trap. My father found his leg caught there."

"Really?" He so rarely mentioned his family. "What does he do?"

"He's a bank clerk. Day after day sitting in a little cage counting other people's money. What a life."

"Well, it's not the life for you."

"Thank God for that. These lads want a bit of a run," he said and kicked Honey into a gallop.

Keeley hissed in frustration but clicked to her mount to match pace. They'd come back to it, she promised herself. She hadn't learned nearly enough about where the man she intended to marry came from.

They rode for an hour before heading back to stable the horses and settle in the rest of her stock for the night. He was half hoping she'd ask him over to the house for dinner again, but she turned to him as they left the stables, lifted a brow.

"Why don't you ask me up for a drink?"

"A drink? There's not much of a variety, but you're welcome."

"It's nice to be asked occasionally." Before he could tuck his hand safely in his pocket, she took it, threaded their fingers together. "You have free time now and again yourself," she said easily. "I wonder if you've heard of the concept of dates. Dinner, movies, drives?"

"I've some experience with them." He glanced at his pickup as they turned toward his quarters. "If you've a yen for a drive, you can climb up into the lorry, but I'd need to shovel it out first."

She huffed out a breath. "That, Donnelly, wasn't the most romantic of invitations."

"Secondhand lorries aren't particularly romantic, and I've forgotten where I parked my glass coach."

"If that's another princess crack—" She broke off, set her teeth. Patience, she reminded herself. She wasn't going to spoil things with an argument. "Never mind. We'll forget the drive." She opened the door herself. "And move straight to dinner."

He caught the scent as soon as he stepped inside. Something aromatic and spicy that reminded him his stomach was about dead empty.

"What is it?"

"What is what?" Then she grinned and sniffed the air. "Oh, what is that? It's chili, one of my specialties. I put it on simmer before my last class."

"You cooked dinner?"

"Mmm." Amused, and very satisfied by his shock, she wandered off into the kitchen. "I didn't think you'd mind, and I knew we'd both be hungry by this time." She lifted the lid on a pot, gave it a quick stir while fragrant steam puffed out. "It's the kind of thing you can just leave and eat when you're ready, which is why it appeals to me. Oh, and I brought over a bottle of Merlot, though beer's never wrong with chili if you'd rather."

"I'm trying to remember the last time someone cooked for me—other than your mother and someone who was related to me."

Even more pleased, she turned to slide her arms around him. "Haven't any of your many women cooked for you?"

"Now and then perhaps, but not in recent memory." Because they were alone, he took her hips, brought her closer. "And I certainly remember none that smelled so appetizing."

"The women? Or the meal?"

"Both." He lowered his mouth to hers, allowed him-

self the luxury of sinking in. "And it reminds me I'm
next to starving."

"What do you want first?" She grazed her teeth over
his bottom lip. "Me, or the food?"

"I want you first. And last, it seems."

"That's handy, because I want you first, too." She
drew back. "Why don't we clean up? I could use a
shower." Laughing, her hands holding his, she pulled
him out of the kitchen.

She'd brought over a change of clothes as well. It
gave Brian a start to see her casually pulling on fresh
jeans. Her hair was still wet from the shower they'd
shared, her skin rosy from it. And, he noted, a bit raw
in places because he hadn't shaved.

But the wild love they'd made under the hot spray
in the steamy room wasn't anywhere near as intimate,
anywhere near as *personal* somehow as her having a
clean sweater lying neatly folded on the foot of his bed.

She reached for it, then glanced over, catching him
staring at her. "What is it?"

He shook his head. There wasn't a way to explain this
sense of panic and delight that lived inside him while he
watched her dress. "I've rubbed your skin raw." Reaching out, he traced his fingertips over her collarbone.
"I should have shaved. You're so soft." He murmured
it, trailing those fingers up over her shoulder. "I don't
know how I manage to forget that."

When she trembled, he looked up into her face. For
a moment she saw the need flash back into his eyes,
glinting like the edge of a sword. "Now you're cold. Put
your sweater on. I've got some ointment."

The hot edge faded as quickly as it came. It was frustrating, she thought as he rooted into a drawer, that the only time he really broke the tether on his control was when they made love.

He got out a tube and since she'd yet to put the sweater on, squeezed ointment onto his fingers and began to gently rub it on her abraded skin. She recognized the scent.

"That's for horses."

"So?"

She laughed and let him fuss. "Does this make me your mare now?"

"No, you're too young and delicate of bone for that. You're still a filly."

"Are you going to train me, Donnelly?"

"Oh, you're out of my league, Miss Grant." He glanced up, cocked a brow when he saw her grinning at him. "And what amuses you?"

"You can't help it can you? You have to tend."

"I put the marks on you," he muttered as he smoothed on the ointment. "It follows I should see to them."

She lifted a hand to toy with the ends of his damp, gold-tipped hair. "I like being seen to by a man with a tough mind and a soft heart."

That soft heart sighed a little, ached a little. But he spoke lightly. "It's no hardship running my fingers over skin like yours." With his eyes on hers, he used the pad of his thumb to spread ointment over the gentle swell of her breast. "Particularly since you don't seem to have a qualm about standing here half naked and letting me."

"Should I blush and flutter?"

"You're not the fluttering sort. I like that about you."

Satisfied, he capped the tube, then tugged the sweater over her head himself. "But I can't have such a fine piece of God's work catching a chill. There you are." He lifted her hair out of the neck.

"You don't have a hair dryer."

"There's air everywhere in here."

She laughed and dragged her fingers through her damp curls. "It'll have to do. Come on, let's have that wine while I finish up dinner."

He didn't know much about wine, but his first sip told him it was several steps up from what might be the usual accompaniment to so humble a meal as chili.

She seemed more at home in his kitchen than he was himself, finding things in drawers he'd yet to open. When she started to dress the salad, he set his glass aside.

"I'll be back in a minute."

"A minute's all you've got," she called out. "I'm putting the bread in to warm."

Since his answer was the slamming of the door, she shrugged and lit the candles she'd set on the little kitchen table. Cozy, she decided. And just romantic enough to suit two practical-minded people who didn't go in for a lot of fussing.

It was the sort of relaxed, simple meal two people could prepare together at the end of a workday. She intended to see they had more of them, until the man got a clue this was exactly how it was going to be.

Satisfied, she picked up her wine, toasted herself. "To good strong starts," she murmured and drank.

Hearing the door open again, she took the bread out of the oven. "We're set in here, and I'm starving."

She turned to put the basket of bread on the table and saw Brian, and the clutch of mums and zinnias he held in his hand.

"It seemed to call for them," he said.

She stared at the cheerful fall blossoms, then up into his face. "You picked me flowers."

The sheer disbelief in her voice had him moving his shoulders restlessly. "Well, you made me dinner, with wine and candles and the whole of it. Besides, they're your flowers anyway."

"No, they're not." Drowning in love she set the basket down, waited. "Until you give them to me."

"I'll never understand why women are so sentimental over posies." He held them out.

"Thank you." She closed her eyes, buried her face in them. She wanted to remember the exact fragrance, the exact texture. Then lowering them again, she lifted her mouth to his for a kiss. Rubbed her cheek against his.

His arms came around her so suddenly, so tightly, she gasped. "Brian? What is it?"

That gesture, the simple and sweet gesture of cheek against cheek nearly destroyed him. "It's nothing. I just like the way you feel against me when I hold you."

"Hold me any tighter, I'll be through you."

"Sorry." He pressed his lips to her forehead to give himself a moment to compose. "I forget my own strength when I'm starving to death."

"Then sit down and get started. I'll put these in some water."

"I…" He had to say something and cast around for a topic where he wouldn't stutter or say something that would embarrass them both. "I meant to tell you earlier, I looked up Finnegan's records."

There, he thought as he sat and began to dish up salad for both of them. Safe ground. "Of course he's registered as Flight of Fancy."

"Yes, I knew that." She tucked the flowers in a vase, and set them on the table before joining Brian. "Finnegan suits him better, I think."

"He's yours to call what you like now. His record in his first year of racing was uneven. His blood stock is very decent, but he never came up to potential, and his owners sold him off as a three-year-old."

"I was going to look up his data. You've saved me the trouble." She broke a hunk of bread in half, offered it. "He has good lines, and he responds well. Even after the abuse he hasn't turned common."

"The thing is he did considerably better in his third year. Some of his match-ups were uneven, and in my mind he was a bit overraced. I'd have done things differently if I'd been working with him."

"You do things different, Brian, all around."

"Ah well. In any case, he went into that claiming race and that's how Tarmack got his hands on him."

"Bastard," Keeley said so coolly, Brian cocked his head.

"We won't argue there. I'm thinking you'd be wasting him in your school here. He was born for the track, and that's where he belongs."

Surprised, she frowned over her salad. "You think he should race?"

"I think you should consider it. Seriously. He's a thoroughbred, Keeley, bred to run. The need for it's in his blood. It's only that he's been misused and mismanaged. The athlete's inside him, and though your school's a fine thing, it's not enough for him."

"If he's prone to knee spavins—"

"You don't know that. It's not a hereditary thing. It was an injury a man was responsible for. You could have your father look him over if you don't think I've got the right of it."

She considered a moment, sipped her wine. "I certainly trust your judgment, Brian. It's not that. You and I both know that a horse can lose heart under mistreatment. Heart and spirit. I just wouldn't want to push him."

"Sure, it's up to you."

"Would you work with him?"

"I could." He ladled chili into bowls. "But so could you. You know what to do, what to look for."

She was already shaking her head. "Not for racing. I know my area, and it's not the track. If I consider running him again, I'd want him to have the best."

"That would be me," he said with such easy arrogance she grinned.

"Is that a yes?"

"If your father agrees to having me work your horse on the side, I'm happy to. We'll start him off easy, and see how he goes." He started to leave it at that, then because he thought she'd understand, hoped she would, finished. "It was in his eyes this morning, when you rode him down to the track. It was there. The yearning."

"I didn't see it." She reached over to touch his hand. "I'm glad you did."

"It's my job to see it."

"It's your gift," she corrected. "Your family must be proud of you." She spoke casually, began to eat again, then stared at him, baffled, when he laughed. "Why is that funny?"

"Pride wouldn't exactly be part of their general outlook to my way of thinking."

"Why?"

"People can't find pride in what they don't understand. Not all families, Keeley, are as cozy as yours."

"I'm sorry," she said, and meant it. Not only for whatever lack there was in his family feelings, but for deliberately prying.

"Sure it's not such a matter. We get on all right."

She meant to let it go, to change the subject, but the words burned inside her. "If they're not proud of you, then they're stupid." When he stared, his next bite of chili halfway to his mouth, she shrugged. "I'm sorry, but they are."

Watching her, he started to eat again. Her eyes were snapping, her cheeks flushed, her jaw set. Why the woman was fuming, he realized. "Darling, that's sweet of you to say, but—"

"It's not. It's rude, but I meant it." Snatching up the wine bottle, she topped off both of their glasses. "You have a real talent, and you've earned a strong reputation—or you damn well wouldn't be here at Royal Meadows. What's not to be proud of?" she demanded, with even more heat. "Your father, of all people, should understand."

"Why?"

Her mouth dropped open. "He's the one who introduced you to horses."

"To the track. It wasn't the horses for my father," Brian told her. He was so fascinated by her reaction it didn't occur to him that he was having an in-depth conversation about his family. Something he absolutely never did.

"They were a kind of vehicle. He admired them, certainly. But it was the wagering, the rush of gambling that called to him. Likely still does. That and the chance to take a few pulls from the flask in his pocket without my mother's silent and deadly disapproval. I told you, Keeley, he's a bank clerk."

"What difference does that make?"

All, was what Brian thought, but he struggled to find a more tangible explanation for her. "He stopped looking through the bars of his little cage years back. He and my mother, they married young, not quite the full nine months, you understand, before my oldest sister came along."

"That can be difficult, but still—"

"No, they were content with it. I think they love each other, in their way." He didn't think about those areas much, but since he was in it now, he did his best. "They made their home, raised their children. My father brought in the wage. Though he gambled, we never went hungry—and bills were paid sooner or later. My mother always set a decent table, and our clothes were clean. But it seemed to me that the both of them were just tired out at the end of the day, just from doing."

Keeley remembered an expression of her mother's. *A child could starve with a full plate.* She understood that without love, affection, laughter, the spirit hungered.

"Going your own way shouldn't stop them from being happy for you."

"My brother and my sisters, they're clerks and parents and settled sort of people. I'm a puzzle, and sooner or later when you can't solve a puzzle, you have to think there's something wrong with it. Else there's something wrong with you."

"You ran away," she murmured.

He wasn't sure he liked the phrase, but nodded. "In a sense, I suppose, and as fast as I could. What's the point in looking back?"

But he was looking back, Keeley thought. Looking back over his shoulder, because he was still running away.

Chapter 11

Keeley decided some men simply took longer than others to realize they wanted to go where you were leading them. It was hard to complain since she was having such a wonderful time. She was making it a habit to go to the track once a week, a pleasure she'd cut out of her life while she'd been organizing her academy.

There were still dozens of details that she needed to see to personally—the meetings, the reports and follow-ups on each individual child. She wanted to plan a kind of open house during the holidays, where all the parents, grandparents, foster families could come to the academy. Meet and mingle, and most importantly see the progress their children had made.

But now that her school was on course, and she'd expanded to seven days a week, she was more than happy to turn the classes over to her mother for one day.

She was thrilled to watch Betty's progress, to see for herself that Brian's instincts had been on target with the filly. Betty was, day after day and week after week, proving herself to be a top competitor and a potential champion.

But even more she was delighted to see Finnegan come to life under Brian's patient, unwavering hand.

Bundled against the chill of a frosty morning, Keeley stood at the fence of the practice oval and waited while Brian gave Larry his instructions on the workout run.

"He gets nervy in the gate, but he breaks clean. You'll need to rate him or he'll lose his wind. He likes a crowd so I want you to keep him in the pack till after the second turn. You let him know then, firm, that you want more. He'll give it to you. He doesn't like running in front, he misses the company."

"I'll keep his eye on the line, Mr. Donnelly. I appreciate you giving me the chance."

"It's Miss Grant's giving you the chance. I smell whiskey on your breath before post time tomorrow, and you won't get a second one."

"Not a drop. We'll run for you, if for nothing but to show that son of a bitch Tarmack how you treat a thoroughbred."

"Fair enough. Let's see how she goes."

Brian walked back to the fence where Keeley stood sipping her soft drink. "I don't know if you made the best choice in jockeys, but he's sober and he's hungry, so it's a good gamble."

"It's not the winning this time, Brian."

He took her bottle, sipped, winced. How the woman

could drink such a thing in the morning was beyond him. "It's always the winning."

"You've done a wonderful job with him."

"We won't know that until tomorrow at Pimlico."

"Stop it," she ordered when he slipped through the split rail fence. "Take credit when it's deserved. That's a horse that's found his pride again," she said as the practice field was led to the gate. "You gave it to him."

"For God's sake, Keeley, he's your horse. I just reminded him he could run."

You're wrong, she thought. You gave him back his pride, just the way you made him your own.

But Brian was already focused on the horse. He took out his stopwatch. "Let's see how well he remembers running this morning."

Mists swam along the ground, a shallow river over the oval. Shards of frost still glittered on the grass while the sun pulsed weakly through the layers of morning clouds. The air was gray and still.

With a ringing clang the gate sprang open. And the horses plunged.

Ground fog tore like thin silver ribbon at the powerful cut of legs. Bodies, glistening from the morning damp, surged past in one sleek blur.

"That's it," Brian murmured. "Keep him centered. That's the way."

"They're beautiful. All of them."

"Got to pace him." Brian watched them round the first turn while the clock in his head ticked off the time. "See, he'll match his rhythm to the leader. It's a game to him now. Out gallivanting with mates, that's all he's thinking."

Keeley laughed, leaned out as her heart began to bump. "How do you know what he's thinking?"

"He told me. Get ready now. Ready now. Aye, that's it. He's strong. He'll never be a beauty, but he's strong. See, he's moving up." Forgetting himself Brian laid a hand on her shoulder, squeezed. "He's got more heart than brains, and it's his heart that runs."

Brian clicked the watch when Finnegan came in, half a length behind the leader. "Well done. Yes, well done. I'd say he'll place for you tomorrow, Miss Grant."

"It doesn't matter."

Sincerely shocked more than offended, he goggled at her. "That's a hell of a thing to say. And what kind of luck is that going to bring us tomorrow, I'd like to know?"

"It's enough to watch him run. And better, to watch you watching him run. Brian." Touched, she laid a hand on his heart. "You've gone and fallen in love with him."

"I love all the horses I train."

"Yes, I've seen that, and understand that because it's the same with me. But you're in love with this one."

Embarrassed because it was true, Brian swung over the fence. "That's a woman for you, making sloppy sentiment out of a job."

She only smiled as Brian walked over to stroke and nuzzle his job.

"That's a fine thing. My daughter and my trainer grooming a competitor."

She glanced over her shoulder, held out a hand for her father as he strode toward her. "Did you see him run?"

"The last few seconds. You've brought him a long

way in a short time." Travis pressed a kiss to the top of her head. "I'm proud of you."

She closed her eyes. How easily he said it, how lovely to know he meant it. It made her only more sad, more angry, that Brian had cause to laugh over the idea of his own father having any pride in him.

"You taught me to care, you and Ma. When I saw that horse, I cared because of what you put inside me." She tilted her head up, kissed her father's cheek. "So thanks."

When his arm came around her, she leaned in, warm and comfortable. "Brian was right. The horse needs to race. It's what he is. I wanted to save him. But Brian knew that wasn't enough. For some it's not enough just to get by."

"You brought this off together."

"You're right." She laughed a little as realization dawned, so clear and bright she wondered how she'd missed it before. "Absolutely right."

She'd canceled classes for the day. It was, Keeley told herself, a kind of holiday. A celebration, she thought, in compassion, understanding and hard work. It wasn't only Finnegan's return to the track, but Betty's first important race. Her parents would be there, and Brendon.

If there was ever a day to close up shop, this was it.

She rode out to the track at dawn, to give herself the pleasure of watching the early workouts, of listening to the track rats, building anticipation.

"You'd think it was the Derby," Brendon said as he walked with her back to the shedrow. "You're hyped."

"I've never owned a racehorse before. And I'm pretty

sure he's my first and last. I'm going to enjoy every moment of this, but… It's not my passion. Not like it's yours and Dad's. Even Ma's."

"You channeled your passions into the school. I never thought you'd give up competing, Keel."

"Neither did I. And I never thought I'd find anything that satisfied me as much, challenged me as much."

They stopped as horses were brought back from the early workouts.

Steam rose off their backs, out of the tubs of hot water set outside the stables. It fogged the air, cushioned the sound, blurred the colors.

Hot walkers hustled to cool off the runners, stable-hands and grooms loitered, waiting for their charges. Someone played a mournful little tune on a harmonica, with the ring of the farrier's anvil setting the beat.

"This is your deal here," she said, gesturing as Betty was led by. "Me, I'm happy just to watch."

"Yeah? Then what're you doing here so early?"

"Just carrying on a fine family tradition. I'm going to act as Finnegan's groom."

That was news to Brian, and he wasn't entirely pleased when she announced her intentions. "Owners don't groom. They sit in the grandstands, or up in the restaurant. They stay out of the way."

Keeley continued strapping Finnegan with straw. "How long have you worked at Royal Meadows now?"

His scowl only deepened. "Since midthrough of August."

"Well, that should be long enough for you to have noticed the Grants don't stay out of the way."

"Noticing doesn't mean approving." He studied the

way she groomed Finnegan's neck and couldn't find fault. But that was beside the point. "Grooming a horse for showing or schooling or basic riding is a different matter than grooming before a race."

She let out a long-suffering sigh. "Does it look like I know what I'm doing?"

"His legs need to be wrapped."

Saying nothing, she gestured to the wrapping on the line, and the extra clothespins hooked to her jeans.

Not yet convinced, he studied her grooming kit and the other tools of a groomer's trade. The cotton batting, the blankets, the tack.

"The irons haven't been polished."

She glanced at the saddle. "I know how to polish irons."

Brian rocked back on his heels. He needed to see to Betty. She was racing in the second. "He needs to be talked to."

"This is funny, but I know how to talk, too."

Brian swore under his breath. "He prefers singing."

"Excuse me?"

"I said, he prefers singing."

"Oh." Keeley tucked her tongue in her cheek. "Any particular tune? Wait, let me guess. *Finnegan's Wake?*" Brian's steely-eyed stare had her laughing until she had to lean weakly against the gelding. The horse responded by twisting his head and trying to sniff her pockets for apples.

"It's a quick tune," Brian said coolly, "and he likes hearing his name."

"I know the chorus." Gamely Keeley struggled to

swallow another giggle. "But I'm not sure I know all the words. There are several verses as I recall."

"Do the best you can," he muttered and strode off. His lips twitched as he heard her launch into the song about the Dubliner who had a tippling way.

When he reached Betty's box, he shook his head. "I should've known. If there's not a Grant one place, there's a Grant in another until you're tripping over them."

Travis gave Betty a last pat on the shoulder. "Is that Keeley I hear singing?"

"She's being sarcastic, but as long as the job's done. She's dug in her heels about grooming Finnegan."

"She comes by it naturally. The hard head as well as the skill."

"Never had so many owners breathing down my neck. We don't need them, do we, darling?" Brian laid his hands on Betty's cheek, and she shook her head, then nibbled his hair.

"Damn horse has a crush on you."

"She may be your lady, sir, but she's my own true love. Aren't you beautiful, my heart?" He stroked, sliding into the Gaelic that had Betty's ears pricked and her body shifting restlessly.

"She likes being excited before a race," Brian murmured. "What do you call it—pumped up like your American football players. Which is a sport that eludes me altogether as they're gathered into circles discussing things most of the time instead of getting on with it."

"I heard you won the pool on last Monday night's game," Travis commented.

"Betting's the only thing about your football I do

understand." Brian gathered her reins. "I'll walk her around a bit before we take her down. She likes to parade. You and your missus will want to stay close to the winner's circle."

Travis grinned at him. "We'll be watching from the rail."

"Let's go show off." Brian led Betty out.

Keeley put the final polish on the saddle irons, rolled her now aching shoulders and decided she had enough time to hunt up a soft drink before giving Finnegan a last-minute pep talk.

She stepped outside and blinked in the sudden whitewash of light. The minute her eyes focused she saw Brian sitting near the stable door on an overturned bucket.

Alarm sprinted into her throat. He had his head in his hands and was still as stone.

"What is it? What's wrong?" She leaped forward to drop to the ground beside him. "Betty?" Her breath came short. "I thought Betty was racing."

"She was. She did. She won."

"God, Brian, I thought something was wrong."

He dropped his hands and she could see his eyes were dark, swarming with emotion. "Two and a half lengths," he said. "She won by two and a half lengths, and I swear I don't think she was half trying. Nothing could touch her, do you see? Nothing. Never in my life did I think to have a horse like that under my hands. She's a miracle."

Keeley laid her hands on his knees, sat back on her heels. Passion, she thought. She'd spoken to Brendon of it, but now she was looking at it. "You made her." Before he could speak, she shook her head. "That's what you said to me once. 'I don't break horses. I make them.'"

"I can't get my head round it just now. This field was strong. I put her in thinking now and then you need a lesson in humility. Time for her to grow up, you know what I mean. Face real competition."

Still staggered, he dragged his hands through his hair and laughed. "Well, she'll never learn a damn thing about humility."

"Why aren't you down with her?"

"That's for your parents. She's their horse."

"You've a lot to learn yourself." She got to her feet, brushed off the knees of her jeans. "Well, Finnegan will be going down shortly. Why don't you come in and look him over?"

Brian blew out a breath, sucked in another, then rose. "I think he'll place for you," he told Keeley as he followed her in. "It wouldn't hurt to wager on it."

"I intend to wager on him." While Brian went in to check Finnegan's leg wrappings, she got papers out of the pocket of the jacket she'd laid aside.

"The wrappings look all right." He flicked a finger over the stirrups. "And you polished the irons well enough."

"Glad you approve. Next time you can do it." She held out the papers.

"What's this?"

"Papers giving you half interest in Flight of Fancy, also known as Finnegan."

"What are you talking about?"

"He was half yours anyway, Brian. This just makes it legal."

His palms went cold and damp. "Don't be ridiculous. I can't take that."

She'd expected him to refuse initially, but she hadn't expected him to go pale and snarl. "Why? You helped bring him back. You trained him."

"A couple of weeks work, on my off time. Now put those away and stop being foolish."

When he started to push by her, she simply shifted to block his way. "First, he wouldn't be racing today if it wasn't for you. And second, you're as attached to him as I am. Probably more. If it's the money—"

"It's not the money." Though a part of him knew it was, to some extent. Because it was hers.

"Then what?"

"I don't own horses. I don't want to be an owner."

"That's a pity, because you are an owner. Or a half owner anyway."

"I said I'm not accepting it."

"We'll argue about it later."

"There's nothing to argue about."

She stepped out of the box, smiled sweetly. "You know, Brian, just because you can make a fifteen-hun-dred-pound horse do what you want, doesn't mean you can budge me one inch. I'm going to go bet on our horse. To win."

"He's not our—" He broke off, swore, as she'd already flounced out. "And you don't bet to win," he muttered. "It's nothing personal," he said to Finnegan who was watching him with soft, sad eyes. "I just can't be owning things. It's not that I don't have great affection and respect for you, for I do. But what happens if in a year or two down the road I move on? Even if I don't—as it's feeling more and more that I'd wonder why I would—I can't have the woman give me a horse. Even a half a horse. Well, not to worry. We'll straighten it all out later."

He shouldn't have been nervous. It was pitiful. It was just another horse, just another race. It wasn't, as Betty was, a shining gift. This was an apple-loving, sweet-natured gelding who'd already broken down once and had lost far more races than he'd won in his short career.

Brian was fond of him, of course, and wanted him to have his day in the sun. But he had no illusions about this one being a champion.

He was simply guiding the horse toward doing what he'd been born for. And that was run his best.

And still nerves danced in Brian's belly.

"The track's dry and fast," he told Larry as they walked past the backstretch. "That's good for him. The field's crowded, and he likes that, too. Blue Devil's the number six horse, and odds-on favorite. There's reason for that."

"I know Blue Devil." Larry nodded and gnashed a mouthful of gum. "He can slither through a pack like a snake. He gets in the lead, he sets a fast pace."

"I expect that's what he'll do today. I need you to feel what Finnegan's got in him. I don't want you over-racing him, but don't hold him back past the first turn. Let him test his legs."

"I'll take care of him, Mr. Donnelly. Here's Miss

Grant come to see us off. He looks fine, Miss Grant. You done good with him."

"Yes." A little breathless from the run back from the betting window, she gave Finnegan a brisk rub. "We did."

When the call sounded for riders up, she stepped back. "Good luck."

"Talk to him." Brian gave Larry a leg up. "Don't forget to talk to him all the way. Don't let him forget what he's there for."

"They look good," Keeley decided. "Here."

"What now?"

"I put fifty down for you."

"You—damn it."

"You can pay me back out of your winnings," she said breezily. "We'd better get to the rail. I don't want to miss the start. Have you seen my family?"

"No. They're around. The lot of you's everywhere." Because she was moving through the crowd, he grabbed her hand. He could imagine her being trampled. "I don't know why you don't go up into the bar where you can watch in civilized surroundings."

"Snob."

"It's not a matter of—" He gave up. "I want you to tear up those papers."

"No. Look they're bringing them to the gate."

"I'm not taking a half interest in your horse."

"Our horse. Who's number three? I lost my *Racing Form*."

"Prime Target, eight to five, likes to come from behind. Keeley, it's a thoughtful gesture, but—"

"It's a sensible one. Okay, here we go." She shot him a brilliant smile. "Our first race."

The bell rang.

They shot out of the gate, ten muscular bodies with men clinging fiercely to their backs. Within seconds they were merged into one speeding form with legs reaching, flying, striking. Silks of red, white, gold, green streamed by in a shock of color. And the sound was huge.

Blindly Keeley groped for Brian's hand and clung.

She lost her breath, and her sense, in the sheer thrill.

Clouds of dust spewed from the dry track, jockeys slanted forward like dolls, and the pack began to break apart at the second turn.

"He's holding onto fourth," Keeley shouted. "He's holding on."

The lead horse edged forward. A head, a half a length. Finnegan bulled up the line, nipping the distance, vying for third. Keeley heard the crowd around her, the solid roar of it, but her heart pounded to the rhythm of hoofbeats.

Those legs stretched, reached, lifted.

"He's gaining." She began to laugh, even as her hand clamped on Brian's, she laughed. From the joy bursting inside her, she might have been riding low on the gelding's back herself. "He's gaining. He's moving up, into second. Would you look at him?"

He was looking, and the grin on his face was wide. "I didn't give him enough credit for guts. Not nearly enough credit. He'll move on the backstretch. If he's still got it in him, he'll move."

And he moved, a big, unhandsome horse at twenty

to one odds with a washed-up jockey in the irons. He moved like a bullet, streaking down the dirt, charging the leader, running neck-in-neck with the favorite while the crowd screamed.

Seconds before the finish line, he pulled ahead by a nose.

"He won." Keeley whirled to Brian. She wondered if the shock on his face mirrored her own. "My God, Brian, he won!"

"Two miracles in one day." He let out a short, baffled laugh, then another, longer. Riding on the thrill, he plucked Keeley off her feet and spun her in circles.

"I never expected it." She threw her arms in the air, then wrapped them around his neck and kissed him. "I never expected him to win."

"You bet on him."

"That was for love, not for reality. I never thought he'd win."

"He did." Brian gave her a last spin before setting her on her feet. "That's what counts."

"We're going to celebrate. Big time."

While Betty's win had left him shaken to the soul by that heady taste of destiny, this was sheer, stupefied delight. He snatched Keeley again and spun her into a quick waltz through the crowd.

"I'll buy you a bottle of champagne."

"Two," she corrected. "One for each of us. We have to get down to the winner's circle."

"You have to. I don't go to winner's circles."

He might behave like a mule, she mused, but he was a man. And she knew which button to push. "You don't have to go for me, or even for yourself. But you have to go for him." She held out a hand.

He wanted to swear but figured it a waste of breath. "I'll go, as his trainer. He's your horse. I don't own any part of him."

"Half," she corrected, trotting to keep up as Brian tugged her along. "But we can discuss which half."

Chapter 12

"Of course I'm seeing to him." Keeley bent to unwrap Finnegan's right foreleg.

"You should be up celebrating."

"This is part of it." She ran her hands carefully up the gelding's leg before pinning the wrapping to the line. "Finnegan and I are going to congratulate each other while I clean him up. But you could do me a favor." She pulled her ticket out of her pocket. "Cash in my winnings."

Brian shook his head. "At the moment I'm too pleased to be annoyed with you for betting my money." With one hand on the horse he leaned over to kiss her. "But I'm not taking half the horse."

Keeley hooked an arm around Finnegan's neck. "You hear that? He doesn't want you."

"Don't say things like that to him."

She laid her cheek against the gelding's. "You're the one hurting his feelings."

As two pairs of eyes studied him, Brian hissed out a breath. "We'll discuss this privately at some other time."

"He needs you. We both do."

The muscles in his belly twisted. "That's unfair."

"That's fact."

He looked so uncomfortable, she sighed. She wanted to throw up her hands, give the man a good thump. But it wasn't the time to rage or demand he take a good look at a woman who loved him.

"We will talk about it." They were going to talk about a great many things, she decided. Very soon. "But for now, we'll just be happy."

He hesitated while she went back to unwrapping Finnegan's legs. "I've been happier in the last few months than I've ever been."

"That doesn't have to change." She finished hanging the wrappings, picked up a dandy brush. "We're a good team, Brian. There's a lot we could do together."

Brian ran a hand down Finnegan's throat. "We've made quite a start here. Would you want to go out after a bit and have some fancy dinner and wine?"

Keeley slanted him a look. "Are you finally asking me for a date?"

"It seems appropriate under the circumstances." Grinning he fingered the betting ticket. "And it seems I've come in to some extra cash."

"Then I'd love to."

"I've got to go check on Betty, make sure she's transported back to the farm."

"If you run into any of my family, tell them where I am, will you?"

"I will. He's had his moment in the sun, hasn't he?" Brian murmured.

Keeley set the brush down, crossing over as Brian opened the stall door. "You've had quite a day, Donnelly."

"I have. I don't know when there's been another like it."

She put her arms around him, resting her head on his shoulder. "There'll be more." *For all of us.* She tipped back her head. "We'll make more," she promised as she raised her mouth to his.

He could have lost himself in her. It was so easy when he was holding her to slip away from the moment and into the dream.

"You're neglecting your horse." He rested his cheek against hers, closed his eyes. "I'll come back for you."

"I'll be waiting."

But he didn't move, only stood with her gathered close while the love inside him pulsed like light. Then he drew back, taking both of her hands and bringing them to his lips. "Don't forget to give him apples. He's fond of them."

"Yes, I know." It felt as though her heart were shaking. "Brian—"

"I'll be back," he said and strode away before the words rising into his throat could be spoken.

"Something's changed," Keeley whispered. "I felt it." She pressed her hands, still warm from his, to her heart. "Oh, it's been a hell of a day. And it's not over yet." She swung back into the stall where Finnegan stood, watching her patiently. "He loves me. He just can't get his tongue around the words yet, but he loves me. I know it."

She picked up the dandy brush again. "We're going to cross another finish line before the day's over. I've got to make myself beautiful. We'll have candlelight and wine, and…"

She trailed off as she heard the stall door open again. Thinking it was Brian come back, she turned. Her brilliant smile faded into ice when she saw Tarmack.

"You think you pulled a fast one, don't you?"

"You're not welcome here."

"Snatched this horse out from under me. No better than a horse thief. Figure you can get away with it 'cause you're a Grant."

"You were paid your asking price." She spoke coolly. She caught the stink of too much whiskey on his breath. And so, she thought, did Finnegan. The horse was beginning to quiver. Calmly, she hooked her hand in his bridle. "If you have a complaint, take it up with the Racing Commission."

"So your father can pay them off?"

Her head came up. Her eyes went from ice to fire. "Be careful what you say about my father."

"I'll say what I want to say." He moved in, his eyes glazed and mean from drinking. "Cheats, all of you, looking down on those of us just trying to make a living. Stole this horse from me." He jabbed a finger into her shoulder. "Said he wasn't fit to run."

"And he wasn't." She wasn't afraid. There were people around, she thought quickly. She had only to call out. But a Grant didn't cry for help at the first tussle. She could deal with a drunk and pitiful bully.

"Fit to run for you, though. To run and win. That purse is mine by rights."

It was only the money, she thought. Just as Brian said, with some, it was all facts and figures, and no feeling. "You've got all the money out of me you'll get." She turned away to brush the gelding. "Now I suggest you leave before I file a complaint."

"Don't you turn your back on me, you little bitch."

It was shock as much as pain that had Keeley gasping when he grabbed her arm and dragged her around. When she tried to jerk free, the sleeve of her shirt tore at the shoulder. Beside her, Finnegan whinnied nervously and shied.

"You look at me when I talk to you. You think you're better than me." He shoved her back against the gelding's side, then yanked her forward again. "You think you're special 'cause your daddy's rolling in money."

"I think," Keeley said with deceptive calm, "that you'd better take your hands off me." She reached in her pocket, closed her fingers, and they were rock steady, around a hoof pick.

It happened fast, a blur of motion and sound. Even as she tugged the makeshift defense free, Finnegan whipped his head and bit Tarmack's shoulder. For the second time Tarmack rapped her hard against the solid wall of the gelding's side, and as he drew back his fist she shouted, leaping to block it from connecting with Finnegan's head.

It skidded over her temple instead, sending a shocking ribbon of pain across her skull, and a haze of pale red over her vision. As she staggered, stumbling around to defend herself and her horse, Brian came through the doors like a vengeful god.

Instinctively Keeley grabbed Finnegan's bridle, to calm him, to balance herself. "It's all right. It's all right now."

But hearing the unmistakable sound of fists against flesh and bone, she ran out.

"Brian, don't!"

His face was blank, a mask without emotion. It seemed all sharp bones and cold eyes. He had Tarmack braced against the wall with a hand over the man's throat, an arm cocked back to deliver another blow. Tarmack's mouth and nose were already bleeding. Keeley grabbed Brian's arm, and hung on like a burr. It felt like gripping hot iron.

"That's enough. It's all right."

Without even a glance, so much as a flicker of acknowledgment, Brian shook her off, rammed a ready fist into Tarmack's gut. "He put his hands on you."

"Stop it." Panting, she grabbed his arm again, and wrapped both hers around it. "He didn't hurt me. Let him go, Brian." She could hear Tarmack struggling for air through the hand Brian had banded around his windpipe. "I'm not hurt."

Very slowly, Brian turned his head. When his eyes, flat and cold with violence, met hers, she trembled. "He put his hands on you," he said again, carefully enunciating each word. "Now step back."

"No." She could hear the shouts behind her, see out of the corner of her eye the crowd already forming. And she could smell the blood. "It's enough. Just let him go."

"It's not enough." He started to shake her off again, and Keeley had an image of herself flying free as he flicked her off like a gnat.

She hadn't feared Tarmack, but she was afraid now.

"What's the problem here?"

She could have wept with relief at the sound of her father's voice. The crowd parted for him. She'd never known one not to. He took one long look at her face, skimmed his gaze over the torn sleeve, and though the hand he laid on her shoulder was gentle, she'd seen the edge come into his eyes.

"Move back, Keeley," he said in a voice of quiet steel.

"Dad." She shook her head, twined around Brian's arm like a vine. "Tell Brian to let him go now. He won't listen to me."

Brian rapped the gasping Tarmack's head against the wall, a kind of absent violence as he once again spoke with rigid patience. "He put his hands on her."

The edge in Travis's eyes went keen, sharp as silver. "Did he touch you?"

"Dad, for God's sake." She lowered her voice. "He'll kill him in a minute."

"Let him go, Brian." Adelia hurried up, took in the situation in one glance. Gently she touched a hand to Brian's shoulder. "You've dealt with him. There's a lad. You're frightening Keeley now."

"Her shirt's torn. Do you see her shirt's torn?" He continued to speak slowly, as if in a foreign tongue. "Take her out of here."

"I will, I will. But let that pathetic man go now. He's not worth it."

Perhaps it was the voice, the lilt of his own country

that broke quietly through the rage. Brian loosened his grip and Tarmack wheezed in air.

"He had her trapped in the stall. Trapped, you see, and his hands were on her."

Adelia nodded. Her gaze shifted briefly to her husband's. A lifetime ago he'd dealt with a drunk who'd had her trapped. She understood the barely reined violence in Brian's eyes. "She's all right now. You saw to that."

"I'm not finished." He said it so calmly, Adelia could only blink when his fist flashed out again and had Tarmack sagging to his knees.

"Stop it." Seeing no other way, Keeley stepped between the two men and shoved Brian with both hands. She didn't move him an inch, but the gesture made a point. "That's enough. It's just a torn shirt. He's drunk, and he was stupid. Now that's enough, Brian."

"You're wrong. It won't ever be enough. You've tender skin, Keeley, and he'll have marked it, so it won't ever be enough."

Tarmack was on his hands and knees, retching. In an almost absent move, Travis dragged him to his feet. "I suggest you apologize to my daughter and then be on your way, or I might let this boy loose on you again."

His stomach was jellied with pain, and he could taste his own blood in his mouth. Humiliation struck nearly as hard as he saw the blur of faces watching. "You can go to hell. You and all the rest. I'm bringing charges."

"Go ahead." Travis bared his teeth in a killing smile. "You're drunk and you're stupid, just as my daughter said. And you touched her."

"He was shouting at her, Mr. Grant." Larry elbowed

his way through the crowd. "I heard him threatening her when I was coming in to see the horse."

Travis blocked Brian's move forward, felt Brian's muscle quiver under his hand. "Hold on," he said quietly, and turned his attention back to Tarmack. "You stay away from what's mine, Tarmack. If you ever lay hands on my girl again, what Brian can do to you will be nothing against what I will do."

Emboldened as he assumed Brian was now on a leash, Tarmack swiped blood from his face with the back of his fist. "So what if I touched her? Just getting her attention was all. She's not so particular who has his hands on her. She wasn't minding when this two-bit mick was pawing her."

Brian surged forward, but Travis was closer, and nearly as quick. His fist cracked, one short-armed hammer blow, against Tarmack's jaw. The man's eyes rolled back as he collapsed.

"Dee, take Keeley home, will you?" Travis glanced at the crowd, one brow lifted as if he dared for comments. "Would someone call security?"

"We shouldn't have left." Keeley paced the kitchen, stopping at the windows on each pass. Why weren't they back?

"Darling, you're shaking. Come on now, sit and drink your tea."

"I can't. What's wrong with men? They'd have beaten that idiot to a pulp. I'm not that surprised at Brian, I suppose, but I expected more restraint from Dad."

Genuinely surprised, Adelia glanced over. "Why?" As worry ate through her she raked her hands through her hair. "He's contained. Now you, I could see you taking a few swings…" She winced. "No offense," she said, then saw that her mother was grinning.

"None taken. My temper might be a bit, we'll say, more colorful than your father's. His tends to be cold and deliberate when it's called for. And it was. The man hurt and frightened his little girl."

"His little girl was about to attempt to gut the man with a hoof pick." Keeley blew out a breath. "I've never seen Dad hit anyone, or look like he wanted to keep right on with it."

"He doesn't use his fists overmuch because he doesn't have to. He'll be upset about this, Keeley." Adelia hesitated, then gestured her daughter to a chair. "Sit a minute. Years ago," she began, "shortly after I came to work here, I was down at the stables at night. One of the grooms had been drinking. He had me down in one of the stalls. I couldn't fight him off."

"Oh, Mama."

"He was starting to tear at my clothes when your father came in. I thought he would beat the man to death. He didn't even raise a sweat about it, just laid in with his fists, systematic like, in a cold kind of rage that was more terrifying than the fire. That's what I saw in Brian's face today." Gently she touched the faint bruise on Keeley's temple. "And I can't blame him for it."

"I don't blame him." She gripped her mother's hands. "This today, this wasn't like that. Tarmack was mad over the horse, and wanted to bully me."

"Threats are threats. If I'd gotten there first, likely I'd have waded in myself. Don't fret so, darling."

"I'm trying not to." She picked up her tea, set it down

again. "Ma, what Tarmack said about Brian. About him pawing me. It wasn't like that. It's not like that between us."

"I know that. You're in love with him."

"Yes." It was lovely to say it. "And he loves me. He just hasn't gotten around to saying so yet. Now I'm worried that Dad... Tempers are up, and if he takes what that bastard said the wrong way." She pushed away from the table again. "Why aren't they back?"

She paced another ten minutes, then finally took some aspirin for the headache that snarled in both temples. She drank a cup of tea and told herself she was calm again.

And was up like a shot the minute she heard wheels on gravel. She got to the door in time to see Brian's truck drive by, and her father's pull in behind the house.

"I missed all the excitement." Though his voice was light, Brendon's eyes carried that same glint of temper she'd seen in their father's. "You okay?"

"I'm fine." Though she patted his arm, her gaze was fixed on her father. She could read nothing in his face as he climbed out of the truck. "I'm absolutely fine," she said again, stepping toward him.

"I'd like you to come inside."

Contained, she thought again. It was impressive, and not a little scary, to see all that rage and fury so tightly contained. "I will. I have to see Brian." Her eyes pleaded with his for understanding. "I have to talk to him. I'll be back."

With one quick squeeze of her hand on his arm, she dashed off.

"Let her go, Travis," Adelia said from the doorway. "She needs to deal with this."

Eyes narrowed, he watched his daughter run to another man. "She's got five minutes."

Keeley caught up with Brian before he climbed the steps to his quarters. She called out, increased her pace. "Wait. I was so worried." She would have leaped straight into his arms, but he stepped back. And his face was glacier cold. "What happened?"

"Nothing. Your father dealt with it. The man won't be bothering you again."

"I'm not worried about that," she said shortly. "Are you all right? I started to think you might be in trouble. I should have stayed and given a statement. Everything got so confused."

"There's no trouble, and nothing to be worried about."

"Good. Brian, I wanted to say that I... Oh, God! Your hands." She snatched them, the tears swimming up as she saw his torn knuckles. "Oh, I'm so sorry. Your poor hands. Let's go up. I'll take care of them."

"I can take care of myself."

"They need to be cleaned and—"

"I don't want you hovering."

He yanked his hands free, then cursed when he saw her cheeks go pale with shock, and the first tear slid down. "Damn it, swallow those back. I'm not in the mood to deal with tears on top of everything else."

"Why are you slapping at me this way?"

Guilt and misery rolled through him. "I've things to do." He turned away, started up the stairs. And fury caught up with guilt and misery. "You didn't want me standing up for you." He spun back, his eyes brilliant with temper.

"What are you talking about?"

"I'm good enough for a roll on the sheets or to help with the horses. But not to stand up for you."

"That's absurd." The tears came fast now as reaction from the last few hours set in. "Was I just supposed to stand by and watch while you beat him half to death?"

"Yes." He snapped, gripped her shoulders, shook. "It was for me to see to. You took that from me, and in the end, handed it to your father. It was for me, two-bit mick or not."

"What's going on here?" For the second time that day, Travis walked in on tempers and shouts, Adelia by his side. And this time, he saw his daughter's tear-streaked face. His eyes shot hotly to Brian. "What the hell is going on here?"

"I'm not sure." Keeley blinked at tears as Brian released her. "This idiot here seems to think I share Tarmack's opinion of him because I didn't stand back and let him beat the man to pieces. Apparently by objecting I've tread on his pride." She looked wearily at her mother. "I'm tired."

"Go up to the house," Travis ordered. "I want to speak with Brian."

"I refuse to be sent away like a child again. This is my business. Mine, and—"

"You don't speak in that tone to your father." Brian's sharp order brought varying reactions. Keeley gaped, Travis frowned thoughtfully and Adelia fought back a grin.

"Excuse me, but I'm very tired of being interrupted

and ordered around and spoken to like a recalcitrant eight-year-old."

"Then don't behave like one," Brian suggested. "My family might not be fancy, but we were taught respect."

"I don't see what—"

"Be quiet."

The command left her stunned and speechless.

"I apologize for causing yet another scene," he said to Travis. "I'm not altogether settled yet. I didn't thank you for smoothing out whatever trouble there might have been with security."

"There were enough people who saw most of what happened. There'd have been no trouble. Not for you."

"A minute ago you were angry because my father smoothed things out."

Brian spared her a glance. "I'm just angry altogether."

"Oh, that's right." Since violence seemed to be the mood of the day, she gave in to it and stabbed a finger into his shoulder. "You're just angry period. He's got some twisted idea that I don't think he's good enough to defend me against a drunk bully. Well, I have news for you, you hardheaded Irish horse's ass."

Now that her own temper was fired, she curled her hand into a fist and used it to thump his chest. "I was defending myself just fine."

"You half Irish, stiff-necked birdbrain, he's twice your size and then some."

"I was handling it, but I appreciate your help."

"The hell you do. It's just like with everything else. You've got to do it all yourself. No one's as smart as you, or as clever, or as capable. Oh it's fine to give me a whistle if you need a diversion."

"Is that what you think?" She was so livid her voice was barely a croak. "That I make love with you for a diversion? You vile, insulting, disgusting son of a bitch."

She raised her own fists, and might have used them, but Travis stepped in and gripped Brian by the shirt. His voice was quiet, almost matter-of-fact. "I ought to take you apart."

"Oh, Travis." Adelia merely pressed her fingers to her eyes.

"Dad, don't you dare." At wit's end, Keeley threw up her hands. "I've got an idea. Why don't we all just beat each other senseless today and be done with it?"

"You've a right." Brian kept his eyes on Travis's and kept hands at his sides.

"The hell he does. I'm a grown woman. A grown woman," she repeated rapping a fist lightly on her father's arm. "And I threw myself at him."

She gained some perverse satisfaction when her father turned that frigid stare on her. "That's right. I *threw* myself at him. I wanted him, I went to him, and I seduced him. Now what? Am I grounded?"

"It doesn't matter how it happened. I was experienced, and she wasn't. I'd no right to touch her, and I knew it. In your place I'd be doing some pounding of my own."

"No one's doing any pounding." Adelia moved forward, laid a hand on Travis's arm. "Darling, are you blind? Can't you see what's between them? Now let the boy go. You know damn well he'll stand there and let you pummel him, and you'd get no satisfaction from it."

No, Travis wasn't blind. Looking in Brian's eyes he saw his life shift. His baby, his little girl, had become someone else's woman. The someone else, he noted, looked about as miserable and baffled by the whole business as he felt himself. "What do you intend to do?"

"I can be gone within the hour."

Amusement was bittersweet. "Can you?"

"Yes, sir." For the first time he knew he'd never pack all he needed, all he wanted into his bag. "Reivers is capable enough to hold you until you find another trainer."

Stubborn Irish pride, Travis thought. Well, he'd had a lifetime of experience on how to handle it. "I'll let you know when you're fired, Donnelly. Dee, we still have that shotgun up at the house, don't we?"

"Oh aye," she said without missing a beat. And wondered if she'd ever been more proud of the man she'd married, or had ever loved him more. "I believe I could lay my hands on it."

Yes, amusement was bittersweet, Travis thought as he watched every ounce of color drain from Brian's face. "Good to know. It's always pleased me that my children recognize and appreciate quality." He released Brian, turned to Keeley. "We'll talk later."

Tears were threatening again as she watched her parents walk off, saw her father reach for her mother's hand, forge that link that had always held strong.

"I've competed for a lot of things," she said quietly. "Worked for a lot of things, wanted a lot of things. But underneath it all, what they have has always been the goal." She turned as Brian walked unsteadily to the steps and sat down. "He won't shoot you, Brian, if you decide you still need to run."

It wasn't the shotgun that worried him, but the implication of it. "I think the lot of you are confused. It's been an emotional day."

"Yes, it has."

"I know who I am, Keeley. The second son of not-quite middle-class parents who are one generation out of poverty. My father liked the drink and the horses a bit too much, and my mother was dead-tired most of the time. We got by is all, then got on. I know what I am," he continued. "I'm a damn good trainer of race-horses. I've never stayed in one job, in one spot, more than three years. If you do, it might take hold of you. I never wanted to find myself fenced in."

"And I'm fencing you in."

He looked up then with eyes both weary and wary. "You could. Then where would you be?"

"Talk about birdbrains." She sighed then walked over to him. "I know who I am, Brian. I'm the oldest daughter of beautiful parents. I've been privileged, brought up in a home full of love. I've had advantages."

She lifted a hand when he said nothing, and brushed at the hair that tumbled over his forehead. "I know what I am. I'm a damn good riding teacher, and I'm rooted here. I can make a difference here, have been making one. But I realize I don't want to do it alone. I want to fence you in, Brian," she murmured, framing his face with her hands. "I've been hammering at that damn fence for weeks. Ever since I realized I was in love with you."

His hands came to her wrists, squeezed reflexively, before he got quickly to his feet. "You're mixing things up." Panic arrowed straight into his heart. "I told you sex complicates things."

"Yes, you did. And of course since you're the only man I've been with, how would I know the difference between sex and love? Then again, that doesn't take into account that I'm a smart and self-aware woman, and I know the reason you're the only man I've been with is that you're the only man I've loved. Brian…"

She stepped toward him, humor flashing into her eyes when he stepped back. "I've made up my mind. You know how stubborn I am."

"I train your father's horses."

"So what? My mother groomed them."

"That's a different matter."

"Why? Oh, because she's a woman. How foolish of me not to realize we can't possibly love each other, build a life with each other. Now if you owned Royal Meadows and I worked here, then it would be all right."

"Stop making me sound ridiculous."

"I can't." She spread her hands. "You are ridiculous. I love you anyway. Really, I tried to approach it sensibly. I like doing things in a structured order that makes a beeline for the goal. But…" She shrugged, smiled. "It just doesn't want to work that way with you. I look at you and my heart, well, it just insists on taking over. I love you so much, Brian. Can't you tell me? Can't you look at me and tell me?"

He skimmed his fingertips over the bruise high on her temple. He wanted to tend to it, to her. "If I did there'd be no going back."

"Coward." She watched the heat flash into his eyes, and thought how lovely it was to know him so well.

"You won't push me into a corner."

Now she laughed. "Watch me," she invited and proceeded to back him up against the steps. "I've figured a lot of things out today, Brian. You're scared of me—of what you feel for me. You were the one always pulling back when we were in public, shifting aside when I'd reach for you. It hurt me."

The idea quite simply appalled him. "I never meant to hurt you."

"No, you couldn't. How could I help but fall for you? A hard head and a soft heart. It's irresistible. Still, it did hurt. But I thought it was just the snob in you. I didn't realize it was nerves."

"I'm not a snob, or a coward."

"Put your arms around me. Kiss me. Tell me."

"Damn it." He grabbed her shoulders, then simply held on, unable to push her back or draw her in. "It was the first time I saw you, the first instant. You walked in the room and my heart stopped. Like it had been struck by lightning. I was fine until you walked into the room."

Her knees wanted to buckle. Hard head, soft heart, and here, suddenly, a staggering sweep of romance. "Why didn't you tell me? Why did you make me wait?"

"I thought I'd get over it."

"Get over it?" Her brow arched up. "Like a head cold?"

"Maybe." He set her aside, paced away to stare out at the hills.

Keeley closed her eyes, let the breeze ruffle her hair, cool her cheeks. When the calm descended, she opened her eyes and smiled. "A good strong head cold's tough to shake off."

"You're telling me. I never wanted to own things," he began with his back still to her. "It was a matter of principle. But when a man decides to settle, things change."

Things change, he thought again. Maybe she had the right of it, and he'd been running for a long time. But in running, hadn't he ended up where he'd been meant to be in the end?

Destiny. He was too Irish not to embrace it when it kept slugging him between the eyes. "I've money put by. Considerable as I've never spent much. There's enough to build a house, or start one anyway. You'd want one close by—for your school, for your family."

She had to close her eyes again. Tears would only fluster him. "Those are the kind of details I usually appreciate, but they just aren't the priority right now. Will you just tell me, Brian. I need you to tell me you love me."

"I'm getting to it." He turned back. "I never thought I wanted family. I want to make children with you, Keeley. I want ours. Please don't cry."

"I'm trying not to. Hurry up."

"I can't be rushed at such a time. Sniffle those back or I'll blunder it. That's the way." He moved to her. "I don't want to own horses, but I can make an exception for the gift you gave me today. As a kind of symbol of things. I didn't have faith in him, not pure faith, that he'd run to win. I didn't have faith in you, either. Give me your hand."

She held it out, clasping his. "Tell me."

"I've never said the words to another woman. You'll be my first, and you'll be my last. I loved you from the first instant, in a kind of blinding flash. Over time the love I have for you has strengthened, and deepened until it's like something alive inside me."

"That's everything I needed to hear." She brought his hand to her cheek. "Marry me, Brian."

"Bloody hell. Will you let me do the asking?"

She had to bite her lip to hold off the watery chuckle. "Sorry."

With a laugh, he plucked her off her feet. "Well, what the hell. Sure I'll marry you."

"Right away."

"Right away." He brushed his lips over her temple. "I love you, Keeley, and since you're birdbrain enough to want to marry a hardheaded Irish horse's ass, I believe it was, I'll go up now and ask your father."

"Ask my—Brian, really."

"I'll do this proper. But maybe I'll take you with me, in case he's found that shotgun."

She laughed, rubbed her cheek against his. "I'll protect you."

He set her on her feet. They began to walk together past the sharply colored fall flowers, the white fences and fields where horses raced their shadows.

When he reached to take her hand, Keeley gripped his firmly. And had everything.

* * * * *

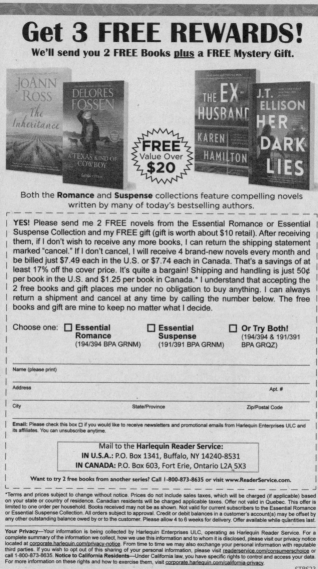

HARLEQUIN
PLUS

Try the best multimedia subscription service for romance readers like you!

Read, Watch and Play.

Experience the easiest way to get the romance content you crave.

Start your **FREE TRIAL** at
www.harlequinplus.com/freetrial.